THE MASQUERADE

Room 2

Club V

EVA HAINING

Copyright

The Masquerade
©Eva Haining 2024

ALL RIGHTS RESERVED

DEVELOPMENTAL EDITING: **RIA ALEXANDER**
EDITING: **BOOKTIQUE EDITING**

Prologue

PIERCE

Thirty Years Ago

"Can you shut the fuck up with that racket, boy?" My daddy is always mad at me. "Lisa, why the hell would you let your mom buy him a toy ambulance with fucking sirens? He's annoying enough without it. Now all he does is sit on the floor and press that fucking button all day long. It does my head in."

"He's four, John. He's only small. Don't be so mean."

Mommy turns to me with a smile as bright as the sun. "You keep playing, baby. Mommy loves to hear her special little man playing doctor. I love you, Pierce." She walks over and pats me on the head before she leaves for work. Mommy works in a bar. I'm not sure what that is, but she says it's 'honest' work, which is 'more than she can say for Daddy.' They say a lot of things I don't understand, but I know their angry voices, and I don't like them. When Daddy shouts at Mommy, she cries, but Mommy shouts a lot when he says mean things about me. She always hides her face with her hair after she shouts at Daddy. She thinks I can't see the marks, but I can. I give her extra cuddles and kisses those days.

As soon as the door closes behind her, my tummy starts to feel squishy. I don't like this feeling. My tummy always does this when it's

1

just Daddy and me in the house. Usually, Grandma comes to see me when Mommy is out, and she plays with me and watches all my favorite cartoons. She gave me my new amb-lance. It's the best thing in the whole world. I vroom it around the house from the moment I finish my cereal in the morning until I crawl into bed at night. I put it nicely on my shelf where I can see it. Mommy makes me laugh when she says 'night, night' to it. She says she has two babies now—me and my amb-lance. She's funny. I can't wait until she gets home from work. Until then, I'll play in my room, away from Daddy.

I can hear him on the phone in our kitchen, so I creep past the doorway as quietly as possible and then run to my room, closing the door behind me. I have a lock on my door, and you need a key as big as my hand to work it. Daddy doesn't know I have it. Mommy gave it to me the last time he was angry. She said that if she's at work, I should use my magic key to lock the door and then hide it until she comes home. I do it exactly the way she told me to—twist it two times toward the picture on my wall. It's of Mommy and me at the park with Grandma. It makes me happy when I look at it, and I feel safe when I know the door is locked.

When my tummy feels normal again, I climb onto my bed and run my hands over the shiny white paint on my amb-lance. I can hear Daddy's voice getting louder. He's saying bad words and throwing stuff. There's a big crashing noise. I press the funny noise harder, over and over, trying to drown out the angry sounds. They scare me.

"Fucking hell! I'll fucking kill you if you don't get this shit sorted out. It's my fucking neck on the line." I press it again. "No excuses, you arrogant little bastard. I'm running this show, so get it done and stop asking questions you don't need the answers to. Christ almighty! If you fuck this up, you're done."

I make the nee-naw-nee-naw noise along with my toy.

"Shut the fuck up, Pierce! I'm sick of hearing that fucking siren."

I'm too scared to stop. Nee-naw… hoping someone will come and help me… nee-naw…

He's coming up the stairs.

"You little shit! I told you to stop that blasted noise."

I watch as the handle on my door turns and shakes. I gulp, holding my breath, happy he can't get in.

"Open the door, you little punk. Where the fuck did you get the key?" The door shakes again as he struggles against the lock. "Open the door!"

My covers are getting wet. I hope Mommy doesn't get upset with me when she comes home. If I just stay in here until she gets back, she'll make everything okay. I know she will.

"Last chance, Pierce. Open the fucking door... *now!*"

Nee... naw. I cower under the covers.

I hear a loud bang right before the door breaks, and I peek out to see Daddy's foot. I jump off the bed and scramble to the corner of the room, hugging my amb-lance and teddy bear, Snoofle. It smells like Mommy. I try to block out the sound of the door breaking piece by piece, making myself as small as I can, hoping I just disappear.

"You're going to pay for this, you little shit. I'm going to make you wish you were never born. Fuck knows *I* wish that. Your mom and I were happy before you came along."

He's inside my room. My tummy hurts really bad, and I can't stop the tears. "Mommy!"

"Your mom's not here, boy. It's just you... and me." He stops at the foot of my bed. I peek out over the top of my teddy to see him looking at my sheets. "You pissed the bed? You're four-fucking-years-old. Are you a little girl, Pierce? Pissed your panties because Mommy isn't here to listen to your bullshit?"

"I want Mommy! I want Mommy!"

I can't see him through my tears, but I feel it when he grabs my amb-lance, yanking it from my arms. "You think this is going to keep you from getting a good hiding for the way you've been acting?" I try to pull it back, but he lifts it too high, and a mean smile creeps onto his face. "You need to learn some respect, boy. When I tell you to shut the fuck up with this racket, you better do it. Better yet, if you don't have this bloody thing, then you *can't* annoy me all the time."

He pulls his arm back and hits my toy against the wall, smashing it repeatedly.

"No, Daddy! No!"

He slowly turns, dropping the broken pieces of my happiness to the floor. "What did you just say to me?"

My tummy hurts so bad now I'm going to be sick. My hands are shaking as I close them tight around Snoofle, breathing in the smell of Mommy as I cry and cry and cry. "I'm... I'm sorry, Daddy. I'll be good. I promise. I love you, Daddy."

"You need to toughen up, you little wimp. I'm going to teach you a lesson."

"Please, Daddy... no." I know what those words mean. A lesson is when you hit someone. I don't like it when Daddy gives me lessons. It makes my skin hurt and Mommy cry.

I quickly crawl under the bed. Daddy's too big to get under here.

"You stupid little fuck."

I bite down on Snoofle to stop myself from screaming.

"Pierce."

His feet are moving. I turn my face away, but all I can see are the pieces of my broken toy all over the carpet. I close my eyes tight and think of Mommy. *Please come home. I don't want Daddy to hit me.* His hands are so big, and it hurts a lot. His fingers tighten around my ankle and pull. I try to hold onto my bed, but he's too strong. His voice gets loud as he grabs me and throws me against the wall, just like he did with my toy. "I'll teach you."

"Pierce!" Mommy, I knew you'd save me.

Daddy makes a weird groaning sound and then stops shouting. He isn't making any noise now. There are funny dots in my eyes, and it makes it hard to see Mommy. But I hear her, and I can smell her perfume as she drops to the floor, pulling me into her arms. The dots get bigger until all I see is black. Mommy sounds far away.

"Pierce... stay with me."

"Mommy."

Chapter 1

PIERCE

"If you're not here to learn, I can't help you. Are you wasting my time? Do you already possess the skills to save this man's life?"

"No, sir."

I hate interns. They come in here cocky as hell, thinking they're ready to wield a scalpel. If I did that as an intern, I'd have been shown the door quicker than the crack of a whip.

"Then please explain to your fellow doctors why you were talking about your dinner plans while I operate on someone's brain. I'm sure this poor man would love to know your burger and fries are more important than his ability to speak, comprehend, and remember his family when I'm done. Please, hotshot, step up and show us how it's done."

Intern—whatever—I don't need to know their names. They come through here every year, and it's the same damn story every fucking time. There's the guy who thinks he has the balls to be a surgeon, who inevitably suffers from micro dick. Then, there's the teacher's pet, who wants to climb so far up my ass they could examine my larynx. My least favorite are the ones who fawn over me. The way a doctor drops in my estimation, is to try and sleep their way through their intern year.

There are no prizes for a good lay. I love to fuck as much as the next man—I'd venture to say much more than the average—but surgery is the one area of my life that isn't ruled by my dick. When I'm in the operating room, I am at my most peaceful. Holding someone's life in my hands is an honor and a privilege I don't take lightly.

"I apologize, Dr. Harrison."

"Don't apologize. Just *be* better." I address the other interns as I prepare to close. "There is no room for apologies when you've got a patient open on the table. You're in the big leagues now. All that book learning means nothing if you don't have what it takes to step up and focus in this room. Until you're ready to take it seriously, you can *all* go and sit in the gallery."

They filter out like petulant children, and I can't see them as anything else. Was I this green when I was an intern? I'd like to think not, but I'm sure my attendings saw me as a cocky young idiot with no concept of what it takes to be the best of the best.

I finish suturing my patient, thankful for another successful outcome. Then comes the best part of my job—telling a family their loved one will be around for birthdays, Christmases, and many years to come. That's what I live for.

"Thank you so much, Dr. Harrison. You are an angel sent from God."

I clear my throat, amused by their observation. It's amazing that I'm an angel in one person's story and a devil in others. All I can do is exist in the space between and find happiness where possible.

"Your husband got through surgery like a champ. He's in recovery right now, awake and responsive. One of the nurses will take you back to see him. I'll be by to check on him before I leave for the night." I offer a firm handshake and a tight smile.

As much as I love giving good news, I don't particularly enjoy interacting with people. I have a few select friends, and I'm good with that.

When my shift is long over and I finish writing up my charts for the day, I decide to head to the club for the rest of the night.

Venom is my safe haven here in Manhattan. It's a place where I can exist outside the hospital, kick back and relax, and it's not a life or death situation. I get to be someone completely different within the walls of Venom, where pleasure is king, pain is consensual, and orgasm is guaranteed.

The moment I walk through the doors, I'm greeted by my small group of friends—people who don't know me as Dr. Harrison, the most prominent neurosurgeon in the country. Here, I'm just Pierce.

"Brother! Come and settle our argument." Flex slings his arm over my shoulder, pulling me toward their table.

"Can I order a drink before you bribe me to pick whatever side of the argument you fall on?"

"Eli!" he shouts. "Send over Pierce's usual."

Apparently, there's no time for niceties this evening. I take a seat alongside some of my friends. Dalton is in with his sub and new wife, Nadia. Flex has his latest sub at the table, and Genevieve seems to be pretty cozy with Ryder tonight.

"What are we all fighting about tonight?"

"Virgins." Holy shit. I came in at the wrong time.

"Sacrificial? Hypothetical? Or is Flex turning up to freshman dorm parties?"

Flex shoves my shoulder. "Thanks for the support. No, in fact, we were just gagging over the fact that Nad and Dalton popped each other's cherries back in the day."

"*What?* Didn't you guys just get together?"

"Have you been living under a rock? They've known each other their entire lives *and* were each other's first." Dalton bristles at his private life being the topic of discussion. I'm surprised he hasn't shut it down already.

"So, what's the question?"

"Do you think virgins can make good submissives? I said no because I'm all about teaching a first-time submissive, but I don't want to explain the fucking mechanics of sex and hold her goddamn hand through the first time. Way too much pressure and not enough pleasure if you ask me."

"Okay."

Dalton continues, "Viv says yes. She likes those virgin boys. Fresh meat."

I look to Dalton. "And what did you have to say about it?" There's a hint of laughter in my voice because I can guess his answer.

"I told him to shut the fuck up about Naddie's cherry before I punch him out."

Flex just finds it funny, and I stifle my amusement.

"Sounds about right."

"What about you?" Flex asks.

"As much as I hate to agree with you, Flex, I think it's a no from me. I don't want to be holding a woman's hand through cashing in her V-card. I was clumsy the first time. Collected a few more cards through med school, and I'm not going to lie, they were not my favorite sexual experiences."

"Okay, but…" Viv interjects, "… think of the potential now that you're a Dom. It's different. I get not wanting a one-night stand to be a virgin, but a sub… think how much easier it would be to train a virgin. No bad habits. No expectations. Definitely less bratty to train." She looks to Naddie with a sly grin. "Sorry, friend."

Dalton wraps his arm around Nadia, pulling her close. "I love you being a brat, kitten. Viv just can't tame a sub the way I can." Genevieve rolls her eyes, laughing as she does.

"Yeah, right. You wish, *Master Callaghan*," she says with an overexaggerated flourish in his direction. "I'm not touching that argument.

"So, what's happening? The new floor seems to be a success. Any plans for further expansion?"

Flex jumps in, more animated than I've seen him in a while. "Yes! Carter and I are working on plans for a training suite right now. Actually, I wouldn't mind picking your brain about a few details."

Now we're talking. As beautiful as the new floor is, I'm not a voyeur for the most part. I don't mind dipping my toe in the water once in a while, but I train submissives. They are short-term, and

I'm strict. I help newer subs find their hard limits as well as their preferences.

"That's what I'm *talking* about," I exclaim.

"I thought you'd be happy," Dalton interjects. "Don't you get tired of training? Training doctors, then training subs in your spare time."

"Could you picture me as a sub?"

"Fuck, no!" they all say in unison.

"Exactly."

We chat back and forth for a few hours, the day's tension dissipating as I sit back and watch my friends, chiming in when I feel like it. Next to the operating room, this is where I feel most myself—here, in this club, with this band of kinksters. There's no judgment when I step through these doors.

Expectation is something that's never really bothered me. When I went to med school, I was different than most. I clawed my way into an Ivy League university, scraping for financial aid and working whatever jobs I could fit around my grueling schedule.

Luxury wasn't in my vocabulary, and no one expected anything more than a basic nine to five from me. After my dad died at her hand, my mom ended up working three jobs just to keep a roof over our heads. In the end, she became an alcoholic, and I was a burden she couldn't cope with anymore. I was put into foster care and learned to depend only on myself.

My mom drank herself to death when I was ten, and the sad thing is, it didn't impact my day-to-day life.

I left the group home the second I could afford to find a shithole apartment to live in until I got a full ride to college through every academic scholarship going, and moved into the dorms at Princeton.

When I found BDSM, it was a lightbulb moment—a way for me to exact control in every aspect of my life. I need order, balance, and, above all, consent. I know my mom was plagued by the abuse my dad subjected her to for years. I don't want any part of relationships, not even with my subs. That's why I train. I'm a safe space for women to explore their sexual desires and figure out what they want in a Dom. When they understand their wants and needs, they move on, and so do I.

I wouldn't have it any other way.

"Earth to Pierce." Flex's voice brings me back to the group.

"Sorry, it's been a long day."

"How can you hack into people's brains all day?" His vernacular makes me laugh.

"If I *hacked*, all of my patients would be dead or in a vegetative state. What I do is poetry in motion, my friend."

"Most guys with your kind of job pressure are subs. It always amazes me that you want control of every fucking minute of your life."

"I had very little control growing up. I'm a walking cliché, Flex. I like everything to be perfect. I teach doctors. I operate. I teach submissives. We fuck. All is right in the world," I say as I drain my drink and signal for another.

Dalton nods in my direction. "Not on call tonight?"

"Nope. I have the weekend off, which virtually never happens."

"Then you can wade in on the training floor tomorrow?"

"Sure. I have a last session with my current sub tomorrow night. I can swing by a few hours early, and you can walk me through it."

"Sounds good to me."

Another round of drinks arrives, courtesy of Dalton. "Are you coming to the masquerade?"

"Did I miss the memo?"

"We're having a masquerade ball for new members and prospective members who've been waitlisted. It'll be a fun night."

"Depends on when it is."

"Two weeks from tonight."

"I'll check my schedule. I have a few subs to interview for training."

"Take a night off, brother. Masquerades are for no strings, no training, no rules fun."

"Does that mean you guys are going to lose yourself in the crowd?" I anticipate Dalton's answer, amused by the furrow of his brow.

"Anyone so much as looks at my kitten the wrong way, they'll require a doctor in the house."

"You're too predictable, Dal."

"Says the robot Dom!" He chuckles.

"Is that what you guys think? That I'm a robot? My submissives would beg to differ. *Literally*."

"I don't think that," Nad speaks up. "I think you can be unpredictable. Sensitive even."

Where the fuck did she get that idea? The only other person who thought I was sensitive was my father, and he was sure to beat it right out of me.

"You've got him all wrong, kitty kat." Flex throws it out there, and I watch as Dalton just about explodes.

"Call her kitty kat again, Flex, and I'll break that pretty face of yours."

"Jesus, bro. You need to calm the fuck down. What happened to easy-going Dom Dal?"

"He packed up and left the building. Kitten is mine."

"God, Pierce, I think you've got it the right way around. Teach 'em and street 'em. This true-love thing has Dal ready to pop a blood vessel over here."

"I'm so glad I have your approval, Flex. How did I ever live without it?"

"A piece of sound advice for you, Pierce... you should have multiple subs on the go. You're so highly strung."

I rub my palm over the scruff on my jaw. "My latest group of interns is pissing me off. They don't know how to do anything."

"Isn't that why they come to you? They have to learn to be doctors," Viv offers.

"Yeah, I'm just fed up today. It's a bunch of rich kids whose daddy bought them a ticket into the program. They're entitled with no skills to back it up right now. They are the bottom of the food chain, mouthing off like the apex predator."

"And we all know you're the predator, Pierce. That's why I love you." Viv gives me that knowing grin. Maybe I'll take her to my private room tonight. She might be a fierce Domme, but we occasionally engage in a little friends-with-benefits action.

Being a trainer affords me the freedom to roam as I see fit. I sign contracts to teach, not for monogamous relationships. It's a one-sided transaction. The sub in training must be faithful only to me. Not because I care if they fuck around, but because learning from a single Dom gives better results.

Leaning back in my chair, I mull over the idea of a masquerade ball. "So this party is for new and prospective members?"

"Yes," Flex confirms.

"Any new submissives?"

"Of course. Everyone will be given the option to wear a tag that'll show their kinks. Doms, subs, voyeurs, teachers, students, toy play, pain, pleasure. A unique QR code you can scan with your phone and know all of the relevant information, except their name and occupation. Hot, right?"

"Wow. QR codes. That's new."

"Nad's friend, Jenna, is a computer whizz kid and has been working on a portal for members. It will allow for contracts, hookups, matching… the whole nine yards."

"Nice."

"You'll like this feature. For trainees, we'll have an application for new subs from various clubs we network with nationwide. You'll have some fresh, shiny new subs to play with." Sounds perfect. Just what the doctor ordered, pun intended.

"I didn't realize Jenna was hopping on the kink train."

"She's not," Nad says with conviction.

I hold my hands up to show innocence. "I get the message. I won't go near her. You made it pretty clear last time." I give it a year max before sweet best friend Jenna starts sniffing around the lifestyle. I have an eye for potential subs, and she'd be a delectable treat to train. Not by me, obviously. I value having my nuts attached to my body, and the way Nad is staring me down is enough to make them wither.

"Good. Anyway…" She giggles. "How are things with your latest sub? Training going well?"

"Yeah, we're pretty much done. She's ready to find a long-term Dom or someone to fool around with who compliments her kinks. She'd be perfect for someone like Mateo, but I think he has a regular right now."

"Maybe she'll find someone at the masquerade."

"I don't see why not. I've trained her well. Whoever makes a contract with her will be a lucky man."

"Wouldn't you ever consider a sub outside of training?" Nad looks lovingly at her Dom, his shit-eating grin saccharin as the rest of us fade into the background while they lose themselves in each other.

"I don't have time. My hours are grueling, and my focus is singular. The club is where I let off steam. I'm not looking to find the love of my life."

Dalton whispers something in Nad's ear, her body shivering before they excuse themselves and head for their private room.

"Good talk, guys," I shout after them.

Throughout the evening, everyone pairs off at different times, leaving me to drink alone at the bar, with only the bartender for company.

"Another scotch neat?" Eli asks as I pull up my latest trainee's number.

"Yes, thanks."

> **Me:** Can you meet me at the club in 30?

> **Sub:** Yes, Sir.

> **Me:** See you then.

I may as well have some fun before I have to find a new sub to play with.

Eli sets my drink down before leaning against the bar, his arms folded over his chest. He talks a big game, but his body language says otherwise.

"So, Eli, how are you enjoying being the manager of this place?"

"It's unlike anywhere else I've worked, that's for sure."

"Yeah, I doubt you had to sign an NDA at your previous job."

"You'd be surprised what Carter expects of his bartenders."

"Really?" I shouldn't be surprised. Carter De Rossi has a reputation for discretion.

"This is definitely next level." He's curious.

"Has it got you wondering what goes on behind closed doors?"

"Me?" He blushes. "No. Of course not. I'm not a Dominant."

"I didn't say you were." I take a sip of my drink, watching him squirm.

"You've never wondered what it would be like to let Genevieve take you to her private room? You might not want to dominate, but I get the feeling you'd enjoy being submissive."

His cheeks flush as he starts cleaning the bar, avoiding my gaze.

"Nah. I'm an old-fashioned guy. A man's man." I think he doth protest too much.

"You'd be surprised by how many 'men's men' enjoy giving over control in the bedroom. High-pressure jobs. Major leadership roles. They take a toll, and for some men, they find an escape through someone like Genevieve. She's very good at what she does."

"How would you know? Aren't you a Dom?"

"Yes, but she and I have worked together. I've trained male submissives before." His eyebrows rise so high they're almost in his hairline.

"Oh. I didn't... it's none of my business."

"Eli, can I give you a word of advice as the weekday manager of V?"

"Of course."

"Lighten up. And I say that as one of the most serious men in this club. I'm a Dom in here and out in the real world. Surgery is high stakes. I mess up, and someone dies. I'm about as tightly wound as they come, and you're stressing me out right now. When was the last time you got laid?"

"Two days ago. Trust me, getting laid isn't an issue."

"Maybe it's not as fulfilling as it could be. It's natural to be curious when you see kink from the outside. I promise you won't burst into flames if you dip your toe in the water."

He rubs the back of his neck, uncomfortable thinking about his obvious interest. "You've got me all wrong. I'm vanilla, and it works for me."

"That's what they all say." I sling back the rest of my drink and drop a twenty on the bar as a tip. "If you ever have any questions, don't hesitate to ask. Sex... kink... don't knock it till you try it."

I leave him to think about what I said. He has submissive written all over him. Genevieve would eat the poor guy alive, but he'd love every second of it.

Entering my private room, I get to work setting up for the arrival of my current trainee. I'm intrigued by Flex's ideas to expand and create a sizable training floor. I already have thoughts on equipment, toys, and a stage for group training. With the number of new members increasing, we have to make sure that patrons engage safely and within the parameters of their contracts. The potential is endless.

Chapter 2
FREYA

My hands are shaking, and the rise and fall of my chest are shallow as we pull up outside what looks like a regular office building.

"I don't know if I can do this."

I've been researching BDSM for a while now, so when I met Celest and found out she's a submissive, I started asking questions, probing her for information. She's not secretive about the lifestyle, but when it comes to her club, she's been tight-lipped about it.

Tonight is a rare occurrence, and I jumped at the chance when she invited me to their first masquerade ball—complete anonymity to explore with no expectation to hook up.

"I can take you home if you're not ready. There's no pressure here, Freya. No one will do anything without your permission. It's just a party."

My stomach churns with excitement, butterflies swarming my chest cavity as I steel my nerves. "I don't want to go home. I've wanted this for a while. I'm just being silly."

"Girl, you look amazing, and no one will know who you are or what you do for a living. Relax," she says, resting her hand on my knee. "I'll be with you."

"Thanks, Celest."

I opted for a lavender floor-length gown tonight, hugging me in all the right places and complimenting my olive complexion. My mask is elaborate and elegant, shielding the top half of my face, the jewels highlighting my chocolate-brown eyes.

Celest leans over, sweeping my hair over my shoulder, its soft curls cascading down my back. "You ready?"

"As I'll ever be." From my fingertips to the tips of my toes, excitement radiates through every cell in my body, vibrating as I step out of the cab, clenching my clutch bag.

"Do you have the invite I gave you?" Celest asks as we step into the lobby. I'm not prepared for how ordinary it looks, and I'm a little crestfallen.

I reach inside my bag, pulling out the sleek black invitation with the time, date, and a golden 'V' embossed on it. Nothing more, nothing less.

"Good evening." The security guard takes the invite before handing us small tags and ushering us to an elevator.

"Are you okay?" Celest asks as the door slides closed.

"It's not what I expected."

"Just wait…" Within seconds, the doors ping open, and my jaw drops. A dark, sumptuous vestibule comes into view. It oozes luxury and a promise of wickedness. She takes my hand, pulling me out of the elevator. "You're going to love it."

As she leads me into the bar, I'm awestruck by the opulence surrounding me—grand chandeliers and a gorgeous dark wood bar that looks to be stocked with anything you could ever wish for. There are tables, booths, and barstools filled with a multitude of people, all with one thing in common—masks obscure their faces.

There are men in tuxedos—obviously tailored—with simple black masks, their lips the only feature unveiled. Some of them have women draped over them, wearing ballgowns that would make a queen look like a serf by comparison. And their masks—intricate and bejeweled in breathtaking colors to match their gowns. Suddenly, I feel completely underdressed, even though this is the most expensive dress I've ever bought.

My pulse is racing, thrumming in my ears as we make our way to the bar.

"What can I get for you ladies?" Even the bartenders are dressed to kill tonight. I wonder if that's normal for a place like this.

"Two French Martinis, please." I need some liquid courage if I'm going to get through tonight. I've wanted to attend a club for years, but being here is overwhelming. When our drinks are set before us, my friend and I lift our glasses, clinking them together.

"Here's to a great night," I say with trepidation.

"Welcome to Venom, Freya. Indulge your desires, my friend. There is no judgment here."

Raising the cocktail glass to my lips, I drink the entire thing before asking for another. My stomach is doing somersaults as I watch everyone interact, missing whatever my friend is saying. I can't look away. Everyone seems so free. I don't know how to explain it, but I want a taste of that feeling.

"Come on, it's time to go upstairs." Celest grabs my hand, dragging me toward a grand staircase on the other side of the bar. I try to take in every detail. Walking past a dark hallway, I wonder what's down there.

"Where are we going?" I don't want to leave.

"They added a new level a few months ago. That's where the ball is."

"Is it like this?" Picking up the bottom of my gown, I make my way up the dark spiraling staircase. It's beautiful down to the last detail, with ornate carvings adorning the balustrade.

"Yes and no. There's a bar up there, but it's a communal gathering space."

"What do you mean? There were lots of people downstairs." As we take the last few steps, it opens up into a lavish ballroom, the décor perfect for an elegant masquerade.

"Not that kind of communal. This area was added for those who enjoy being watched or watching others."

"While they have sex?" My voice comes out an octave higher than usual.

"Oh, my sweet, innocent friend." She links her arm with mine, pulling me into the crowd.

"What about that hallway?"

"The voyeur hall. Private rooms for patrons but with viewing windows. You wouldn't know if people are watching or not." Heat pools at the apex of my thighs. I've never considered anything like this, and I'm a little ashamed to think it might be something I'd enjoy.

"And out here?"

"Patrons can engage with one partner or several at a time. Before now, the club has only had one room downstairs for orgies and one for voyeurs. Any kind of sexual contact is strictly prohibited in the bar downstairs."

"So they must have a lot of members who enjoy *that*."

"You can say it, Freya," she coaxes.

"People who enjoy orgies." I trip over the words, wondering if I made the right decision by coming here tonight. Celest picks up on my unease.

"It's all about consent here, Freya. Relax. No one will have their wicked way with you unless you expressly tell them otherwise."

I breathe out a sigh of relief, but it's mixed with a hint of disappointment. I'm not sure if I can push myself to ask for what I want. It feels like it would be easier just to let it happen. To have someone else take the reins.

The music stops, and all eyes go to the stage where a ridiculously handsome man stands at the microphone, his mask in one hand and a drink in the other.

"Hello, everyone. I'm Dalton Callaghan, one of the club owners. Most of you know me, but I'm aware we have many new and hidden faces tonight. Please enjoy the facilities, respect the rules, and welcome to Venom. Let the masquerade begin."

He fixes his mask in place and walks off stage into the arms of a beautiful woman. Her mask obscures most of her face, but I can tell she's gorgeous. There's something in the way he gazes at her with complete adoration.

The music starts up again, and a buzz of excitement ripples

through the crowd as people start chatting, drinking, and dancing. It's like a fairy tale if Cinderella wanted to be chained up and whipped.

"Is your Dom here tonight?" I ask Celest.

"Yes, but I told him I won't be leaving you to the wolves, so don't worry. I'll be by your side as long as you want me."

"Thanks. I'm a little overwhelmed."

Everyone around me seems so confident and carefree. I'm not used to having doubts. I am a self-assured woman in every other aspect of my life, but when it comes to sex, I've always known I'm different and what I want from a man.

I think.

Maybe.

"Come on. It's time to put our tags on, and we'll get you another drink. You don't have to have sex tonight, Freya. We're out having a girl's night. You were curious. Don't let any preconceived ideas ruin your night. Promise me."

"Okay." I blow out a long breath before following her through the crowd toward the bar. When we get there, I reach into my purse and pull out the tag we received when we arrived.

"You don't even need to wear that if you don't want to. Or you can take it off whenever you feel like it. Did you complete the information in the portal?"

"Yeah, but the extent of my likes and dislikes were 'I have no idea what I want.' "

She presses a reassuring hand on my shoulder. "That's where we all start, Freya. I guarantee there are others in this room who said the same thing. Don't be shy. It's okay not to know. Plenty of men here would be more than willing to explore with you."

A thrill courses through me at the thought, and I attach the small tag to my gown. I can do this. When we have a fresh drink in hand, Celest and I start to mingle. She introduces me to a few of her friends as we navigate the crowd, her Dom zeroing in on her in a sea of people. Even in a mask, he can pick her out, and I realize this is what I came here for. I want a man who will know my body and can find me in a crowd, even with a mask on my face. Is it too much to ask for a man like that? It would seem so with the men I've dated of late.

I dip in and out of various conversations, my eyes roving over every detail of the club. It's enchanting. I can't help coming back to the hallway Celest mentioned, knowing what people could be doing right now. There's a man leaning against the wall—tall, muscular but lean, dirty blond hair, and his eyes—he's looking at me.

My body heats under his gaze. Even from this distance, I can tell his focus is on me alone. My breath is shallow as I stand frozen to the spot, entranced as he casually makes his way through the crowd with a confident gait to his stride, his eyes never leaving mine.

Celest is talking to me, but I don't pay enough attention to answer, transfixed by the man walking toward me. When he comes to a stop, he's a foot away from me, and it feels like too little and too much all at once. We stand for what feels like the longest time, his emerald gaze fixed on mine. His lips are sensuous, his jaw peppered with stubble, and I'm flooded by the thought of how it would feel against my skin.

"Hello." His voice is a low rumble, gravelly and dripping with sex. The scent of his cologne invades my senses, and my mouth goes dry.

"Hi."

"Would you like to dance?" Holding out his hand to me, I shove my drink and purse at Celest without breaking eye contact with my mysterious suitor.

I don't speak. I can't.

Instead, I slip my hand into his, letting him lead me to the dance floor, his arm wrapping around my waist, pulling my body flush with his. Every nerve ending in my body sparks to life, the rapid rise and fall of my chest giving me away as we begin to sway to the music. Electricity courses through every fiber of my being, and I feel alive in a way I never have before.

He doesn't speak, and his eyes remain fixed on me as if I'm the only person in the room. My body is on fire where his hand holds tight on my waist as I gaze up into his eyes. I could get lost in their depths, everything else fading away as I let him lead me around the floor.

The music is ethereal, as enchanting as my dance partner. One song bleeds into the next and the next, and still, we don't exchange words. He spins me with ease, clearly an adept dancer. It makes me wonder if he does this often, sweeping women off their feet without more than a simple *hello*, and yet I find I don't much care. Tonight, I'm the woman in his arms, and suddenly, the night is full of possibilities. The unsettling nerves I felt when I walked through the door give way to a different kind of nervous energy.

My body reacts to this man—a masked stranger—in ways it never has before. As the song finishes, his hand shifts from my waist, sliding up my side, across my shoulder, and into my hair as he leans in, his gaze flitting from my eyes to my lips and back again. A silent question. A plea for permission which I freely give with a slight nod.

His lips brush mine, sending a shiver down my spine, my nipples hardening as his tongue darts out to lick the seam, asking for entrance. He tastes like scotch and a hint of mint, his stroke firm and slow as our tongues tangle in a sensual dance. His hand fists in my hair, holding me firm as he deepens our kiss. When he pulls back, I'm left panting, my senses in overdrive as he presses his lips to mine once more before he speaks.

"Come with me." It's not a question. It is a command, and it makes my body sing with anticipation. He releases my hair, his hand caressing down my spine until it reaches the small of my back. It's almost territorial, sending a jolt of desire straight to my core.

He navigates the crowd easily, finding his way back to the edge of the voyeur hallway where I first caught him watching me. Opening one of the many doors, he guides me inside before locking it behind us.

"Do you want the window left open to whoever may be on the other side, little one?"

"I…" I can barely catch my breath. Am I really going to do this with a perfect stranger?

"Don't be afraid. Tell me what you want, and I'll make it so."

My heart is hammering so hard in my chest, my pulse whooshing in my ears as his eyes rake the length of me.

"Open," I whisper, my voice unrecognizable.

He runs his fingertips down my arms, goose bumps spreading across my skin, my head swimming as his lips find mine once more.

His touch is tender yet fierce, but as his hands move into my hair to release my mask, I panic.

"Leave it on," I beg.

He pulls back, leaving me bereft. "I won't do anything you don't want, little one. You can keep it on if you so wish."

"Yes, please."

"Do you want me to keep mine on, or do you want to see my face as I bury it between your thighs?" Holy Mother of God.

"Keep it on," I choke past my nerves, desperate for more of his touch.

"Then you will call me Sir. Understood?"

"Yes."

He leans in, his lips caressing the shell of my ear. "That's your first mistake, little one. I think you meant to say *yes, Sir.*" My heartbeat goes wild.

"Yes, Sir," I pant in a breathy whisper.

"Good girl." His fingers trail down my arm until they interlace with mine, and he leads me to a bed in the center of the room. "Sit on the edge."

I do as I'm told, my eyes glancing at the blacked-out window on the wall. A two-way mirror?

"Last chance to close the curtains." He drops to his knees in front of me. "Tell me what you want."

"Leave them open… Sir."

"Well done, little one." He leisurely slips his hand under my dress, caressing my calf as he makes his way up to my knee. "Now, tell me your safeword."

"I don't have one." He stops his ascent, pinning me with his gaze.

"I could tell you're new to this, but you're brand new, aren't you, little one?"

"Yes. Yes, Sir."

"That's okay." Every cell in my body is focused on where his warm hand grips my leg. "Choose a word. Something easy to remember. If you want me to stop what I'm doing, you use that word, and I will cease everything." I read about this, but I didn't plan ahead.

"Um… lavender."

He starts drawing circles with his fingertips, his striking green eyes staring up at me from behind his mask. "Lavender. Beautiful. Now, tell me you understand. You are in complete control. You say your safeword, and I stop. No matter what."

"I understand, Sir."

I'm mesmerized as he licks his lips, his other hand now under my gown, pushing it up over my knees. My body is trembling, nerves swarming my stomach as he slides his fingers up my thighs before hooking them under my panties and slowly easing the lace down my legs and dropping them to the floor.

My masked Dom trails soft kisses up my legs, savoring every inch as he gets closer to the apex of my thighs. Pushing my gown up toward my waist, his eyes drop to where I ache for his touch. I've never done anything like this before, but I want him.

"So beautiful. You're already wet for me. Shall I see how you taste?" I feel my cheeks blush as he kneels between my legs, pushing them apart until I'm on display for his eyes only. From here, he's careful to shield me from anyone watching.

"Yes, Sir."

He groans in approval as he holds my gaze, dipping his head to where I need him at this moment. The second his lips brush against my sex, my entire body quivers, the rapid rise and fall of my chest giving away just how much I desire his mouth on me.

Pressing open-mouthed kisses to my most tender flesh, he darts his tongue out, tasting me in one long, languorous kiss, making me moan. I know I should be embarrassed, but it feels so good.

"That's it, little one. Let me hear you." He continues his ministrations, moving one hand up to my stomach, holding me in place as he licks, nibbles, and kisses me until all I care about is where our bodies meet.

"Oh God... yes... yes..."

"You taste so fucking good. I could eat you for hours, little one. You're sweet like honey." His breath is warm against my skin, making me even wetter. "Such a good girl." He kisses me. "Do you want me to show whoever is watching this pretty pussy of yours?"

My back arches off the bed, a slick sheen of sweat coating my body as he flicks his tongue over my clit.

"Yes, Sir."

Without another word, he grabs my dress and shoves it up to my waist, displaying me for anyone to see, causing a blazing inferno at my core.

"You're so wet for me, little one. Are you a dirty girl? You like knowing that any number of people are watching me fuck you with my tongue right now."

"Yes... oh God, yes... Sir."

"Yes, little one. Be a good girl and spread your legs as far as they'll go." His eyes remain fixed on mine as he quickens his pace, his tongue doing wicked things to me as I start to move my hips, desperate for more of him.

"Such a perfect pussy."

When I can barely stand it, I fist my hands in the sheets, trying to crawl away and yet wanting more. Grabbing my ankles, he pulls me right to the edge of the bed before setting a punishing rhythm, sending me to the brink of release.

"Oh God..."

"He's got nothing to do with your pleasure, little one. Tonight, you're mine. Come for me. *Now.*" His tongue circles my clit as he sends me crashing headlong into an orgasm, my entire body coming to life like it never has before. I shamelessly ride his face, his stubble rubbing against my sex, making it all the more deliciously wicked.

"Yes... Sir... *Sir!*"

Chapter 3
PIERCE

My dick is so hard it hurts, straining against my suit pants as she comes hard on my tongue, her delectable body convulsing under my touch. I let her ride out the aftershocks, unfastening my belt, ready to fuck her so hard she won't remember her name. Shit, I don't even know her name, but I want her pleasure, and I don't care who knows it.

Her cheeks are flushed, the color creeping under her mask, her deep brown eyes glazed over in a post-orgasmic haze. She tastes divine, and I can't wait to sink balls deep inside her. It takes every ounce of self-restraint to calm myself enough to get up and walk over to the tall dresser in the corner, grabbing a few condoms from the top drawer.

"Take off your dress, little one. I want to see every inch of you as you take every inch of me."

She hesitates as I stalk toward her, chewing on her bottom lip while slowly sliding the straps of her dress off her shoulders.

"Don't make me ask you again unless you want to be punished. Is that what you want?"

"I'm not sure." She catches me off-guard. I assume she's here tonight to explore a fantasy or some intrigue she has regarding her kinks, but the way she hesitates and her gaze flits to the two-way mirror has me questioning myself.

"If you're not sure, then I won't touch you. Pain doesn't have to be a part of our evening."

"I don't want to leave."

"You don't have to, little one, but you do need to take off that dress. It'll look so much better puddled on the floor at your feet."

As I stalk toward her, I watch her body stiffen.

"Lavender." She fixes her straps back in place, slips her shoes into her hand, and jumps to her feet. "I'm sorry. I can't do this."

Before I get another word out, she's at the door, leaving me hard as a rock and aching for release, her taste still fresh on my tongue. I move to go after her, but I stop myself, realizing that I have no claim to her. There's no contract in place, so I can't force her to stay as much as I would like to.

It doesn't escape me that she used her safeword. She'll make a good trainee.

I've had the week from hell and needed a release tonight. Now, I'm more wound up than I was when I got here, aching for an orgasm.

Adrenaline courses through me with nowhere to go, so I do what any self-respecting man would. Pulling my dick out of my pants, I stride over to the two-way mirror. May as well give them a show. Fisting my hand around the base of my dick, I stare into the darkness, biting down on my bottom lip. My lavender little one's cum on my lips is all I need, and the memory of the way her pussy reacted under my touch. Fucking perfect.

I don't close my eyes or look away as I stroke my dick, letting her scent do all the work as I take my time with slow, measured movements. There could be no one behind that mirror, or there could be a hundred. It's part of the thrill as I pick up the pace. She might have gotten away tonight, but she'll be back. They always are. I imagine how fucking glorious her tits will look when I come all over them. How tight her pussy will be when it contracts around my dick as she orgasms harder than she's ever done in her life. It's going to be so fucking sweet.

My balls tighten, and I brace my hand on the wall, steadying myself as my orgasm pulses through me, my cum spilling onto the floor. Such a waste. I'll find her soon enough, and when I do, she'll take my cum like a good little girl.

When I'm done, I get cleaned up, return to the party, and seek out my friends.

"Anyone seen Flex?" I question as I down a shot.

"He's in the voyeur hall. Why?" Genevieve asks.

I can't help laughing. "Shit. He's probably off in a corner crying at how inadequate he is."

She looks at me with a questioning furrow in her brow. "What?"

"I just gave whoever is in there a prime view of my dick." I chuckle.

"Lucky them." Her eyes flit to my groin as she bites down on her lip.

"Don't you have a companion for the evening?" She looks set to devour me whole.

"They have the night off. I wanted the freedom to roam the masquerade, but I could be persuaded otherwise." My dick twitches.

"As much as I would normally take you up on a little mutual release, I have another woman's cum all over my face. Even I'm not enough of an asshole for that."

"I've licked your jaw clean of another woman's cum before, Pierce," she says with a wicked grin.

"That was different. You were sucking her tits when I made her come."

"True." She pouts as she reaches for her drink. "Why are you looking for Flex?"

"I want him to find out whose cum I can still taste."

"What happened?"

"I buried my head between her legs until she screamed herself hoarse. Then I told her to strip, and she freaked out. Said her safeword and ran."

"A newbie?"

"I'm ninety-nine percent sure, but I didn't get her name. Fuck, I have no idea what she looks like. She kept the mask on."

"I'm intrigued."

"Me too. I want Flex to use the security cameras to super sleuth for me."

"Was her pussy really that good? You don't usually go chasing your trainees."

"Yes. There was something about her, Viv. Fucking edible."

"You just want what you can't have. Whoever she is, she gets it. Leave you wanting more."

"I don't think so. She seemed almost shy."

"Didn't you say you were in the voyeur hallway?"

"I can't explain it. I just have a feeling."

"Well, your *feeling* is sending you home with blue balls."

"Aww, Viv, thanks for the concern, but I saw to myself with everyone watching. I'll survive until I find her."

"You gave yourself a hand job?" I love the surprise in her voice. "You're a Dom. Do I need to remind you that we do not need to get ourselves off?"

"I'm well aware, but I have my reasons. If you see Flex, tell him I'm looking for him." I press a quick kiss to her cheek before downing my drink and melting into the crowd. If the lady in lavender is still here, I'll find her.

It's been two weeks since the masquerade ball, and Flex hasn't been able to get me a name. I've taken myself in hand more times than I can count, the image of her slender legs spread wide for me to feast on is all I can think about. I work, and I fist my dick like a high schooler with his first porno magazine.

With my last trainee ready for a Dom, I should be interviewing new potential subs, but I've been putting it off, waiting for *her*.

The club is busy tonight as I nurse my third scotch. I lost a patient today, and I just couldn't stay home all night replaying it on a loop. Their chance of survival was in the single-digit percentile, but it never gets easier. I take on the almost impossible cases, and sometimes there's nothing I can do, but I always take the losses to heart. People say the best surgeons leave their feelings at the door. For me, I believe the opposite. I may not outwardly show my compassion, but it's in every stitch and every surgery. I'm at the top of my field *because* I care about every patient. Their families look to me for hope, and I give it where I can, offering my deepest condolences when I can't prolong the inevitable.

Flex is sitting at the bar with his latest sub, his expression turning to a shit-eating grin at the sight of me. "The man of the hour! Welcome, my friend. You're going to love me, the bearer of good tidings." He never fails to make me laugh.

"Okay, I'll bite. Why are you so happy tonight?"

"A woman in a mask was here earlier." My pulse starts whooshing in my ears.

"Is she still here? What did she say? What did she look like?"

Flex takes a long swig of his drink. "Calm down. The answers are *no, not much,* and *she was wearing a purple mask.*"

I rake my hands through my hair. *Fuck.* "Great. Just fucking great."

"She left something for you. Not specifically. She said she wanted to leave it for a masked Dom. That narrows it down to ninety percent of the guys who attended the masquerade."

"What did she leave?"

He reaches into his suit jacket pocket and pulls out a lavender mask—the one she was wearing that night. He holds it out to me, taunting me with his conspiratorial grin. "Check the back."

I snatch it out of his hand, lifting it to my face, inhaling the soft scent of her perfume that still lingers. My dick twitches at the memory of her coming all over my tongue, and I quickly turn it over to find a phone number scrawled on the inside of the mask.

That's it, little one.

I immediately pull out my phone and input the number, saving it under *Lavender.* She came back. I'd almost given up hope of seeing her again or finding out who she is and what she needs.

"I don't think I've ever seen a guy look happier about getting some random girl's number. Was the sex *that* good?"

"A gentleman never kisses and tells."

"Exactly. How good was it?"

"I've got a few things to do in my room."

"Seriously, bro? Don't become another Dalton. You guys are killing all the fun with your obsessive fawning."

"Not the same thing. I train, I fuck, and it's done."

"Tell yourself whatever you need to, Pierce. You're a goner." He shouts after me as I head to my private room.

Once inside, I take out my phone and start typing, writing and deleting the message repeatedly.

> Me: Hello, little one.

The elusive dancing dots don't appear, so I start pacing the room, my mind going over every moment of that night as I run my fingers over the intricate lines of the mask. After a few minutes, my phone vibrates with a message from her.

> Lavender: Hello, Sir.

God, my cock gets hard at the sight of what a good girl she is.

> Me: Why did you leave your number for me? You made your feelings clear when you left.

> Lavender: I'm sorry. I have no right to ask, but I want to see you again. If that's something you would be open to.

> Me: I had to take myself in hand after you left.

> Lavender: I know.

My heartbeat thumps in my chest. Viv questioned why I would do such a thing, but she should know better. I *always* have a reason.

> Me: You watched me?

> Lavender: Yes.

> Me: Did you enjoy the show?

> Lavender: Very much, Sir.

Fuck. This woman does something to me.

> Me: That's what you did to me, little one. I could taste you on my lips as I stroked my dick. You had that effect on me.

> Lavender: I wish it were my mouth giving you pleasure.

Holy shit. I let out an audible groan as my dick turns to steel.

> Me: Then why didn't you wrap those pretty lips around my dick? All you had to do was ask.

> Lavender: I've never done that before. That night was my first at a BDSM club.

> Me: I guessed as much. Are you still curious, little one?

> Lavender: Yes. Though I'm sure you already have a submissive.

> Me: Would it matter if I did? Would you still want to suck my dick?

> Lavender: I should say no.

> Me: Tell me what you want from me.

A few minutes pass by before she replies.

> Lavender: I don't know, but I can't stop thinking about that night.

> Me: Have you been slipping your hand between your legs, little one? Imagining it's me touching you there? Did it feel good to remember my tongue fucking your sweet pussy while any number of strangers watched?

> Lavender: Yes. I've touched myself every night, but it doesn't feel as good.

> Me: Of course it doesn't. You crave something darker, little one. Something you can't find elsewhere. I can do things to your body you could never imagine. Is that what you want? For me to show you how good it can be?

> Lavender: Yes, Sir. I want to learn.

> Me: Then come to the club. I'll teach you to be a good little sub. A dirty girl who isn't afraid to ask for what she wants. Would you like that?

It takes her a while to respond, and I find myself pacing the room again, eager for her reply. It's been a long time since I've felt the thrill of the chase. Subs come and go, and I retain a calm equilibrium, but this woman—she's different.

> Lavender: I would. But I want to stay anonymous. Would that be okay... Sir?

Oh, my girl has some kinks to explore. We can play this game, but eventually, she'll show me her face. I tap out a quick message.

> Me: I'm sure we can come to an agreement. Be at the club next Wednesday night at eight. Ask for access to Room 2. Your instructions and contract will be waiting. What happens from there is up to you.

> Lavender: I have to check my work schedule.

> Me: I won't wait around for you, little one. This is your second chance. There won't be a third.

> Lavender: Understood. What should I wear?

Good girl. Asking questions. Who am I kidding? Saying this is her last chance? This woman has me intrigued, and that is worth its weight in gold. I'd have her come right now and ride her with no apology. The date I set is arbitrary, something to convince myself I wouldn't walk over broken glass for another taste of her cunt.

> Me: It doesn't matter. Whatever you wear will look just as good on the floor of my playroom. Don't be late. Goodnight, little one.

> Lavender: Goodnight, Sir.

I toss the phone down on the bed and move to the chest of drawers, pulling out my standard contract for subs in training. There are some changes necessary, and I want to be prepared. My room has been restocked for a new submissive, but I have some ideas of additions for my new little Lavender.

When I've written out the requests for my room, I set to work on adjusting the contract. I plan to take it slow with this one. Three months won't be enough to train her. Most subs I train have at least some experience, but from the way she reacted to me, she has no idea what she wants. There are so many kinks to explore for her, and I'm going to show her every last one, loving every fucking minute of her pleasure.

~

"Time." I've been on my feet for God knows how long.

"Eleven hours and sixteen minutes, Dr. Harrison."

As I prepare to close, I heave a sigh of relief, thanking everyone for their hard work and dedication today. They've all been on their feet as long as I have, helping and monitoring in a collective effort to save this patient's life.

When I place the final stitch, a wave of satisfaction washes over me. It's the privilege of my job. It is so much more than a paycheck to me.

"Great work, everyone."

Another day done and closer to the beginning of a blissful six months of training. When I get home, I practically fall into the shower, letting the steaming hot water pummel my shoulders. Eleven hours of surgery take their toll on the body. Bracing my hands on the wall, I let the day's stress wash away. I've not had the release of a good sub over the past few weeks, and I'm feeling it.

I don't know how long I stand under the spray, but by the time I step out of the shower, the pads of my fingers have begun to prune. Wrapping a towel around my waist, I grab my phone off the counter to find a new message.

> Lavender: Will you be wearing a mask?

A smile tugs at the corner of my lips. My girl is thinking about me, her anticipation building with every passing day, just the way I want.

> Me: Is that what you want, little one?

> Lavender: To begin with. Is that okay?

> Me: For now. But there will come a time when you'll beg to see my face as I fuck you.

> Me: Now go to bed and think of me as you caress your slick cunt.

> Lavender: Yes, Sir.

God, I can't wait to hear her call me Sir again. So innocent but desperate to be wicked. If that's what my little one wants, then that's what she'll get. Only two days until she's mine. Two days until I bury my face between those pretty little thighs once more.

Chapter 4

FREYA

He's all I think about, night and day. I dream of him, counting the minutes until I meet him at the club. It's wrong on so many levels—wanting to have sex with someone whose face I've never seen. A stranger who kissed my most intimate flesh like it was his own personal feast and gave me the best orgasm of my life.

"Are you sure about this?" Celest asks as we wait for our coffee orders. "You don't even know his name."

"That's part of the excitement."

"I can find out which Dom it is. It wouldn't be that difficult. The head of security, Flex, will know. Just to make sure he's a good guy." She's right. I probably should know his name, but every time I think about the fact that he's a total stranger, heat pools deep in my core, making my panties wet with anticipation.

"I'm not even sure if I'll go."

"Bullshit. It's written all over your face. You're usually so…"

"Boring. Predictable. Safe."

There's a hint of pity in her eyes. "Not at all. You're amazing, smart, and completely kickass. I just worry that you're jumping the gun with this, and you have no idea what you are getting yourself into."

"I need something more."

"How do you know that, Freya? Why not dip your toe in before you dive off the highest springboard headfirst?"

"I can't explain it. I just… know."

"Okay, then I'll be as supportive as I can. How does that look at the club? Am I allowed to be your friend there, or does the mask apply outside the private room?"

"I…" Shit. I didn't think this through. Having Celest there would give me away almost immediately. I don't want anyone to know who I am, and I do not want to know the identity of my Dom. The plan is to learn, not socialize. I don't need a boyfriend. I want a man to teach me about BDSM and myself.

"Yeah, see the gaping hole in your idea now?"

"I won't be anywhere other than the Dom's private room. In and out. I won't be sitting at the bar making small talk with people."

"But you should. What better way to learn about BDSM than to make some friends? There is so much more to it. So many fun kinks to discover and explore."

"I know. That's why I want a man who can help me figure out my kinks, but I'm not ready to be known. You must understand my reluctance."

"Not really. Venom is an elite club with NDAs signed by everyone who walks through the door. Staff and patrons included. It's a safe space to express your wildest desires, Freya."

"That's great, and maybe somewhere down the line, I will take full advantage of it, but for now, I want to remain anonymous."

Celest shrugs, rolling her eyes as she grabs our coffees, and we head out for a walk around Central Park. The weather is beautiful this time of year, and the city is full of possibilities. A thrill courses through me as we leisurely stroll past other people enjoying their day. He could be anyone. We might have been in the same place at the same time in the past few weeks and been none the wiser.

There's something so naughty about it, and I love it.

When I'm done with my coffee, I discard the cup in the nearest trashcan and pull my phone from my pocket, typing out a quick message as Celest talks about her plans for the weekend.

> Me: Hello, Sir. I was just thinking about you.

I'm not expecting those three little dots to appear so quickly, my heart skipping a beat. I saved his number with a contact name that excites me.

> Sir: Is that right? Exactly what were you thinking, little one?

> Me: How you could be anyone. That we might have walked past each other on the streets of Manhattan or admired the same flowers in Central Park.

> Sir: Does it make you wet thinking that you don't even know what I look like? That I've tasted your arousal as you bucked against my face?

> Me: Yes.

My sex responds to his words, the memory of his warm, sexy voice coaxing me to orgasm that night.

> Sir: Have you forgotten your manners already?

> Me: No, Sir.

Why does it turn me on to have a stranger demand I call him Sir?

> Sir: I want you to take your panties off and keep them in your pocket for the rest of the day, little one.

> Me: I can't. I'm not at my apartment. I'm out in public, Sir.

> Sir: There would be no fun in it if you were at home. Are you wearing a skirt?

Me: Yes, Sir.

Sir: Then be a good girl and find somewhere to. Take. Them. Off.

I feel my cheeks flush as I read his text, a tingling warmth spreading throughout my body.

"Are you even listening to me?" Celest interjects.

"Sorry, what?"

"Who are you texting? Is it him?"

I'm suddenly shy. "Maybe."

"You're blushing. Are you sexting?" She reaches for my phone, but I slide it back in my purse.

"No."

"Then why do you look guilty as hell right now?"

"He… he asked me to do something for him, but I can't."

"Tell me."

I pull in a ragged breath, so turned on I can barely control the rise and fall of my chest. "He asked me to take off my panties. But I can't. We're in a public place. One wrong gust of wind and I'd be showing my sex to all of Manhattan."

"First of all, you have to stop calling it your *sex*. You can say pussy. It's hot. And you can absolutely take them off. Just run behind that tree and do it. It'll only take a second. The thrill is in the fact that you could get caught. The breeze will feel so good, Freya. Trust me."

We are not having this conversation right now. "You've done it before?"

"Of course. Nothing builds anticipation like a little pre-scene fun."

"Is that what he's doing? A scene."

"I don't know, but I wouldn't keep him waiting."

"I can't."

"Yes, you can. I'll keep watch." We find a quiet spot in the trees, adrenaline pumping in my veins as I slip my hands up under my skirt and pull my panties down my legs. I scrunch them in my

40

hands and snap a picture on my phone before slipping them in my purse.

When I emerge sans panties, Celest pins me with a wickedly sexy grin. "Doesn't that feel better?"

The breeze kisses my skin, a jolt of desire going straight to my core. "I feel…"

"Naughty."

"Yeah, and I kind of love it."

She links her arm with mine, but I quickly pull it free when my phone buzzes. I have messages from *him*.

> Sir: Have you done it yet?
>
> Sir: I don't like waiting, little one. If I message you, I expect a response, especially when I've given you an order.

> Me: I'm sorry, Sir, I was talking with a friend.

I select the photograph of my panties in my hand and press send.

> Sir: Good girl. I see you're outside. Every time the breeze caresses your cunt, I want you to imagine what I'm going to do to you. Text me when you get home.

> Me: Yes, Sir.

"What did he say?"

"That I should imagine what he's going to do to my… *cunt* the next time he sees me."

I blush at the use of the word. I've never been good at cussing, and I've never referred to my sex as anything vulgar before. Except that it doesn't feel vulgar when he says it. I like it when he says it. So possessive, raw, and masculine.

"Girl, you are in for a treat. I want all the details after you've been to his playroom."

"I'm nervous." I would only admit that to Celest.

"Don't be," she says as she loops her arm with mine once more. "You're going to have a night to remember. Just don't overthink it, Freya. You are in complete control, and he will do *anything* to please you. It's a feeling like no other."

We spend an hour enjoying a stroll through Strawberry Fields and Poet's Walk before I have to leave.

"As much as I'd love to stay, I need to go into work for a few hours. My boss was riding me about paperwork, and I have a few things to finish up that I didn't get to last night. It was a busy day."

"So, you're working even on your days off? That's such bullshit!"

"It's par for the course. I knew it would never be a strict nine-to-five job. Anyway, I'm more concerned that I have to go in there with no underwear on."

Celest wiggles her eyebrows suggestively. "Maybe you should show your boss, and he could *ride you* about something else."

"And I just threw up a little in my mouth. Thanks for that, Cel. I'll see you on Sunday." I give her a quick peck on the cheek and make my way out of the park and through the bustling streets, my body in a permanent state of arousal with every step.

Thankfully, my afternoon goes by quickly as I get my notes written up and check my schedule for the rest of the week. Just as I'm about to leave, my boss appears in the doorway.

"Are you up to date with everything?"

"Yes. Just finished. Is there anything else you need, sir?" He smirks as I hand him the files.

"I need you to stay on top of this in the future. I don't have time to baby you. This is important work. I expect excellence because I won't waste time on anyone who cannot meet my standards. Am I wasting my time with you?"

"No, sir. It won't happen again."

He eyes me warily. "We'll see. I have an interesting case tomorrow. Read up on it tonight and present first thing. If I'm satisfied, you can assist." He drops the file down on the desk.

"Thank you, sir. I will do my due diligence. You won't be disappointed."

He disappears without another word. In fact, this might be the longest conversation we've ever had. My boss is a man of few words, and he chooses them carefully for maximum impact. I guess I have some studying to do tonight, but first, I have a man I do want to talk to. One that has been on my mind all afternoon as I sat with my sex naked under my skirt. At times, I found myself opening my legs, feeling dirty even though no one was around to see.

I wanted to touch myself, to alleviate the ache between my thighs, but I didn't. I couldn't. Not in public. My thoughts go back to that night and the two-way mirror, wondering if anyone could see me. He was careful to shield me from view, but when I stood there and watched him pleasure himself, I didn't care if someone had seen him pleasure me.

When I get home, the first thing I do is pull my phone—and panties—out of my purse and type a message to the man who consumes my thoughts.

> Me: I'm home.

> Sir: Hello, little one. How was the rest of your day? Were you a good girl and kept your panties off?

> Me: Yes, Sir.

> Sir: Mmm, just the thought of your pretty little cunt makes me hard. Tell me, how did you feel?

> Me: Dirty.

> Sir: And did you like being my dirty girl?

> Me: I did like it. I thought about you all afternoon.

Should I tell him?

> Sir: I was thinking about you too. How wet I knew you would be. I think you enjoyed being naked beneath your skirt.

> Me: I did.

I want him to know.

> Me: I spread my legs at my desk.

> Sir: Spreading your legs like a filthy little sub. Tell me, did you touch yourself?

A thrill courses through me that he thinks I'm dirty.

> Me: No, Sir.

> Sir: Are you sure you haven't done any training as a submissive?

> Me: None. I have no experience, but I'm hoping you will help me fix that.

> Sir: Oh, I will, little one. You must be frustrated.

> Me: Yes, Sir.

> Sir: I'll make an exception this once. Usually, I wouldn't let you touch what's mine, but you were such a good girl today. You should be rewarded for spreading those beautiful legs of yours. I want you to go and lie on your bed. Hitch up your skirt and tell me when you've done it.

My pulse is racing as I walk to the bedroom, my breathing shallow as I crawl onto the bed and pull my skirt up to my waist. I've done this so many times before, yet it feels brand new, as if he's in the room with me.

> Me: I'm on the bed.

> Sir: Good girl. Now, spread your legs as wide as they'll go, the way you did for me at the club.

Me: Done.

Sir: Slide your hand down your body until you reach that perfect pussy. Tell me how it feels.

I do as he asks, about ready to detonate when my fingers make contact with my sex.

Me: It's warm and wet.

Sir: Of course it is. Your cunt is ready for me, even now. Be a good girl and push one finger inside, then put it up to your mouth and taste how fucking sweet you are.

My cheeks blush as I do exactly that, my sex clenching around my finger, making it slick with arousal. I've never tasted myself before, and it feels forbidden.

Me: What next?

Sir: How do you taste?

Me: Like honey, but almost metallic on my tongue.

Sir: Your cunt tastes divine, little one. I'm looking forward to feasting on you again. Now, insert two fingers, making sure you coat them well before slipping up to your clit. Soft circles. Lazy. Like you have all the time in the world to enjoy every fucking ounce of pleasure.

Me: I wish it were your hand.

Sir: It'll be my cock soon enough.

I can't contain the groan of delight and anticipation. I want to know what it feels like to have him grinding his hips into me, filling me with that beautiful cock. I've dreamed of it every night since I watched him jerk off at the club. My phone buzzes at my side, and I grab it one-handed, desperate for more of him.

> Sir: That's it, little one. It's my hand caressing your clit, pushing you closer to the edge.

> Sir: Feel how wet you are for me. Imagine the head of my cock pressing into you. You'll take every hard inch like a good little girl, won't you?

> Me: Yes, Sir. I'm so close.

> Sir: Open the voice recorder on your phone. I want to hear you come for me, little one.

I do as he asks, my hand trembling as I drop my phone on the bed, my entire body undulating as I circle my clit, the bed wet with my cum as I crash over the edge, moaning for him, wishing he was here with me. Touching me. Driving me wild.

"Yes… oh God, yes… Sir… you feel so good, *Daddy*… yes!"

It takes me a couple of minutes to compose myself, riding out the aftershocks before grabbing my phone. I can't send this to him, especially not the end. I don't know why I said that. It's so wrong.

> Sir: I'm waiting. Send it to me now. It's not a request. I'd hate to have to punish you on your first night as my submissive in training.

My sex pulses at his words. How does he know what I'm thinking? I open the voice memo, listening back to me screaming for him. I crop it before I said *it*. I can't believe I'm doing this. Sending him the sound of me coming. I've never made myself come this hard before, a sheen of sweat covering my body. Once I've sent it, I head for the bathroom and fill the tub, adding a generous amount of bubbles.

He doesn't answer right away, leaving me embarrassed, wondering if he didn't enjoy what he heard. Maybe real submissives are better at this. I never question myself in any other aspect of my life, but this—sex—I have trouble being confident.

I'm submerged in the tub, my hand drifting between my legs once more when my phone vibrates, pulling me out of a pleasure haze. I nervously open his message.

> Sir: You are not to touch yourself again unless I say so. Understood?

> Me: Yes, Sir.

When he doesn't elaborate, I start to worry.

> Me: Was I bad?

> Sir: Yes.

My heart drops into my stomach.

> Sir: You altered the recording, didn't you? I know what you sound like when you come, little one. I've been playing it on a loop in my head for weeks. You cut it off before you were done.

> Me: I'm sorry. I was embarrassed.

> Sir: We'll discuss this further at the club.

> Me: Okay.

I sink beneath the surface, hating how vulnerable I am at this moment. I displeased him, and I don't like the way it feels. My phone vibrates.

> Sir: Don't be embarrassed. You never have to feel that way with me. You're fucking resplendent when you come. Your pleasure is mine from here on out. Got it?

> Me: Yes, Sir.

> Sir: Good girl. Now, get some rest. You're going to need it.

> Me: Goodnight.

> Sir: Goodnight, little one.

Resplendent. My heart is full as I clean up and get ready for bed. I'm like a kid at Christmas. Two sleeps left until I'm his.

My hands tremble as I tie my mask in place in the elevator. I bought a new mask in a similar lavender hue as I wore to the masquerade ball. Tonight, I'm wearing a black bodycon dress and my favorite heels, hoping they'll give me the confidence to strut through this club like I belong here.

As the doors ping open to the Venom lobby, my breath catches, anticipation unfurling deep in my core. *I'm going to see him tonight.*

There's a gentleman dressed all in black—some kind of security guard, I guess.

"Hello." I almost squeak.

"Good evening, ma'am." He doesn't seem phased by my mask, and it has me wondering if other people conceal their identity here.

"I wonder if you can help me. I'm supposed to go to room two, but I don't know where that is."

"Follow me." He doesn't crack a smile, and I fall in step behind him, my heart racing when he stops outside a door with a simple gold '2' marked on it. Handing me a key card, he turns on his heel. "Have a pleasant evening."

I stand frozen to the spot, staring down at the matte black card with an embossed 'V' on one side. Taking in a shaky breath, I hold it to the handle, listening to the soft click before pushing my way inside.

He's not here yet. A pang of disappointment hits, but it allows me to take in my surroundings. There's a cross on one side of the room with metal cuffs hanging from each spar. A massive bed sits against the opposite wall, big enough for more than two people. I can't help wondering if he's had more than one person in here at a time. *Will he expect that of me?*

There is a large chest of drawers close to the door, and a bouquet of red roses sit atop it with a note. The sumptuous red matches the décor—decadent and luxurious. I make my way toward it, the penmanship elegant.

Little One

You'll find everything you need on the bed. I left some lingerie for you to wear and instructions on how I want you waiting for me.

I'll give you some time to get ready.

My gaze snaps to the bed. I didn't notice the underwear. It's black, the same color as the bedding. I would describe it as a few scraps of lace—barely enough to cover my breasts and even less to cover my sex. *My pussy.* Celest told me to stop calling it my 'sex.' Apparently, it will give me away as inexperienced.

I place my purse on the nightstand before gripping the hem of my dress and dragging it up my body. I change clothes at the gym in a locker room full of women all the time, and yet stripping for no one in this room has my body vibrating. Dropping my dress to the floor, I slip out of my heels and slide my panties off. I wasn't wearing a bra, so I find myself completely naked, and my pussy is already throbbing with anticipation.

The lingerie fits perfectly, and I take in the sight of myself in an ornate, full-length gilded mirror in one corner. I look—

Reading his instructions has my pulse racing, my eyes shooting to a corner of the room with black ropes hanging from the wall. I make my way over to them, running my fingers over the self-tightening ropes. Facing the wall, I slip my hands through them before lowering my knees to the floor and sitting on my heels.

The loops tighten around my wrists, holding my arms above my head with just enough bite to be uncomfortable. My heart is hammering in my chest as I follow the last of his instructions, dropping my head and lowering my gaze to the floor.

Now, *I wait.*

Chapter 5

PIERCE

The security guard informed me that my little one arrived forty-five minutes ago, right on time. I had him take her directly to my room, bypassing the bar in case she didn't arrive wearing her mask. Taking her request seriously, I want to wait until she's ready to show me her face.

It's taken all of my self-restraint to leave her to explore my room and situate herself. We have so much to talk through tonight, and I need to keep a clear head. If I had my way, I'd chain her to the wall and devour her cunt for hours, but if she's to be my submissive in training, we have to set the ground rules. Tonight will be a testament to self-control.

Downing the last of my drink, I reach into my pocket as I navigate through the bar, stopping outside the door to my private room. When I've secured my mask in place, I hold my key card to the door handle, take a deep breath, and enter.

Holy fuck.

I've imagined this moment since that night in the voyeur hall, but she is even more breathtaking. Her ass is fucking perfect as she sits on her heels, unable to see me with her head down and arms roped above her head.

My cock stirs in my pants, already getting hard at the sight of her, waiting and ready for me. She flinches as the door clicks shut, and I flip the lock. I loosen my tie before discarding it on the chest of drawers and roll up the sleeves of my crisp white shirt. The rapid rise and fall of my chest betray my usually calm, collected nature when I'm in this room. It's something akin to nerves, and I'm not accustomed to it.

She looks edible, and all I can see is her back, the scrap of the lace thong I had her put on, highlighting her cheeks to perfection. Walking toward her, I hear her sharp intake of breath as I get closer until I'm standing at her back.

Reaching out, I ghost my fingers over her shoulder. "Good evening, little one," I say, caressing her neck before slipping my hand under her chin. "You may look at me." I force her head back to look up at me.

"Good evening, Sir." Her voice is dreamlike as if she's in a haze from waiting patiently. She's drunk on submission, and it's so fucking beautiful. She licks her lips, her eyes dropping to my mouth.

"Do you have any idea how stunning you are?" She tries to look away, but I keep a firm grip on her chin and dip my head down to kiss her forehead. "Don't be shy, little one. Not in here and not with me."

"Yes, Sir."

"You follow instructions well."

"Thank you."

"In the future, this is how you will wait for me in this room." She gives a small nod as I let go of her chin. "Do you enjoy this position?"

"Yes, Sir. I want to please you." I have to stop from groaning at her words.

"Should I check if it aroused you, little one?"

"Yes, please."

Kneeling behind her, I reach around her waist. "Spread your legs for me like a good girl."

She does as I ask, and I let my hand travel down to the apex of her thighs, my fingers gently caressing what's mine.

The lace is drenched in her arousal. "You're soaked. Did it turn you on to sit and wait for me?"

"Yes, Sir."

I nuzzle her long, elegant neck as I press soft circles against her clit, the lace the only thing that separates us. "Are you going to run away this time?"

"No, Sir," she moans as she tilts her head, giving my lips full access. She smells so fucking good, and it only makes me harder.

"Did you enjoy watching me fist my dick because of you?"

"Yes. I wished I could've been the one to satisfy you."

"You will, little one, but not before we sign a contract." I slip one finger under her lace panties before putting it up to her mouth. "Taste what I do to you."

She licks my finger clean, sucking it into her mouth, teasing me with how good it's going to feel when I slip my dick between her lips and make her take every hard inch. Her soft mewls of pleasure are almost enough to make me abandon my plan for the evening and lose myself in her, but I leave her wanting more as I get to my feet and set about loosening the ropes. Reaching out my hand, I help her into a standing position before taking a moment to admire how she looks in the lingerie I picked out. Her tits are full, heavy, and perfect for fucking.

All in good time.

I lead her over to the bed and sit down, gesturing for her to sit in my lap which she does with such ease as if she's done it a thousand times before.

"Before we go any further, we need to discuss the rules. Have you done any research on Dominant/submissive agreements?"

"Yes, Sir, but I thought we were going to… be physical tonight." There's such hesitation in her voice. She's too bashful to ask for what she wants.

"You mean you thought I would fuck you?" She shivers, unable to meet my gaze.

She nods, her eyes fixed on the floor.

"If you can't voice what you want from me, this won't work."

"I'm embarrassed. I've never done anything like this before."

"That's okay. I'm a submissive trainer, little one. Do you want me to teach you how to ask for what you want?"

"Yes, Sir."

I rest my hand on the small of her back, loving how she relaxes into my touch, nestling her head against my chest.

"Okay then, I want you kneeling before me. Now."

She does it without hesitation, and as she looks up at me through hooded lashes, her face obscured by a lavender mask, I find myself aching to kiss her pretty pink lips.

I have a file on the bed with all of the relevant information we need to get started.

"Good girl. You look beautiful on your knees."

She wets her bottom lip before biting down on it. She's gorgeous, and I haven't even seen her full face.

"I want you to answer my questions honestly so that I know how best to train you. Understood?"

"Yes, Sir."

"Then we'll begin." I open the file of papers and start at the beginning.

"I have a questionnaire here. Some basic information I require. You can leave your name blank... for now. I would usually create a three-month agreement with a prospective submissive, but I get the feeling I am your first foray into the lifestyle. Am I right?"

"Yes, Sir. I have no experience." A wave of pride rushes through me at the knowledge. I'll be the one to find every last one of her kinks.

"I am proposing that we have a six-month contract. You need time to explore your likes and dislikes. Your soft and hard limits. I will be your safety net. Put your trust in me, and I'll help you become the submissive you crave to be." My pulse is racing as I put forward my desire for more time. This is a first for me, but I already know three months won't be long enough.

"I'd like that."

"Here." I hand her the first sheet of paper. "You will take this home, take your time to read it over, and complete it to the best of your ability. This first page is standard."

I watch as her eyes go wide as saucers when she starts reading.

"Sexual history, birth control, STI testing. They are all items that need to be discussed prior to any physical contact."

Her shoulders slump. My girl is disappointed. "We've already had physical contact." Her voice is barely above a whisper.

"That was an error on my part. Parties don't generally require contracts. I got carried away. I apologize, especially given your inexperience."

"I liked it." Her shy smile cracks me wide open.

"So did I. That's why I want to make sure you feel comfortable every step of the way."

As I hand over the next page, I'm hesitant. I don't want to overwhelm her.

"This is a list of possible activities... preferences. It's not an exhaustive list, so if there is anything you would like to try, just add it at the bottom. You can have as many or as few as you choose."

I hand over the next sheet. "This page is meant to ascertain what you *do not* want to do. They are generally categorized as soft and hard limits."

"What is the difference? How will I know which is which?"

"Soft limits are things you don't necessarily want to try but would trust me to show you if I think you will like it. Hard limits are activities that you will not participate in at all. As your Dominant, I will never cross that line or force you to do anything you explicitly tell me not to."

"Okay."

"This is a lot of information, little one."

"Yes, Sir." God, I want to kiss her.

"That's why I want you to take it home and consider it well before we move forward. Shall I continue?"

"Yes." The way her eyes sparkle through her mask—so innocent and wicked in equal measure.

"This..." I say, handing her the final paperwork, "... is the legal contract. It's standard practice, but if you want to keep your anonymity, I can have a lawyer look at it and tell us how to proceed."

"Is it necessary to have a legal contract? I... trust you."

Fuck me. She undoes me, and I lean down, capturing her lips with mine in a long, sensual kiss. I would never consider proceeding without a binding contract, but with her, I find myself breaking the rules before we've even started.

"Let me speak with the lawyer, and we can discuss it further."

Reaching into my pocket. I pull out a phone and hand it to her. "This is the phone you will use to contact me from this point on. I don't want it used to speak with anyone else. Understood?"

"Yes, Sir. Can I ask why?"

"You can, and thank you for addressing me correctly. You're doing so well, little one." Her cheeks blush as I praise her, and she shifts on her heels, squirming as she patiently waits. "I have set up the Venom portal on this phone. Once you have read up on everything I'm sending you away with tonight, you can input as much information into your profile... the one you set up for the masquerade ball. I also had them create an email address for you. Anything to do with our relationship as trainer and trainee will be sent to this address. I also took the liberty of having the head of security ensure you can send anything I may ask of you, and it will be completely secure. As much as I enjoyed the voice memo you cut short, I wouldn't want it to fall into the wrong hands."

"What kind of things might you ask of me?"

"It would spoil the fun if I told you ahead of time," I say with a conspiratorial wink. "Just know that I wouldn't ask if I weren't certain that the phone is secure."

"Okay." She sits quietly with it in her lap, so fucking beautiful I physically ache to be inside her.

"Good. You've done well tonight, little one. I saw that you arrived on time and executed my requests perfectly. You will come to understand how spectacular you are to me when you submit. You were a vision in the rope restraints."

"Thank you, Sir."

"If you choose to proceed, I have linked our calendars so we can create a schedule that works for us. I have so much to teach you, little one."

"I'm eager to learn." Her voice is like silk, tantalizing my senses.

"Do you have any questions for me before we adjourn for the evening?"

With her eyes on the floor, she tucks a loose tendril of hair behind her ear. "Will you... touch me tonight?"

"As much as I want to, I need you to look over all of this information and really think about whether or not this is what you want."

The look of disappointment in her eyes fucking breaks me. Submissives have always existed to please me, yet I find myself wanting to please her, even though I don't know her name.

"Give me your hand." She sets the phone on the floor and holds out her right hand for me. I slide it onto my crotch. "Do you feel what you do to me, little one?"

A soft smile creeps at the edges of her mouth. "Can I make you feel good?" Jesus, she's making this difficult.

"I'm not going to make you come tonight, little one. You misbehaved when you cut the audio of your orgasm short. Why did you do that?"

"I listened to it afterward. I was embarrassed. I said something I shouldn't have."

"That's not your decision to make. Not if you're going to be mine. I want to hear you scream for me, and you need to be confident in your effect on me. Your pleasure isn't something to be shy or ashamed of. When you're here with me, nothing is off-limits."

"Yes, Sir. I understand that I can't come, but I would like... I mean if you wanted me to..."

"Spit it out, little one. Tell me what you want and say it with conviction."

"I..." she hesitates. I grab her chin, forcing her to meet my gaze.

"*Say it.* I know what you want, but I want to hear you. Say. It."

"I want to taste you."

"Say please."

"Please, Sir. Can I taste you the way you tasted me? I've imagined your cock in my mouth since I watched you pleasure yourself that night." My breath catches, a lightning bolt of desire striking me where I sit. Fuck me, she knows how to make me want her.

"Unbuckle my belt, unzip my pants, and pull my dick out," I growl like a feral animal. "Then sit back on your heels until I say otherwise."

Her slender fingers make short work of my pants, and the second she slides her hand under the waistband of my underwear, I fucking hiss at how good it feels to have her wrap her fist around my dick. I drop my head back as she lets my erection spring free, and I can barely contain myself when she sits back on her heels like a good little girl, licking her lips as she stares at every rock-hard inch of me, relishing what she does to me.

I slowly unbutton my shirt and discard it on the bed. My little one likes what she sees, her greedy gaze making my dick twitch.

"How much do you want this?" I ask, taking myself in hand, stroking my dick as she watches my every move.

"I dream of your cock, Sir. Your big, beautiful cock. Of how it will feel when you fuck my mouth."

"Open wide, little one." She complies like a perfect submissive. I wrap her long black hair around my fist. "Sit up."

I guide her head to the tip of my dick, holding her gaze as I slip the tip over her lips, my heart pounding as I give her another inch, the warmth of her tongue sliding up the shaft. *Jesus Christ.* It feels too fucking good.

She moves to brace her hands on my thighs, but she won't be setting the pace tonight. "Hands behind your back."

I grip her tight, forcing her to take more of me. Her pretty little mouth won't be able to take all of me, but I push until the crest of my dick hits the back of her throat. She swallows past her gag reflex. "You're a greedy little thing, aren't you?"

She hums as her tongue strokes the length of me before circling the tip. *Holy shit.* My girl is fucking stunning with her lips wrapped around my dick.

"That's it, little one. You feel so fucking good. I can only imagine how much better your cunt will be with my dick filling it."

I circle my hips, keeping a steady rhythm as her wet warmth

drives me to the edge of madness. As my thrusts get harder, I can feel her body tensing.

"Relax your throat. That filthy mouth of yours can take a little more." She's so fucking responsive. "Good girl. Now, spread your legs. I want your cunt slick with arousal and aching the same way I did when you walked out."

Her knees push apart as I continue to hold her head in place, thrusting my dick faster and harder, the beginnings of my release building, my balls tight as I set a punishing rhythm. She's completely at my mercy, and it's a thing of beauty.

"That's it, little one. Keep your eyes on me." It takes every ounce of restraint not to shoot my load and make her swallow like the dirty girl she is, but not tonight. I want to know she's mine when she's lapping up my cum, begging for it.

My hips are bucking off the edge of the bed as desire consumes me. I need to come. She feels so good it hurts, straddling the line between ecstasy and agony as my orgasm starts to pulse the length of me. Pulling out of her mouth, I fist my hand around my soaking wet dick and pump it twice before I come on her chest, mesmerized by the sight of my cum dripping between her tits.

"Fuck... your mouth was made for sin." I draw in a slow, steadying breath as she sits back on her heels.

"Did I please you, Sir?"

"Yes, little one. You've had your taste. Now, stand and take off your panties."

I'm entranced by the rapid rise and fall of her chest as she steps out of the tiny sliver of lace, her cunt on display.

"Give them to me." She bends down, keeping her dirty little eyes on me, biting down on her bottom lip. They are soaked with her arousal, making me groan as I slip them into my pocket.

"What now?"

"Take off the bra. I want to see every inch of your body, knowing I'm going to claim each and every one."

As she stands before me, gloriously naked, I grab her hips and pull her toward me, pressing my lips to her belly button. My hands roam up to her breasts, smearing my cum over her tightly budded nipples, making her moan, leaning into my touch.

"You're so fucking beautiful."

She drops her head back, closing her eyes behind the mask. I want to rip it off and see her face, but I'll give her this small piece of mystique for now. I will see her face when my cock is buried deep inside, thrusting so hard she can't help but scream my name. *My name.*

With my cum coating my hands, she grabs me, pulling my index finger to the edge of her lips, darting her tongue out to taste me. *Holy shit.* She sucks it into her mouth, licking it clean as her eyes hold my gaze. For a woman who says she doesn't have experience with kink, she's a fucking siren.

I watch, enraptured and awestruck.

"That's enough, little one. You can get dressed now." It takes everything in me not to bend her over the bed and fuck her into submission. I'm always so controlled in this room, but she makes me want to toss it aside and lose myself in her for hours.

When she's dressed, her hair is a tangled mess from my fist as I fucked her mouth. I cup her face in my hands, leaning in to brush my lips over hers. "Do your research and contact me when you're sure this is what you want."

My eyes search hers, entreating her to want this—to trust me even though she has no reason to and to want me as much as I want her right now.

"We'll speak soon. You did so well tonight, little one."

"Thank you, Sir."

"I'll have a driver take you home."

"I can walk. I don't want to be any trouble."

"Not if you want to be mine. I won't have you out walking alone at night." A soft smile tugs at the corner of her lips.

"Okay."

I kiss her one last time, knowing I need more and fearing I may never get enough.

Chapter 6

FREYA

Between work and trying to research everything Sir gave me, I'm emotionally and physically spent. I've been slammed at work this week, and when I finally make it home, I can't stop reading and rereading the paperwork. It scares and excites me. Everything I read turns me on with no release. He told me I'm not allowed to pleasure myself, and as much as I want to every time I think of him, I have such a burning desire to please him.

We speak daily on the phone he gave me at the club, and there's something so comforting about his voice. He doesn't push or pressure me, answering any questions without judgment, yet I still haven't put pen to paper.

The moment I step foot inside my apartment, I peel off my clothes and head straight for the shower. It's been a long day. One of those days that you physically need to wash it away before you can relax.

When I'm clean and my hair is towel-dried, I grab a sandwich —the dinner of champions—and reach for my Dom phone. Just thinking it is crazy. Me. *Freya.* I have a phone that's just for a Dominant whose name I don't know and whose face I've never fully seen. As ridiculous as it sounds, I can't help myself. My whole body has pulsed with a low, thrumming arousal since the first time he touched me, his lips brushing mine on the dance floor.

> Me: That's me home for the night. Tucked up in my bed.

He likes to know I'm safe, even though he barely knows me, and I like that someone cares. Manhattan can be a lonely place when all you do is work. I've never had much time for a social life, and until now, it hasn't bothered me. It wasn't until I started looking into the lifestyle that I made the decision to make time for a life, and since meeting Sir, I crave his attention. I shouldn't. I pride myself on not being one of those women who needs a man, but there's something about him.

> Sir: Lucky bed. I'll call you in five. Just finishing up something.

A thrill courses through me. What would it be like to have him in my bed? He doesn't know where I live. We know next to nothing about each other.

When the phone rings, I immediately pick up, and any pretense of being cool, calm, and collected evaporates. I just want to hear his voice.

"Hello, little one." The low rumble sends a shiver down my spine.

"Hello, Sir."

"You were out late tonight."

"I was working. It's been a long, stressful day."

"I'd come and de-stress you, but then I'd have to know some personal details about you."

A pang of fear prickles my skin. "I'm not ready for that."

"Do you have any questions for me tonight? I see you haven't updated the portal yet. What's holding you back, little one?" There's something so genuine in his words. It's how I've always pictured a boyfriend treating me—kind but authoritative. Except he's not my boyfriend and doesn't even know my name.

"Did you speak to your lawyer friend about a contract without names?"

"Yes. You and I can sign separate contracts and have her keep them. She will need your legal name to write it up, and obviously, she already knows mine. You can still shield your face and let me know your name, little one. Or you could show me your face and keep your name hidden. Why are you so afraid for me to know who you are?"

"The things I want you to do to me. Depraved things. The last guy I dated…"

"Let me stop you there for a moment. I'm not like the boys you've been with before. I'm a man who knows what you need. Whatever you desire, I will give you the opportunity to explore in a safe space with me."

"But what if we don't like the same kinks?"

"Let me worry about that, little one. My job is to help you solidify what you do and don't like."

"I'm just a job."

"No. Not at all. I never train people I don't find attractive or have a connection with."

"What happens if I don't sign the paperwork?"

"I really hope that's not what you choose because we can't move forward without it."

"But we've already had some form of intimacy."

"Yes, and that was again a weakness on my part the last time you were here. I'm drawn to you, little one, but as much as you have wants and needs, so do I. I need you to sign the paperwork if I'm to train you properly."

"Six months? That's how long you want me?"

"Yes. I'll make sure you have the best sex of your life, little one. All you have to do is fill out the forms and sign on the dotted line. You can do this. *We* can do this."

"If I complete them tonight, when can I see you next?"

"I've put my schedule on the calendar I created. Check it

tonight and see when you have time. We can take it from there." My heartbeat picks up, galloping to new heights at the thought of seeing him again.

"Okay."

"Say yes, little one. I promise you won't regret it."

"Okay." It's all my brain can manage while enthralled by every word that leaves his lips. The memory of how those lips felt at the apex of my thighs has me panting.

"Is my girl frustrated?"

"Yes, Sir." If he were here with me, the rapid rise and fall of my chest would give me away.

"Tell me, have you been a good girl? I told you not to touch what's mine."

"I've been good, Sir." Just speaking those words to him makes me squirm in my bed. Why do I crave his approval? He would be none the wiser if I slipped my hand between my legs to ease the ache I feel whenever he's on my mind.

"You'll be rewarded the next time you come to my private room."

"Do you usually use the voyeur room?"

"That was the first. It's a new floor of Venom."

"What about..." I stutter over my words.

"Are you asking if people have watched me having sex before?" I don't respond, too nervous to speak. "The answer is yes. I've explored a lot of kink, and I know what I like now."

"Will you expect me to have sex in front of people?" I'm not sure which answer I want him to give.

"That depends on you, little one. If it's a hard limit, then no, I would never ask you to do that. If it's something you want to try, then I'll make it happen."

"Do I have to decide right now?" Butterflies take flight in my stomach, swarming as arousal builds. I look over the papers in my hand, thinking I might let this man do anything he wants to me. That I want him to make the decisions for me because something is holding me back, and I'm certain I am getting in my own way at this point.

"Of course not. First, you need to complete the forms. Then, we take it one lesson at a time. If and when you feel comfortable enough, you can choose where we have sex and who's watching."

Holy Mother of all that is good and pure. I want this man more than my next breath.

"Thank you, Sir."

"It will be my pleasure. We'll talk soon, okay?"

"Yes."

"Goodnight, little one."

"Goodnight, Sir."

My pulse is racing when the call ends, already starved for his attention. I want it all. Setting the papers out in front of me, I start filling them out, one by one.

Sexual History

An STI test is required by both parties prior to any sexual interaction. Please attach results.

Have you previously had an STI? *No*

If yes, please state:

Date of your last period: *12 months ago*

Is there a chance you're pregnant? *No*

Are you currently on birth control? *Yes*

If yes, please state: *Pill*

Further discussion may be required regarding birth control methods approved by both parties.

That one was easy. If there was a box to tick if you're the most basic vanilla bean, it would be me. No pregnancy scares. No orgasms unless they were by my hand. Not even a really great first-date kiss in a long time.

I can only imagine how experienced Sir is if he trains submissives. Would he think twice about teaching me if he knew how woeful my sexual history truly is? An abandoned fumble on prom night that left me somewhat disillusioned with the whole thing, a college date who didn't know his ass from his elbow, and one boyfriend a few years back who wasn't exactly open to ideas.

Sex is such a vulnerable act to share with another person, and when you put your trust in someone like that, it's crushing to be mocked and shamed by the time you hit third base.

I realized pretty soon after that my tastes lie outside the norm, and that's when I started my research. In every other aspect of my life, I'm meticulous to a fault—methodical, rational, and always in control.

With one form complete, I steel myself for the next. This won't be so easy to fill out.

Sexual Preferences

Read the following list and mark as appropriate. This list is not exhaustive and can be added to.

Section 1

French kissing - *Yes*
Vaginal sex - *Yes*
Anal sex - *Maybe*
Oral sex – receiving - *Yes*
Oral sex – performing - *Yes*
Unprotected sex (with BC) - *Maybe*
Anal toys - *Yes*
Vaginal toys - *Yes*
Nipple clamps - *Yes*
Clitoral clamp - *Maybe*
Leg restraints - *Yes*
Wrist restraints - *Yes*
Spreader bars - *Yes*
St. Andrew's Cross - *Yes*
Ball gag - *Maybe*
Mouth ring - *Maybe*
Mask play - *Yes*

Finger play - _Yes_
Fisting - _No_
Blindfold - _Yes_
Sensory deprivation - _Yes_
Shibari - _Yes_
Multiple partners - _Maybe_
Additional male - _Maybe_
Additional female - _Maybe_
Group Sex - _No_
Voyeurism - _Maybe_
Exhibitionism - _Maybe_
Punishment (complete section 2) - _Yes_
Degradation - _Maybe_
Praise - _Yes_
Pet - _Maybe_
Daddy - _Maybe_
Withholding release - _Yes_
Ingestion of body fluids (cum) - _Maybe_
Golden shower - _No_
Wax play - _Yes_
Training demonstrations - _Maybe_
Club V submissive - _Yes_
Bedroom submissive - _Maybe_
24/7 submissive - _Maybe_

Section 2

Cat of nine tails - _Maybe_
Paddle - _Yes_
Cane - _Maybe_
Flogger - _Yes_
Whip - _Maybe_

Additional Information:

_N/A_

. . .

Reading the list has me wet with arousal, moaning as I squeeze my thighs together to try and alleviate the growing ache. I've never even heard of some of these practices. The golden shower was an eye-opener. I can gladly say I *never* want to try it. Sir is sexy as hell, but it turns out I do have a line I won't cross. I hope it's not something he requires of his submissives.

Thinking about him with other submissives causes a knot deep in the pit of my stomach, and I consider the contract. It mentions fidelity of both Dominant and submissive. That means if I give myself over to him for six months, then he's mine and mine alone for that same time.

I move on to the next sheet of paper.

Limits

Safeword: *Lavender*
Safe signal: *clenching her fist three times*
Hard Limits: *fisting, group sex, golden shower*
Soft Limits: *pet*

It's easy enough, assuming the limits can be determined as my training moves forward. Now, onto the contract.

1.Contract

This agreement is entered into as a consensual training contract between _____the Dominant, and _____the submissive, to ensure respect and understanding is observed at all times. The nature of this contract is to provide the submissive with a safe place to train and explore her role as a submissive, under the tutelage of the Dominant. This includes exploration of her sexuality in accordance with the list of hard and soft limits provided, together with a list of sexual preferences. This agreement permits the Dominant to exercise control in a trusting environment with the submissive, allowing him to help ascertain her wants and needs. The submissive's well-being, both in and out of the playroom will be respected at all times. Modifications to this agreement will be permissible if both parties agree. Revised documents would then be provided and signed. Should either party find themselves unfulfilled by this agreement, or they wish to terminate this training agreement for any reason, then either party may do so by written or verbal communication to the other.

The Dominant and submissive will be sexually exclusive to each other for the duration of the training contract unless a third party has been agreed upon by both parties.

Current date: _____

Contract duration: _six months_____ .

2. Limits

The submissive will provide The Dominant with a list of soft and hard limits. The submissive agrees to the use of the safeword _"Lavender"_ and will use it responsibly. In case speech isn't possible during a scene, the safe signal _"clenching her fist three times"_ will be implemented. The Dominant will respond accordingly where a safeword/safe signal is used, and all activity will cease. The Dominant will hold no resentment toward the submissive for enacting her safeword/safe signal, and no punishment shall be administered following the responsible use of the safeword/safe signal.

If a safeword/safe signal is not used, but the Dominant sees signs of distress, training for the evening will cease. The Dominant will then explain his reasoning to the submissive in order that she understands his decision as part of her training.

The Dominant will provide the submissive with a list of soft and hard limits. This is to ensure _both_ parties are comfortable with all activity and are given equal respect.

See attached list of soft/hard limits provided by both parties.

. . .

3. Roles and Responsibilities

The roles and responsibilities of the Dominant and the submissive will be as follows:

The Dominant

The Dominant will always be honest, clear, and concise with the submissive. He will be sensitive to the submissive voicing her opinions and any concerns regarding her training, encouraging her to express her feelings without fear of reproach.

The Dominant hereby commits to undertaking the responsibility to train, discipline, and punish the submissive as he deems appropriate. The Dominant may use the submissive as he sees fit, but only in a healthy, rational state of mind. Punishment will never be administered from a place of anger.

The Dominant will maintain a healthy, positive attitude regarding the submissive's life outside the playroom. He will be open to discussion regarding any concerns in her private life only when requested by the submissive. He will not isolate her from friends and family unless she is in a dangerous situation or has voiced concern.

The Dominant will respect the submissive at all times, unless the terms of this agreement are breeched.

The submissive

The submissive will use a safeword/signal to communicate her boundaries, ensuring they are maintained at all times. (see attached lists of sexual preferences and limits)

The submissive will be honest with the Dominant at all times to ensure he can effectively meet her needs. If the submissive is found to be dishonest, putting her training in jeopardy, the Dominant is within his rights to immediately terminate this agreement without further discussion.

The submissive agrees to trust the Dominant within the bounds of this training agreement, and will obey his rules in accordance with a consensual Dom/sub relationship.

The submissive will respect the Dominant at all times, unless the terms of this agreement are breeched.

. . .

4. Consent Between Both Parties

I, _____, as The Dominant, have read and understood this contract in its entirety. I accept the submissive's submission in a consensual training agreement.

Signed: _____
Date: _____

I, _____, as the submissive, have read and understood this document in its entirety. I agree to submit to The Dominant in a consensual training agreement.

Signed: _____
Date: _____

With everything completed and signed, I move on to entering all of the relevant information into my Club V profile. When I'm done, I type out a quick message.

> Me: I've completed everything, Sir.

It's a few minutes before he answers.

> Sir: Good girl. And naughty girl. You're supposed to be sleeping.

> Me: I'm sure you'll find a way to punish me the next time we meet.

> Sir: You can count on it. Tomorrow, I'll send you my profile so you can get acquainted with my preferences and limits. Should you have any questions, message me. Once you have all the necessary information, you can set a date for our next meeting, little one.

> Me: Can't you send it now?

> **Sir:** Patience is a virtue. You'll learn. Go to sleep.

> **Me:** Ugh. Fine. Goodnight, Sir.

> **Sir:** Goodnight, little one. Dream of me.

My heart takes flight at his tender words. Can I dream of a man I've never seen? Maybe he *is* my dream *because* I have never seen his face. As I burrow beneath the blankets, arousal gives way to something much more sinister—something akin to affection. I fall into a fitful sleep, plagued by a knight in shining armor, unafraid to wield his sword and have me beg on bended knee. He wears a mask, and yet I know it's *him*.

Sir's profile was enlightening. He has a wide variety of tastes. Some I'm hesitant to learn, and others I will gladly and whole-heartedly submit to. We've set a time for our next date. That sounds so pedestrian. It's not like we're grabbing dinner and a movie. We are going to perform explicit, kinky acts on one another, with me submitting to his every whim.

My day has been grueling, to say the least. I'm overworked, underpaid for the hours I put in, and most definitely underappreciated by my boss. He has this way of talking that makes me feel one inch tall sometimes. Today was one of those days. I missed something, and I knew as soon as it happened. It was fixed in a matter of seconds, but he chewed me out in front of my coworkers, and I hated every second of it. I'm counting the days until I can leave and work somewhere else.

All that gets me through the day is knowing I'll speak to Sir before I go to bed. He's seen my profile by now, and I hope he's pleased with what I've written. There's a part of me that worries he'll judge me for the acts I want to try, and maybe he won't want me after reading it. I know that's ridiculous—he's a Dom. He wants to participate in this with me. To teach me how to please him.

I'm lost in thought as I grab my jacket and purse to head home, only to find one of my colleagues staring at me. "What? Do I have something on my face?" I swipe at my cheeks.

"No," he says with a voice so smooth it should be illegal. "You seem different lately."

"Do I? Nothing has changed. Work, rinse, repeat. You know the drill."

He crosses his arms, eyeing me with a stare that makes me uncomfortable. Is it written on my forehead? *Kinky slut.*

"I don't believe you. You're getting laid. I can tell. You have that pep in your step."

He and I have been friends for a while, and he's always on me to date more, but I don't want to share Sir with him or anyone else.

Schooling my face, I try to play it off as nothing. "I think you need some vacation time. You're clearly so overworked you're delusional."

"Deny it all you want, but I'll get it out of you eventually."

"Good luck with that." I head for the door, hoping I'm not blushing at the thought of Sir. "I'll see you tomorrow."

"Bright and early, Freya. Don't stay up too late riding the D train."

"I feel bad for you. I hope you have the good sense to be embarrassed about that last statement."

"Not my finest hour."

"Goodnight, Shane."

The moment I hit the street, I reach for my phone.

> Me: Hello, Sir.

As I walk the couple of blocks to the subway, every step is heavier than the last. I don't remember the last time I got a full night's sleep. I work, and I wait. Wait for the next time Sir and I will be together in his playroom.

> Sir: Hello, little one.

Chapter 7

PIERCE

"What are you going to do about it, you little shit?"

I wake in a cold sweat, thrashing against my inner demons, tangled in the sheets as I fight the invisible memories of my father. My heart is hammering in my chest, my pulse racing as a spike of adrenaline courses through every cell in my body.

"Fuck." I fell into bed tonight after a long day at the hospital. It wasn't that I had challenging surgeries, but sometimes a case comes in that hits a little close to home. An emergency patient landed in my operating room today—she'd been beaten to within an inch of her life, her body covered in defensive wounds. She had blunt-force trauma to the head and suffered a brain bleed. It was touch and go for a while, but my team and I managed to save her life.

The police were eager to get a statement, having taken her asshole husband into custody. He was found at the scene just before finishing the job. Thankfully, a neighbor heard the commotion and called 911. Another five minutes and she'd have died in the ambulance.

Domestic violence cases always burrow their way under my skin, but it's been a while since I've taken it this hard. It took me decades to get past frequent nightmares as a kid. My mom never really acknowledged the fact that I rarely had a night of uninterrupted sleep. She was too busy drinking to curb *her* nightmares.

I know I'm not going to get any more meaningful sleep tonight, needing an outlet for the adrenaline, my muscles vibrating with the necessity to move. When I look at the clock, I pull in a deep, steadying breath. It's two a.m. This is the reason I put a home gym in my apartment. It helps when my body is fighting against the memories of my four-year-old self.

Shrugging into a pair of gray sweats, I pad down the hall to the kitchen, grabbing a bottle of water before heading for the gym. I'm hoping thirty minutes on the rowing machine might tire me out, but I won't hold my breath.

My dream plays on a loop—the last memory of my father. He wasn't the only one who died that day. Something in my mother broke beyond repair. Looking back, I think I believed that once my dad was gone, my mom and I would have a better life. How fucked up is that? To think as a fucking child that life without my dad was going to be a nicer experience.

No matter how much I push myself, my mind can't shut off. The sound of bone cracking as my mom hit him over the head. The way my tiny body ached, like an agonizing pulse ran through every muscle. Then it all went black, and that was the last time the mother I knew held me in her arms.

I think she resented me for forcing her hand. She loved my father, even when he hurt us. It was impossible for her to walk away, but in the end, she knew she had to protect me. That doesn't mean she didn't hate me a little for being the reason she took a life—the life of the man she loved.

When I'm dripping with sweat, my hair plastered to my forehead, I give up trying to tire myself out and decide to take a shower.

As I wander through my apartment, I stop at the floor-to-ceiling windows in the living room, watching the city that never sleeps, wondering where my masked submissive is and *who* she is. She'll be sound asleep somewhere, alone in her bed, her face uncovered.

Once I've settled on the couch, I pull up the Venom portal on my phone and look over her completed profile. I can't wait to get her back in the playroom. There is so much I want to teach her and so many scenarios to explore. I click the message icon in the portal and type out a quick text. I don't want to disturb her by texting her phone. She'll see a Venom message in the morning.

> Me: Hi, little one. I can't wait to get you in my private room this week. Now that I know what you do and don't want to try, we can really have some fun. I couldn't sleep, and I'm thinking of you. Talk later. Your Dom.

Within minutes, my phone rings. It's her.

"Hello, little one. I wasn't expecting you to be awake. Sorry if I disturbed you."

"I'm wide awake. Why aren't you asleep, Sir?"

I consider my answer, not wanting to show any sign of weakness. "I'm a night owl, always working."

"Me too."

"Good to know. Maybe the next time we can't sleep, we can spend some time at the club. I have a bed that's meant for anything *but* sleep."

"I remember it well. The last time I saw it, I had your..." She hesitates.

"My dick in your mouth. You can say it, little one."

"I'm shy when it comes to stuff like this. That sounds ridiculous, considering I don't know your name, and I'm talking about giving you a blow job." There's something so sweet in her admission.

"I like that you're shy. Although, you didn't seem so bashful when I had my head between your legs and a group of people on the other side of a mirror watching you."

"I'm so embarrassed." I can just imagine her cheeks blushing and wonder what her face looks like without that mask.

"Don't be. Everyone has a kink or two. Some of us just have more than others."

"Do you really believe *everyone* has a kink? Maybe some people are basic vanilla."

"You're not."

"No, I'm not, and I don't know how to feel about it." I hate that she's torn between meeting society's idea of 'normal' and choosing what makes her happy.

"Well, how did you feel that night? Letting a veritable stranger kiss you there."

"I loved it. I don't know how to explain it. I know I shouldn't want to do stuff like that, but…"

"Who says you're not allowed to want kink?"

"People." Her voice becomes small.

"Boyfriends?" The thought makes my jaw tense. How any man could deny her whatever she wants is beyond me. One fool's error is my gain.

"Yes." The line goes quiet.

"Current or ex?" I didn't think to ask when we first met. I'm ninety-nine percent sure I know the answer, but just to be on the safe side.

"Ex. I'm not seeing anyone. I haven't in a long time."

"I am glad I'm not stealing you from another man. Don't get me wrong, I still fucking would, but I'll sleep easier knowing you're mine."

I hear her breath catch, and it's so goddamn satisfying.

"Is that what I am now that I've signed the contract? I'm yours."

"Yes, little one. You're mine now."

"Feminists are spinning in their graves right now," she says with a nervous giggle.

"Does it bother you?"

"No, but I feel like it should. Women have fought tooth and nail to have the same rights as men. To be independent. And here I am *wanting* to hand over my autonomy to a man I don't even know. It seems wrong, yet I want to submit to you with every fiber of my being. What does that say about me?"

"It tells me you are truly an independent, powerful woman."

"Really?"

"Submission isn't about giving away part of yourself, little one. You'll come to learn that it takes strength to ask for what you want and be confident with it. As a submissive, you have complete control when you're in my private room."

"Other people won't see it that way."

"Who gives a fuck what anyone else thinks? All that matters is how you feel about it. If you don't enjoy your training, at least you'll walk away from this experience knowing you were brave enough to explore your sexuality. Do you have any idea how many women crave what you're asking of me but are too scared to try? When I read through your paperwork, I was so fucking proud of you, little one."

"Proud... of me?"

"Yes. You're mine now, and if I teach you nothing else in the next six months, I will teach you to be confident in your sexual desires."

"I want that. With you."

"Do you understand I will need to know what you look like at some point? That I want to know whose name to fucking growl when I come inside you."

She doesn't say anything for the longest time, and I wonder if I went too far.

"Yes, Sir. I just feel like my anonymity makes asking for what I want a little easier."

"I understand, but when I deem it to be the right time in your training, I expect you to comply."

"I will do my best, Sir."

"Good girl. I appreciate your honesty. Never promise anything you feel you may not be able to fulfill."

"Sir, why do you want to train me? Why reach out to *me* in the middle of the night?"

"I want to train you because I see your potential. You will be a breathtaking submissive, little one. I've taught enough women to know. I didn't even need to see your face to be completely in awe of your beauty at the masquerade. As for contacting you at this hour, I enjoy our chats. Is it so difficult to believe that I could be attracted to more than your body?"

"Yes." Her response cuts like a knife.

"Who hurt you, little one?" I clench my jaw as my body stiffens.

"How do you know that?"

"Because a woman like you doesn't have such a lack of self-awareness in your sexuality and sensuality unless someone has told you it's wrong."

"I shouldn't let it get to me. I hate that it still affects me years later."

"Never berate yourself for how you feel. There is no set way to deal with your emotions."

"Thank you."

"For what?"

"For understanding me in a way no one else does." My heart grinds to a halt, knowing how difficult it is to exist in a world where it feels as if no one understands you. Until I found the lifestyle, I was truly alone. It's a hard place to be.

"We've only scratched the surface. I want to know everything about you, little one."

"Difficult when you don't know my name."

"I plan to remedy that as soon as possible. Tell me something, anything about you."

She considers my request for a moment. "I like to help people."

"Go on…"

"My favorite color is pink. A cliché, I know, but I'm a girly girl. What's your favorite color?"

"I recently became fond of lavender."

"Smooth talker."

"I try my best."

"Do you have any hobbies?" I wasn't expecting her to show interest in my personal life.

"I enjoy painting, though I don't have much time for it these days. Work takes up ninety percent of my time, and the other ten I plan to spend lost in you."

"My job is demanding too. It's hard to have a social life. I find that friends don't understand, so they stop asking me to hang out."

"Their loss."

"What about you? Do you have time for friends?"

"All of my friends frequent Venom, so I see them as often as work allows. Anyway, let's get back to you. What do you do for a living?"

She hesitates, deciding how much to share with me.

"Too personal."

"You're a funny little thing. I plan to make every last one of your sexual fantasies come to life, and yet your career choice is too personal?"

"I'm scared." I can just imagine her chewing on her sumptuous bottom lip.

"Of what?"

"That I won't be able to go through with this if I know too much. Or if you know too much about me. I've been judged for not being normal in the past."

"You don't have to explain your reasons, little one. We'll go slow, and when I think you're ready, we can learn more about each other."

She heaves an audible sigh of relief. "Thank you, Sir. Did you see my updates on the calendar?"

"I'm looking at it now. We both have Sunday night free. Be in my room at seven sharp."

"Yes, Sir."

"You better go to sleep now, little one, because you won't be getting any sleep on Sunday." A thrill rips through me, the anticipation of sinking my dick into her wet cunt too much to take.

"Goodnight, Sir."

"Goodnight, my little one." I hang up, the silence of my apartment suddenly so acute.

I've always relished living alone after so many years in group homes after my mom passed, but on nights like this, when shadows of my past rear their ugly head, I wonder if it might be nice to have someone to share my space.

Going back to bed, I imagine what it would feel like to have my little one here with me. I never bring submissives I'm training to my home, but I know without a doubt I want to have this woman in my bed. It's fucking crazy because I know next to nothing about her.

～

This week has been like wading through molasses. I'm sleep deprived—the nightmares happening like clockwork. It's the same every night. I wake up around two a.m. in a cold sweat and workout until I'm so tired my body gives in and lets me sleep for a few hours before I have to get up for work.

There are two things that have been getting me through this week. Knowing that I'll have my little one ready and waiting in my private room tonight, and one of my residents who shows real promise. Perrington is my new protégé, and they are few and far between in neurosurgery. The dexterity needed for microsurgery isn't something that all surgeons possess.

I was the last person at this hospital who excelled in the field, so I'm enthused to be the one to nurture someone else's talent. I love to teach, as evidenced by my extracurricular activities.

"Dr. Harrison."

Speak of the devil.

"Dr. Perrington. Great work today. You were a valuable asset in the operating room." It's rare that I hand out compliments, as evidenced by the shocked look on Perrington's face.

"Thank you. It's an honor to assist you."

"Have you declared a specialty yet?"

"No, but I've narrowed it down."

"I hope neuro is on the shortlist. You've got amazing hands."

"It's at the top of my list."

"Excellent. I'm going to have you put on my service."

"Thank you, Dr. Harrison. Shall I read up on your upcoming cases?"

"Yes, and my current ones. You'll be with me as of tomorrow."

"Consider it done."

"Good. I'll see you tomorrow, Perrington." Without another word, I head for the locker room for a quick shower. I have a play-room to set up.

~

When I reach the club, Flex and Ryder are propping up the bar, a woman sitting in each of their laps.

"Good evening, gentlemen."

"What have you done with the real Pierce? He's six foot four and grumpy. I don't understand this expression on your face." Flex thinks he's a stand-up comedian.

"Witness the shit-eating grin, boys. I have a delicious new sub to teach *and* a great resident at work to impart my wisdom on."

They exchange glances before Ryder interjects. "Oh, fuck. He's going to be insufferable. Do we need to widen the door to your private room to accommodate your ever-growing ego?"

"Possibly, but when you have the goods to back it up, it's called confidence."

I signal Eli for a drink. I have a little time before I get the room organized.

Taking a seat, Flex and Ryder's lady friends excuse themselves, leaving us to shoot the shit for a while.

"Dalton coming in tonight?"

"Are you kidding? He's going to need a snorkel if he doesn't come up for air sometime soon. He and Nad are at it twenty-four seven. I have no earthly idea how they hold down jobs. We shouldn't have built him a suite of rooms upstairs."

Flex sounds a little jealous that his best friend is occupied with his wife.

"Speaking of the expansion, have you started on the training floor yet?"

"Should be up and running in two months. We'll throw another party and have you and Logan do some demonstrations if you're cool with that?"

Logan is a Master Dominant like me, except he gave up training years ago when he met his wife, leaving me with his share of subs to train. It's hard work, but someone's got to do it. Usually, I'd be happy at the thought, but for the first time, I don't want to think about moving on to the next trainee. I've barely begun with my little one, and yet I get this weird, uncomfortable constriction in my chest at the thought of handing her over to another Dom.

"What's got you looking like that?" Flex interrupts my disturbing daydream—more like a nightmare.

"Like what?"

"Like you're chewing a bee."

"Nothing. I'm fine." The minute Eli sets my drink down on the bar, I drain it in one gulp. "I just have some prep to get done. I'll be back."

My little one is bringing the signed paperwork with her tonight, and it has my pulse racing as I step into my private room. The second we get that out of the way, I'll start with lesson one—patience. I plan to kiss every last inch of her body tonight before sinking balls deep in that pretty little cunt of hers.

Running my fingers over the cuffs attached to the St. Andrew's cross, my dick twitches, getting hard knowing she'll be naked and splayed open for me on this in an hour. She's going to look so fucking perfect.

I set the new lingerie I bought for her on the bed with a matching white lace mask. She still wants to shield her identity, and I'll indulge her for now. It's hot, but I'm a greedy man, and I want her complete submission. She has two months before I insist on knowing her name and seeing her face. If she still evades me, I'll be forced to terminate our contract.

When everything is laid out just the way I like it, I head back out to the bar with my mask tucked into the back pocket of my jeans. Flex is nowhere to be found, but Ryder is still chatting with Eli, no sign of the woman who was in his lap before I left.

"Can I grab another drink, Eli?"

"Coming up."

I take a seat next to Ryder. "How's the new sub working out?" he asks before sipping his drink.

"She becomes my submissive tonight."

"What? You haven't signed the paperwork already? The Pierce I know would never lay a finger on a sub without a signature."

I consider his statement, and it sits uneasy in my chest. I've broken my own rules with this woman, and I don't even know her name.

If I don't get myself in check, I'm so screwed.

Chapter 8

FREYA

As I slip out of my clothes, my panties are soaked with anticipation. Thankfully, Sir won't know because he left a beautiful La Perla thong for me to change into. It's jaw-dropping and fits perfectly, and tonight he's given me a mask to match. There's something so freeing about remaining anonymous with him. I'd be lying if I said I'm not intrigued to see his face, his panty-melting smile is only one feature of what I know is a handsome face.

Once I'm dressed in the minute lingerie, I fix the delicate lace mask in place and make my way to the corner. Tonight, the ropes that hang waiting for me have been changed to white, and my stomach does somersaults at his attention to detail. He takes such care to ensure every last aspect of our interaction is perfect. Sliding my hands into the loops, I lower to my knees, sitting back on my heels as my arms are suspended above me, the ropes tightening around my wrists. I cast my gaze to the floor and wait, my pussy beginning to ache for his touch.

By the time I hear the door open and the soft click as it closes, I'm already on the brink of orgasm just knowing his eyes are on me. I'm not allowed to turn and look at him, and the restraints would stop me even if I could. Anyone could have walked in right now, and I'd be none the wiser—except I can *feel* his masculine energy fill the room, consuming the air around me.

"Such a good girl." The low rumble of his voice sends a shiver down my spine as his footsteps get closer. "Did you bring the signed paperwork?"

"Yes, Sir. It's on the dresser." His hand fists in my hair, pulling my head back to meet his gaze.

"Are you ready to submit, little one?" His piercing green eyes are a stark contrast to his black mask, his luscious full lips dipping to press a kiss to my forehead.

"Yes, Sir." He walks away, relinquishing his hold on me, leaving me wanting more.

I listen intently as he strides across the room, the rustle of papers telling me he's looking over our contract.

"Do you understand that I expect your complete submission in this room?"

"I do, Sir."

"I will teach you to be a good submissive. I'll help you discover your sexual preferences and kinks. You may not like everything I do to you, but it's the only way you'll learn. Are you willing to give me control?"

My body vibrates at his words, my arms shaking, still tied above me. "Y-yes… Sir."

"You don't sound too sure of yourself."

I clear my throat and say it with conviction this time. "Yes, Sir."

He makes his way back to me and loosens the restraints, my wrists aching almost as much as my pussy. Reaching out his hand, he steadies me as I get to my feet, my legs shaking from sitting on my heels.

"I want you against the cross, arms and legs spread." His tone is commanding, darker than before and full of wicked intent.

My heart is hammering, my pulse racing so hard I can hear it thrumming in my ears. As I take my place against the cross, I hesitate before setting my feet apart and opening my arms, completely exposed but for a scrap of lace.

Every touch of his hands as they secure me in restraints only fuels my desire. My breathing is labored, the rapid rise and fall of my chest making my breasts heave. He tightens my wrists first before kneeling at my feet, wrapping the cuffs around each ankle. His eyes are fixed on mine, his fingers working deftly as if he's done it a thousand times before. Probably more.

His green eyes darken as he stands, his knuckles gently stroking my face as he leans in, a hairsbreadth from me. I can feel his breath on my mouth as he speaks.

"You're mine now, little one. Mine to punish, to pleasure, to *fuck* as I see fit."

"Yes, Sir." I pant, desperate for his touch.

"Where to begin." He runs his fingertips down my neck to my breasts, pinching one nipple, sending a jolt of electricity straight to my core. "Patience..." his hand moves lower, circling my belly button before traveling lower, stopping just shy of where I need him, "... or punishment?"

I can barely contain a moan as his hands travel back up, cupping my face.

"Sir..."

"Did I say you could speak?"

"No, Sir."

"Then keep your mouth shut, or I'll gag you." The command in his voice has me weak at the knees, not that I could drop to them even if I wanted to.

"Yes, Sir."

"Tonight, we will start with patience." He stalks to the other side of the room, pulling a chair to sit in front of me, just far enough to drive me crazy with the need to reach out and touch him. He takes a seat, his legs spread casually as he drinks me in, his gaze devouring every inch of my body. Suddenly, I feel so vulnerable, unable to move and on display for this man.

I cast my eyes to the floor, letting my head drop. I can't bear to meet his stare.

"Tell me, little one, why now? Why this club? Why *me?*"

"I..."

"Look at me when you talk."

"Sorry, Sir." My skin heats as I scramble for what I hope is the right answer.

"Good girl. You may continue."

"I don't really fit into the normal dating scene. I've known for a long time that I wanted something more. One of my friends frequents this club and brought me to the masquerade."

"And why me?"

"Because…" I hesitate. "Because I'm drawn to you. When you kissed me that night, I felt *alive*."

"And yet you ran out on me, only to watch me jerk off. Do you know how often I take myself in hand at this club?"

"No, Sir."

"Never." My heart stutters to a halt. "You tasted so fucking sweet you made me desperate for release. I wanted to come in your perfect cunt. Now, you can't run, little one."

He runs a flogger between his fingers as his eyes drop to the lace panties he had me put on.

"I'm sorry, Sir."

"Patience is *not* a virtue I possess."

He drops the flogger and stalks over to me, grabbing the sides of my panties before ripping them off me. I'm so wet for him I can hardly stand it. I'm desperate for his touch, yet he leaves me wanting, returning to the chair. He picks up the flogger, running it across his palm.

"Tonight, I will take what I want, and if you're a good girl, I might let you come before I fuck you so hard you'll be sore tomorrow. How does that sound?" Fireflies run riot in my chest at his words. I know I'm wet for him, the growing ache becoming unbearable.

"It sounds wonderful." My voice is almost dreamy, anticipating what he'll do to me.

He stands from the chair and steps into me, letting the flogger's soft leather run up the inside of my thigh before snapping it against my pussy, eliciting a scream.

"I think you forgot who you're talking to."

"I'm sorry, Sir."

"Good girl," he growls as he caresses between my legs with the flogger. After a moment, he lifts it to show me the glistening leather. "Oh, you like that, little one. You're fucking soaked."

I moan as he reaches down, sliding his fingers over my entrance before putting them to his lips. "Even sweeter than I remember."

The scent of his cologne mixed with leather is a heady cocktail, intoxicating my senses as he drapes the flogger over my breasts and flicks his wrist, catching my nipples with it. They instantly pebble, tightening as desire washes over me. It's a pleasurable pain as he administers lash after lash, switching between my breasts and pussy.

"You will learn patience in this room. Your pleasure is mine to bestow or withhold. Understood?"

"Yes, Sir."

"You will not come unless I give you permission."

"I… don't know how to stop it, Sir."

A low, rasping chuckle escapes him as his eyes meet mine. "It's not yours to control. I can take you to the brink of fucking ecstasy and pull you back. You'll learn to come on command, little one. You'll beg me to let you come all over my fingers, face, and dick. Is that what you want?"

"Yes, Sir." My voice is unrecognizable—a breathy whisper of wanton desire.

I'm rewarded as he drops to his knees and darts his tongue out to circle my clit. I can't help the moan that escapes me.

"That's it, little one. Let me hear how much you want to ride my face."

"Oh God, yes, Sir."

"So fucking wet and greedy for me. How many times have you gotten yourself off to the memory of my mouth on your pretty little cunt?" His breath is warm on my skin as he presses open-mouthed kisses to my folds before tasting me with one long, languorous lick.

I let my head rest against the hardwood cross, my brain scrambled by such intense pleasure.

"Answer me."

"A lot, Sir. But not after you told me not to touch myself."

"Such a good little girl." He continues to kiss and lick my pussy, reaching up to grab my breast in his large, strong hand.

When he stops, I cry out in frustration as he stands, running his fingertips up my body until he cups my face. "Do you want to taste how fucking sweet you are when you're aroused, little one?" His lips are almost touching mine, making me gasp, hungry for his kiss.

"Yes, Sir."

His lips crash down on mine, his hands gripping me, forcing me to taste myself on his tongue as they twist and tangle in a frenzy, his groan pushing me to the edge of madness.

"Please... more."

"Are you frustrated, little one?"

"Yes, Sir."

He moves his lips to the shell of my ear as he whispers, "Good."

Continuing his ministrations, I'm overwhelmed by the softness of his tongue, a stark juxtaposition from the stubble on his chiseled jaw. It feels too good. His hands grip my thighs, and at this moment, I would sell my soul for an orgasm.

"Oh God... yes... I'm so close."

"Not yet, little one."

"I..." My words die on my lips as he pushes me to the brink before pulling back. He leaves me writhing against the restraints, over and over again until I'm begging for release.

He takes a step back, his eyes roving over every inch of my body as he begins to unbutton his shirt, exposing his broad shoulders and lean, muscular abs, a mouthwatering V dipping beneath the waist of his pants.

"See something you like?" His panty-melting smile sets me on fire.

"I want to see all of you, Sir." He slowly unbuckles his belt, pulling it from the loops before running it through his hand.

"Patience, little one." Setting the belt on his chair, he removes his shoes and socks, and even his feet are sexy. When he picks the belt back up, my stomach drops with fear and exhilaration.

He takes his time, running the leather up my legs, ghosting it across my pussy, his eyes following the trail, burning into me like a blazing inferno.

"So greedy for more. All in good time, little one. Tonight isn't about punishment. We'll get to that... soon. I'd be lying if I said I haven't fantasized about spanking your beautiful ass until it's a bright shade of red. Would you like that?"

"Yes, Sir." My breathing is shallow, rapid, and filled with need.

"Are you ready to beg for release yet?"

"I'll do anything, Sir."

"Would you swallow my dick like a whore?"

"I will do whatever you ask of me, Sir."

He drops the belt to the floor and unbuttons his pants, tossing them aside, standing before me in only his boxers. Still teasing me, I will gladly beg him for more.

"Please, Sir, I want to see all of you. I'll suck your cock. I promise I'll be good."

"Oh, I'm sure you will, little one, but it's not your mouth I'll be fucking tonight."

With his eyes on me, he slips his fingers under the waistband of his boxers, achingly slow, and lets them fall to the floor, his large cock hard as he steps into me, his hand cupping my pussy.

"Yes... Sir!" I try to grind against his palm, needing more, my desire to come radiating through every cell in my body. "Please... please... I want you."

"So fucking wet. You enjoy begging for dick, don't you?"

"Only for yours, Sir."

His lips crash down on mine. I struggle against the restraints, desperate to touch him and wrap my legs around his waist to ease the ache that's been building all night. I want to run my fingers through his messy hair.

My heart is beating wildly, my pulse racing as he positions his cock at my entrance and pushes into me with one hard thrust, forcing a cry from my lips. Tears spill over my lashes onto my mask as he fills me like no man ever has, groaning as our tongues twist and tangle, his hand fisted in my hair, further anchoring me in place as he forces me to take more of him.

"You're so fucking tight," he growls as he hammers into me, my body screaming against the size of his cock. My pussy aches but in the most wicked of ways.

"Oh God… *yes*… please… *Sir!*" He swallows my words, his kiss so ferocious his stubble burns my skin.

"Such a greedy little cunt. Wet and begging for more." He sets a punishing rhythm, his hands grabbing my breasts, rough and oh so good. I can't move, and the harder he fucks me, the more I need to touch him.

"Please… I'm begging you… let me touch you."

"Ask like a good little girl."

"Please, Sir, let me touch you."

"Maybe next time." He fists his hand in my hair once more. "Tonight is about patience."

"I've waited my whole life for this, Sir. For you."

His kiss grows desperate as he grips my ass and hammers into me. It's so painful and yet so amazing. I'm overwhelmed with emotion.

"You're going to scream for me, little one." He slips one hand between us, his thumb circling my clit as he continues to fuck me harder and harder.

My body starts to tingle all over, a slick sheen of sweat covering every inch of my skin, the beginnings of an orgasm taking hold.

"You feel that, little one? That's your cunt fucking begging for me. For what only I can give you."

"Yes… Sir."

He picks up the pace, chasing his release, taking me right along with him. "Come for me, little one. Let me hear you scream."

I let go, my voice growing hoarse as I spiral out of control, pain and pleasure tearing through my body as his cock pulses inside me.

"*Fuck… little one… you're fucking mine! Say it.*"

"I'm yours, Sir" I pant. I'm boneless and breathless—the restraints are all that hold me up at this point.

He drops his forehead to mine, our masks hitting against each other. "You did so well, little one. Fucking breathtaking."

"Thank you, Sir."

"Now, I'm going to watch my cum drip down your thighs like a good little slut."

I wince as he pulls out of me, his gaze dropping to between my legs. His sated grin turns to horror as he takes in the sight of me, his eyes snapping to mine.

"Sir... I..."

"Were you a virgin? You're bleeding. Tell me you just got your period." He runs a hand over his anguished face. "Tell me I didn't just take your virginity."

I can't look at him, so ashamed of his disgust for me. When I refuse to meet his gaze, he drops to the floor, unfastening the restraints, and taking care to massage my ankles. He averts his gaze as he stands to loosen the restraints around my wrists, my body slumping against his involuntarily. I couldn't stand up if I tried right now. Slipping one arm under my legs and the other around my back, he cradles me as my head rests against his chest.

I've never felt more vulnerable, afraid of what he'll say.

He doesn't speak.

Laying me down on the bed, he tugs the plush comforter back before crawling in next to me, wrapping his strong arms around me. His touch has changed from rough and ready to soft and careful. It's as if he suddenly sees me as fragile, and I'm confused by how it makes me feel. Is it wrong of me to have kept my virginity a secret?

Sir tucks a loose tendril of hair behind my ear. It's such a gentle caress—a stark juxtaposition to the storm I see in his eyes.

"Why didn't you tell me? I would've done things very differently tonight." His voice is clipped, and I can feel him struggling to keep his composure.

"I was scared you'd refuse to teach me. Am I wrong?" I trace lazy circles in the smattering of hair on his chest, breathing him in.

He grabs my hand, stopping me from touching him. "You're not wrong. I thought you were inexperienced when it came to kink and being a submissive. I make it a rule not to teach virgins."

My heart sinks. "Was I bad, Sir? Are you not satisfied?"

I wait what feels like an eternity for him to speak, and I'm caught off guard by the way he gently places his finger under my chin, forcing me to meet his gaze. "You were exquisite, little one. I don't even know your name. I haven't seen your face. This isn't how it's supposed to be."

His words are saying one thing, but his body says another.

"It..." I'm not sure how to explain myself. "It was everything I wanted it to be, Sir."

His hold on me tightens. "I'm not the type of man to waste your virginity on, little one. You deserve so much better than me."

"Every one of my girlfriends has stories of losing their virginity to some guy who peaked in high school. Who had no idea what they were doing, and it didn't even cross their mind to make it pleasurable for her. The way I see it, this was a better memory."

"This relationship is built on trust. You lied to me. Fuck, I called you a slut."

"And your good girl." I love the thought of being his for as long as he'll have me.

He scrubs his hand over his jaw, his body still tense beneath mine. "I'm not sure if this can work. You don't trust me enough to show me your face, and yet I had faith in you, but tonight just tells me that you're not ready for this."

"So what, you just take my virginity and see you later?"

"I didn't know I was taking it to begin with."

"You said you enjoyed it."

"Enjoyment isn't relevant here. I'm a submissive trainer. I need your absolute trust, and until you're ready to give me that, I don't see a way forward. I can teach you about kink, but I won't fuck you. It's your choice."

Chapter 9

PIERCE

My heart is hammering in my chest, betraying the façade of measured control. I've already broken my carefully constructed rules for this woman, and I unwittingly broke another. I don't fuck virgins. I don't train them. Jesus, I was so fucking rough with her, so eager to sink balls deep inside her cunt.

Pent-up anger radiates through every cell, threatening to push me over the edge. With anyone else, this would be over already. I don't tolerate lying, even by omission. I get off the bed and start pacing the room, trying to ignore the fact that my cock is hard for her, even now.

"Sir..."

I scrub my hand over my face as I try to process what I've done and what she did.

"You signed the contract. How could you neglect to mention that you wanted to try something as simple as *sex* for the first time? God, the stuff I asked you about. I'm fucking livid right now. If you had any experience before now, I'd be chaining you up and punishing you for such a massive error in judgment. In fact, I would terminate the contract immediately."

"Please don't do that. I didn't think it was a big deal."

"Don't lie to me, little one. If you thought it was nothing, you'd have told me straight out the gate. For God's sake, I ate you out in the voyeur hall." There's a weight on my chest—frustration, anger, and fucking lust.

"I enjoyed it... Sir."

"Fuck." I continue to pace, fighting the urge to fuck her into submission. I'm a castrated Dom right now. I've always prided myself on my rules. At work. In my playroom. I'm the master of every domain I inhabit, but this little one—she confounds me. I know I should walk away right now, but I couldn't leave this room if it were on fire.

"I'm so sorry, Sir."

"You shouldn't have to apologize for losing your virginity. But can you understand why I'm furious?" I never lose control. I'm always level-headed. I hate how angry I am at this moment. We barely know each other, and yet I *want* her trust.

"I didn't want the fairy tale. I waited for it and overthought every aspect. I let guys do the foreplay thing, and I knew it wasn't what I wanted."

"How can you say that? Guys being inept at proper foreplay isn't reason enough to let a guy like me fuck you."

"Guys like you?"

"Yeah, guys who use women to satisfy their sexual needs without any commitment."

"You committed the next six months of your life to me. That's more than most women get in a relationship."

"Why are your standards so low?" I don't understand why she's being this way.

"I'm nothing special." Her words are a dagger through my chest. I've spent several hours with this woman, and I already know she's different.

"You have no idea how spellbinding you are, little one." I strut back over to the bed and slide in beside her, holding her in my arms. This shouldn't even be a discussion. I've never had a submissive lie to me on this scale. When it comes to this lifestyle, omission is as good as lying. I should've listened to my gut when she said she wanted to remain anonymous. Venom provides discretion unlike any club I've ever been to. This place is locked down tight.

I should let go of her and leave, but I can't relinquish my hold, something in me unable to bear this being her lasting memory of losing her virginity. It's a big responsibility, which is why I don't take on submissives without at least vanilla sexual experience.

"I'm sorry, Sir."

For a woman to reach her age and still be a virgin is rare these days, and I didn't just *take* it from her—I ripped it from her body. I have no words. No wisdom to bestow in this moment.

"Please, Sir, say something." Her voice is barely a whisper, breaking my heart as she begs for my approval. The way she addresses me—how she purrs 'Sir'—has me wanting to make this better for her. I can give her tenderness if only for tonight.

"What do you want me to say, little one?"

"That you forgive me. That I can be your good girl."

I reach down, cupping her cheek, our eyes fixed on each other. "You were so good, little one. Absolutely beautiful in your submission."

"I can't explain it, but I know you're the right Dominant to teach me."

I trace lazy circles on her back, at war with myself over what to do. I know what I want and what I should do are two very different things.

"You're not ready. It kills me, little one. Believe me."

"Please, Sir." She pushes herself up and presses her lips to mine. Her kiss is electric, setting my whole body on fire.

Tangling my fist in her hair, I hold her close, darting my tongue out to meet hers in a slow, sensual fuck. My resolve dies on my lips at the sight of tears welling in her eyes. Rolling her onto her back, she moans into my mouth. I convince myself I'm making it right, giving her the tenderness she deserves on the night she lost her virginity, but I know it's selfish of me.

She melts under me, her legs spread wide, wrapping around my waist as I position myself at her entrance, slowly working my way in. She's wet and eager to take all of me, but I know she's hurting. If this is the last I have of her, I want her to know there can be a gentleness to submission. A tangling of two souls if only for one night.

"Oh God... Sir," she whispers, her hands wrapping around my back, digging into my shoulders as I rock in and out of her sweet pussy. I take my time, kissing her with a tenderness I never afford my submissives in training. She feels so fucking good, taking every hard inch of me as we lose ourselves to the soft sensation, our bodies intertwined. At this moment, we're lovers. I'm not her Dominant. We move in sync, her hips rising to meet every thrust, her moans of pleasure driving me to the edge of madness. I want her more than my next breath, and as a silent, powerful wave washes over us, we find release in each other's arms.

When she's breathless in my arms, our limbs tangled together, I press my lips to hers in a plea for forgiveness. She might not see it right now, but when she does, she'll hate me for taking her virginity in such a cold, hard, and calculated way. This is the least I could do to make up for it in some small way.

Guilt is an unfamiliar emotion for me, and yet it weighs heavy in my chest.

"That's how it's supposed to be, little one. Loving, caring, everything you deserve. Not a guy like me, who'll fuck you up and spit you out. Do you understand?"

She doesn't answer, her breaths soft and even asleep in my arms. My little one looks so peaceful, and all I want to do is untie her mask and gaze at her blissful face.

It's been three days since I deflowered my mystery submissive, and I've thought of virtually nothing else. The only time I get a reprieve is in the operating room. I have been channeling my desire to teach into my new residents. They are benefiting from my sexual frustration.

I set out the rules for my little one after we spent the night at the club—a first for me. She was so beautiful as she slept. I couldn't bring myself to wake her up, even though I never sleep with submissives. Having a woman in my bed has never been for anything other than sex. Sleeping—actually sleeping—is a foreign concept to me. I spent my years of medical training grabbing an hour here and there in on-call rooms, too tired and dedicated to bother making a home for myself.

Yes, I have an amazing apartment that overlooks Central Park, but it's not what I think a home should be. For me, it's all fairy tales and whimsical notions born of a childhood spent in and out of group homes. I've never known what it truly feels like to have a family and a place that gives me a sense of belonging.

Now that I'm an attending, I spend more time at my apartment, but I usually pass my waking hours at the club. The past three days, I've had too much time to think about *her*, fighting the urge to summon her to my room at Venom and do all manner of wicked things to her body.

In truth, I'm not sure how to proceed at this point, and that's unlike me. I make decisions based on all relevant information and move forward in all things with conviction. This woman has me floundering.

After setting my phone down on the nightstand, it pings with a message.

> Lavender: Good evening, Sir.

It's shameful how my dick instantly hardens for her.

> Me: Hello, little one.

> Lavender: I'm sorry I didn't tell you I was a virgin. I hate that you don't trust me. It's been eating away at me.

> Me: Have you decided how you want to move forward?

> Lavender: I still want you to be my Dominant for the agreed time.

My pulse quickens at the thought of bringing her back to my playroom.

> Me: Are you ready to be open with me?

> Lavender: Can we take it slow?

> Me: Of course. I'm going to send you some reading material. It contains more information about praise kink and degradation. Based on your responses the last time we were together, I believe you favor one over the other, but some submissives like both, which can be more challenging. Read up and reach out when you're done.

> Lavender: Yes, Sir.

> Me: Goodnight, little one.

> Lavender: Goodnight, Sir.

Unfortunately, I have to work this weekend, so meeting my little one is out of the question. To add insult to injury, I'm expected to attend the hospital's annual fundraiser. Black tie. Very fancy. No kink allowed. It's my idea of a penance. I get paraded around to all the wealthy benefactors. I'm basically the hospital's whore for the evening. There's a reason I got into medicine—surgery specifically. I want to save lives with as little interaction as possible.

The last time I went to a party was at the club, and it ended with my head between a woman's thighs. She would definitely make this fundraiser more bearable. Although, I'd have to know who the fuck she is in order to invite her to join me.

The second I get my little one back in the playroom, I'll have her begging to tell me her name. I will make sure of it.

～

I've said hello to hundreds of guests as I make the rounds. My only saving grace is the drink in my hand and the promise of a delicious dinner.

"How are your residents shaping up this year, Pierce?" My Chief of Surgery and mentor, Dr. Joseph Milligan, loves these events. I'm his finest protégé, and he'll tell anyone who'll listen. He got a kick out of teaching and passing on his expertise. I'm not so enthusiastic when it comes to my residents. It's a necessary evil as far as I'm concerned.

"You want my honest opinion?"

"Of course."

"Perrington is the only one who has what it takes for neuro." It's unusual for me to consider taking someone under my wing, but maybe this year is different.

"High praise from you, Pierce. You have standards that few could live up to. Imagine if I'd done that with you."

"We'd still be where we are now. I'm extraordinary, and you know it."

"I see you're still an arrogant son of a bitch."

"It's not arrogance when you have the skill to back it up."

He chuckles. "Well, channel all that skill into creating another you. I need more surgeons of your caliber."

"I'm great, but I'm not a miracle worker." I slap him on the back before heading to the bar for another drink.

"Scotch neat, thanks."

"Dr. Harrison," says a familiar voice at my side.

"Perrington? You scrub up well. I don't think I've ever seen you out of surgical scrubs." I find myself lost for words. It's amazing how different we all are outside of the hospital. I live a double life. It stands to reason that others do the same.

"Thank you."

"Can I get you a drink? Pick your poison."

"Gin and tonic, please."

I flag down the bartender and order for my new shadow, standing in awkward silence until our drinks arrive.

"So, Perrington, have you thought about our last conversation? Your prospective specialty."

"Yes, sir."

"Walk with me. Dinner is about to be served." Following me like a puppy, we take our seats.

"I came into residency with cardio in mind, but the more I have learned, the more interested I've become in neuro."

"I don't want to waste my time teaching you if you're not sure." It's the story of my life right now.

"I understand, Dr. Harrison. I've put a lot of thought into it, and I would consider myself lucky to work under you." My cock twitches. My little one has me on edge and turned on every minute of the day. Anything sounds dirty to me right now. I'm turning into Flex with the perpetual humor of a fifteen-year-old boy.

"You are lucky to work under me, Perrington. You have no idea."

"Yes, Dr. Harrison."

"So tell me, where did you go to school?"

"I was top of my class, pre-med at Stanford." Impressive. "Then I went on to Harvard Medical School. I graduated summa cum laude."

"Any other doctors in the family?"

"No. My dad was never in the picture, and my mom worked three jobs to put food on the table."

"I'm impressed. How did you put yourself through college?" I'm not usually this inquisitive, but summa cum laude at Harvard is something to be praised.

"I worked as many jobs as I could growing up. I started saving for college when I was ten and started mowing lawns in my neighborhood."

"You don't strike me as the outdoor type."

"I'm not, but I was determined to become a doctor. I wasn't handed everything on a silver platter." I track Perrington's gaze, taking in the opulence and wealth in this room.

"I respect that."

"Are you from a family of doctors?"

"No. I grew up…" I stop myself. I don't share my life story with anyone, never mind a work colleague. A resident. "Enough about that. We need more drinks. Can I get you another?"

"Yes, please."

"I'll be right back." I stand and make my way through the tables back to the bar. I never let myself slip like that. It's no one's business but mine as to how I got to where I am today. It leaves an uneasy feeling in my chest. I don't do well when I don't have absolute control in any situation.

Pulling my phone from my pocket, I type out a quick message. I need to compose myself, and this is a sure-fire way to do it.

> Me: Are you at home?

> Lavender: No, Sir.

> Me: Then go to the restroom and remove your panties.

She hesitates before answering.

> Lavender: Sir, why do you want me to do that?

> Me: It's not your place to question. If you want to come back to my playroom, you'll do as you're told, little one.

I shove my phone back in my pocket, grab our drinks, and head back to the table, stopping to say hello to some of my fellow attendings. I know the head of cardiology is going to be pissed that I'm stealing their best potential resident. I can't say I feel bad about it. I will always do what's necessary when I want something.

A few minutes later, I get a text.

> Lavender: Done.

Good girl.

Me: I'll call you when I get home. Do not touch yourself.

Lavender: Yes, Sir.

Dinner is enjoyable, and I find myself deep in conversation with my new protégé. It turns out not all residents are a royal pain. I don't bother speaking with any of the others trying to kiss my ass. If you can't show me your skill in the operating room, I have no desire to hear about your cat, kids, or your bog-standard-vanilla life.

I don't think I could ever live the cookie-cutter lifestyle. Becoming a Dom saved me from myself. When you grow up like I did, you have to find ways to connect with people. I'm sure a shrink would go to town on why I was drawn to **BDSM** and don't even get me started on the fact that I train rather than having a long-term submissive. I'm all kinds of fucked up, but none of that matters when I operate.

Patients don't care if I'm a warm and fuzzy human being. In fact, I think it's often comforting that I'm focused on providing them with the best care possible rather than being their buddy. That's what I tell myself when I keep my distance with patients. In truth, I don't think I could do this job if I took on emotional attachments to every single person I operate on. Yes, it may make the wins even better, but the lows—emotional detachment is the only option to keep functioning and moving on to help the next person. I'm not saying I never get attached, but I try to remain professional at all times.

I'm not sure if Perrington has what it takes to remain professional with a difficult case, but we'll find out soon enough.

By the end of the night, all I want to do is lose myself in my little one, but I can't show weakness when it comes to her. She needs a firm hand and proper guidance. Going easy on a submissive in training does nothing to help her become a good sub.

When I arrive home, I head straight to my closet to get out of this penguin suit. I'm down to my boxer shorts when my phone rings. It's *her*.

"Hello, little one."

"Hello, Sir."

"How was your evening?"

"Torture." I love the bite in her voice. She's got moxie.

"You didn't enjoy being a dirty girl?"

"I loved it, but I was working. I felt like everyone was looking at me. Like they *knew*."

"Maybe they did. Would it really matter?"

"Why do you frequent a club that requires an NDA? People judge the lifestyle harshly. Of course it matters."

"Tell me, little one, what do you do for a living? Where do you work?"

"Details that do not need to be divulged."

"You put so little faith in me. How can you trust me with your submission but not with the most meager of details regarding your person?"

"I…"

"Lost for words, little one. I should put that mouth of yours to good use."

"Does that mean you will allow me back into your playroom, Sir?"

"That depends entirely on you. Come to me when you're ready to divulge at least your first name."

"But, Sir…"

"That is my final decision. As much as I crave your submission in the bedroom, I desire your trust more. Goodnight, little one."

I end the call, not to punish her, but to stop myself from giving in. I cannot ask her to meet me at Venom. As much as it pains me, she needs to come back of her own volition, willing to afford the small mercy of her name. Until then, I will throw myself into teaching elsewhere.

Chapter 10
FREYA

It's been a week since I last spoke with Sir. I miss our interactions, and my body craves his touch. Work keeps me busy, but in the rare moments of silence, I find myself at war. I promised myself I wouldn't let my personal life encroach on my choice to pursue becoming a submissive.

I didn't take into consideration that I would grow attached to my Dom outside of the playroom. My naivety clearly extends to more than my virginity. I thought it could be a simple transaction. A contract devoid of feeling. I never imagined I would enjoy submitting to Sir in my day-to-day life.

I pride myself on being an independent, self-made woman. Anyone who truly knows me understands how much it means to me. My work is my identity—my reason for breathing in and out.

Growing up, I didn't fit in. No one thought me special except my mother, but that's her job. Moms love you unconditionally. I was the reason she lost my father, and yet she never once held it against me. He wanted nothing to do with her after she told him she was pregnant.

My mother picked herself up, refusing to fall apart over a man who could overlook his own daughter. She taught me never to give a man so much power over my life in any capacity. I have never given a man control, and yet that's what intrigues me most about becoming a submissive. I'm different from other women. I've never been one to consider relationships with men a priority. The few I have tried to connect with wanted one thing while professing something else.

Sir offers no such complications. I offer my body freely, without emotional entanglements. At least, that's what I've told myself up until now. This past week has felt almost unbearable without our interactions. I have loved them as much as I loved being in his playroom. I want to please him and hear him praise me for being a *good girl*.

Giving my name may seem like such a small ask, but it's what comes after that scares me. First my name, then my mask will be gone, leaving no barriers between Sir and me. I fear that when I set eyes on his face, it will only make me crave him more. Until today, I've been steadfast in my resolve to do the right thing and keep my distance.

It's been a long and grueling day, and as I stand under the showerhead, letting it all wash away, I find myself wanting to hear his voice. Yes, I need to feel the way he made my body sing, but I'm just as anxious to let his words caress me.

With my mind made up, I get out of the shower and wrap a towel around myself before reaching for my phone. *His* phone. He's the only number saved to contacts. I hit call and wait.

Ring! Ring! Ring!

I expect it to go to voicemail, ready to hang up when his dark, delicious voice speaks into my ear.

"Hello, little one. It took you longer than I anticipated to call." He knew I wouldn't be able to stay away. Part of me is excited by how well he knows me. It's ridiculous when the reason we haven't spoken is my reticence to give him my name.

"Did you miss me, Sir?"

"You haven't earned the answer to that, little one." A thrill courses through me.

"And what would I have to do to earn such an answer?"

"You need only tell me your first name. Baby steps."

"Would it earn me a trip back to your playroom?"

"Most certainly, however, it would be for your punishment."

"My... punishment?" I swallow hard as I contemplate the idea, squeezing my thighs together.

"Yes. You didn't tell me you were a virgin, and you've taken a week to contact me."

"I'm sorry, Sir. It was never my intention to displease you."

"I meant what I said. I won't have sex with you again until you reveal your face or your name to me."

"Why?"

"It is not for you to question. You might try addressing me appropriately. You've just added two to your punishment."

"Two of what, Sir?"

"That's for me to know. Are you going to do what's necessary to reenter my playroom?"

My heart is hammering in my chest, my pulse galloping like an untamed stallion. What's the worst that could happen? My first name gives nothing away.

"What if I keep wearing the mask?"

"Then I will only teach you. Clearly, you have much to learn. When you ask me a question, I expect you to call me Sir."

"What does that mean... Sir?"

"Let me worry about the details. First things first, will you agree to telling me your first name?"

I hesitate, a pregnant pause hanging on the line between us. It's not because I'm unsure of my decision. It's because I *know* I would do almost anything to experience his punishment. To bask in the glow of his playroom once more.

"Well, little one, what's it going to be?" Butterflies take flight in the pit of my stomach as he caresses my name.

"I like when you call me, *little one*. I don't want that to change, Sir."

"If that is your preference, I will continue to do so. One doesn't negate the other."

"Okay." He waits me out, my voice croaking as I continue. "My name is Freya."

"*Freya.*" I swear I could come just hearing him purr my name. I wasn't expecting it to spark my desire, making me wet as I sit on the edge of my bed, clutching my towel tighter. "A beautiful name, my little one."

"Thank you, Sir." It comes out as barely more than a whisper.

"Isn't that better? I've eaten you out in public and taken your virginity in private, and yet it feels like meeting you for the first time. My name is…"

"Don't," I squeal. "Not yet."

"You just added another three to your punishment."

"When will you punish me, Sir?" Even I hear how eager I sound.

"Pull up the calendar. Now." His commanding tone sends a shiver down my spine. I do as I'm told, excited when I see our availability. The stars have aligned and are screaming my name.

"Tomorrow night."

"Eager little thing, aren't you?"

"Yes, Sir."

"I've missed you, little one." My heart takes flight.

"Really?"

"Is it that hard to believe?"

"Yes. You are… amazing."

"As are you. I don't want to hear you question my taste in submissives. If you are down on yourself in my playroom, you will be punished. I see great potential in you, little one."

"Thank you, Sir."

"Tell me, are you confident in your career, Freya? In other aspects of your life?"

"Yes." I don't have to think this one through. "I excel outside of… relationships."

"You are fulfilled by your work?"

"Yes, Sir. I love my job, and I'm good."

"I'm sure you're more than good. I venture to think you're great."

"I will be."

"What do you mean?"

"I have goals. I'm not at my peak yet."

"That's not a bad thing. Better to build a solid foundation."

"Exactly." Sir is so easy to talk to. I'm about to address my lack of success with relationships when he interjects.

"Be in the playroom tomorrow at seven," he commands.

"Yes, Sir."

"And, little one, do not touch yourself tonight."

"But I'm naked and wet from the shower." I'm not sure why I say it, but I'm rewarded by a deep rumble.

"That's two more added to your punishment." I poked the bear, and it has me so riled up, I desperately want to touch myself.

"Why, Sir?"

"You know why, you little minx. If I have to endure knowing you are ready for me right now, then you must pay for it."

"I didn't realize it would affect you, Sir." There's no conviction in my voice.

"No lying, little one. It will only result in sexual frustration for you. You think it's bad that you can't touch yourself tonight... you have no idea what I can do to your body. I'm going to enjoy punishing you tomorrow."

"I think I'll enjoy it, too, Sir."

"I am certain you will. Be on time and make sure you're in the position when I arrive."

"Yes, Sir."

"Goodnight, Freya."

"Goodnight, Sir." The line goes dead, and all I want to do is slip my hand between my legs to satisfy the ache Sir's voice alone caused. My mind is racing with ideas of how he may punish me. I've read a lot about various kinks, and pain has always intrigued me. I'm giddy with excitement and so turned on I can hardly stand it.

I usually sleep in sweats and a baggy T-shirt, but tonight, with Sir's voice fresh in my mind, I lean into the frustration. I stand and let my towel fall to the floor, leaving me completely naked and acutely aware of my arousal, my thighs wet as I climb into bed.

The sheets glide over my naked flesh, goose bumps spreading across my entire body. My nipples pebble as the cotton sweeps over them as I lie back and think of tomorrow. The ache between my thighs intensifies, and I spread my legs, letting the sheet settle against my pussy.

I'm making it worse, but I continue to tease myself. I've never slept naked before, and it feels forbidden somehow. Knowing I'm not allowed to pleasure myself is a rush. I'm not sure how I'll get through work tomorrow with Sir on my mind.

When the ache is so bad, and I can think of nothing else, I push the sheet down to my waist, letting the ceiling fan caress my breasts, my nipples so tight they're on the edge of painful—just the way I want it.

Eventually, I pull out my phone and reread some of my research on pain, kinks, and delayed release, only making it harder for me to fall asleep. Tomorrow can't come fast enough. My first *punishment*.

Shit! Shit! Shit!

I'm used to work getting in the way of my attempts at a social life, but I needed today to be the exception. There's no way I'm going to make it to Venom tonight. I wait until the last possible moment to contact Sir, wishing for a miracle to get me into his playroom.

> **Me:** I'm so sorry, Sir. I have been delayed at work.

> **Sir:** Is it a life or death career emergency?

> **Me:** Yes. Trust me, I am devastated that we cannot meet tonight.

> Sir: It's okay, little one. I'll look at our calendar and reschedule. Don't fear, you'll still get your punishment.

> Me: Promise?

> Sir: I promise. My cane is twitching. I'll let you get on with your work. Let me know you get home safely.

> Me: Yes, Sir. Thank you for being so understanding.

> Sir: You're welcome, little one.

Did he just mention a twitching cane? Desire sparks deep in my core, a bolt of lightning, setting my body on fire. If he's serious, a cane is will smart for sure. My pulse quickens as I slip my phone back in my purse. I've got a long night ahead, and I need my mind to be focused on the task at hand. Not in a playroom with Sir and his cane.

I take a few moments to calm my breathing, only to be interrupted by my boss. He's imposing, intimidating, and brilliant.

"Are you sure you're up for this?"

"Yes. I won't disappoint you."

"I saw you flinch earlier when I stated the details of this case. I need your A-game."

"Always." I never bring less than my best, and I don't plan to change that tonight. Maybe I was right before when I dedicated every breath I took to my work. Relationships complicate things, and my current contract with Sir was supposed to be simple—an exchange of like-minded people.

I want to know if I have what it takes to be a submissive. I don't do anything half-heartedly. If I'm going to enter this lifestyle, then I want to be well-informed. I need to learn about my kinks and train to be an excellent submissive. Being a *good* sub isn't enough for me. I strive for perfection in all things. Why should this be any different?

Taking a few minutes to meditate, I calm my mind as I do before any big case. I can do this. I'm a strong, confident, more than capable woman. I go through all the steps, playing it out in my mind. Each action has an equal and opposite reaction. One decision creates a knock-on effect, dictating the next move. You have to be prepared in life. Otherwise, you can be blindsided. That's how I feel when I think of Sir—caught completely off guard by how deeply he affects me.

Eight hours later, I emerge under the cover of darkness, my body tired, my mind exhausted, and my heart full at a job well done. Hailing a cab, I jump in and pull up the calendar on my phone, eager to find the next time I can meet with Sir.

It's only as I think of him that I realize I may have given him my first name, but I refused his offer. *What does he think of that? Do I even want to know?* I add my availability for three days from now and type out a quick message to Sir.

> **Me:** I updated the calendar. Does Thursday work for you, Sir?

I almost sent that without addressing him as Sir. I'm a little disappointed that I won't be adding to my punishment.

> **Sir:** That works. Why are you up at this time, little one?

> **Me:** Long night at work.

> **Sir:** Did you take a cab home? I don't like the idea of you walking around Manhattan alone in the middle of the night.

> **Me:** I'm in a cab, Sir. I knew it would displease you if I walked the couple of blocks to the subway.

> **Sir:** Good girl.

Why do I crave his approval? I barely know the man, yet my mind is consumed with the desire to please him.

Me: Thank you, Sir.

Sir: Are you prepared to be punished?

Me: Yes, Sir. I'm looking forward to it.

The moment I hit send, I regret it. I shouldn't admit such a thing. Who *wants* someone to hurt them in pursuit of sexual gratification? It's a rhetorical question, of course. I've done extensive research on the matter, and Venom is full of people who enjoy punishment.

Sir: You say that now, little one. Wait until your body is shaking, your ass burning from the sting of my cane. You might think otherwise.

Me: I trust you, Sir.

I really do. I trust him with my pleasure and conversely with my pain. He's shown me tenderness, and there is something in his eyes —a discernment I admire. When you look at someone behind a mask, their gaze is magnified, distilled with a clarity that's refreshing. It's as if I truly *see* him and him me.

Sir: Trying to get on my good side?

Me: Always, Sir.

Sir: Good answer. Are you home yet?

Me: No, Sir.

Sir: Let me know when you're home safe with the doors locked. If you're going to be working these hours regularly, I'll have a town car pick you up.

Me: Then you'd know far too much about me, Sir.

> Sir: Safety comes before anonymity. I'll figure it out. Let me worry about the logistics.

> Me: Yes, Sir.

By the time the cab driver pulls up at my apartment building, moving my limbs is hard work. I'm so tired. Once I'm safely inside, I let Sir know I'm home and crawl into bed, sleep instantly settling over my weary body, my mind taking me to a certain playroom, a set of piercing forest green eyes staring back at me.

"Hello, little one."

The bite of the restraints against my wrists is deliciously wicked as I sit on my heels in the position Sir requires of me. Waiting for him like this is the greatest form of torture. Tonight, he set out sumptuous wine-red lingerie—a stunning basque lace thong and a matching jewel-encrusted mask. The ropes that currently hold my hands above me are the same deep shade of red.

"Hello, Sir." My voice is barely above a whisper, my breathing shallow as my pulse races.

"Are you ready for tonight's lesson?"

"Yes, Sir." I'm already wet for him, and he hasn't even touched me yet.

"Let's be clear on the rules of this evening. After every point I'm about to list, I need your verbal acknowledgment that you understand and consent to everything that's going to happen."

"Yes, Sir." My nerves burst into a thousand fireflies, swarming my chest.

"You can stop at any time. All you need do is say your safeword. You will not be gagged, so your safe signal will not be required. What is your safeword, little one?"

"Lavender. I understand, Sir."

"Good girl." The fireflies multiply.

"Tonight is a lesson in punishment. What did you do to require punishment?"

"I didn't tell you I was a virgin, Sir. I have also forgotten to address you correctly at times… Sir."

"Yes. This punishment is predominantly for your lie of omission. Also, I will not fuck your beautiful little cunt this evening." My heart sinks.

"Understood, Sir."

"If you take your punishment like a good little girl, you will be rewarded because you offered your first name, Freya." I could detonate right now at the way my name drips with sex from his lips.

"Thank you, Sir."

"I haven't told you what that reward will be. You might not want to thank me yet, little one."

"Sorry, Sir."

"When I release your restraints, you will stand, keeping your gaze on the floor, and make your way over to the table. Bend over with your arms outstretched to be secured in the leather cuffs."

"Yes, Sir."

"You will count each lash, continuing to address me correctly."

"Gladly, Sir. I want to be good for you."

I feel him at my back, the scent of his cologne invading my senses, casting a haze of arousal with every brush of his fingertips up my arms. I tremble at his touch. My entire body sings as he loosens the ropes, gently massaging my wrists before stepping back.

"Get up." His deep, growling command courses through my veins as I get to my feet. It takes everything in me not to meet his gaze. All I can see are his bare feet and the bottom of his jeans. I want to look at him so badly it's an ache in my chest.

I do as I'm told, stopping at the narrow ebony table, which is at waist height. Bending over, I splay my arms out to either side of me. He makes his way to the other side of the table. "You may look at me while I restrain you, little one."

I greedily take in the length of him as he reaches for my left hand, pulling it into the leather cuff and buckling it tight. He's wearing nothing but his mask and jeans, his lean, muscled chest on display, his happy trail dipping beneath the waistband, the top button undone. He's teasing me with that button. I want to rip the rest of them open and drop to my knees for him.

He takes my right hand and buckles the leather cuff tightly around my wrist, leaving me completely at his mercy, a thrill coursing through me.

"See something you want?" he says with a wry grin, following my gaze to his crotch.

"Yes, Sir."

"Shall that be your reward, little one?" he asks, stepping closer. The table is just wide enough for my head to be perfectly positioned should he decide to fuck my mouth, and I squeeze my thighs together, desperate to suck his cock.

"Yes, please, Sir."

"Oh, we can't have you alleviating the ache between your legs. That would make this too easy." He moves out of my line of sight before dropping to grip my ankle. "Lift." He runs his hand up my calf before positioning my foot to secure a leather cuff around my ankle, shackling me to the table leg. He does the same thing on the other side, leaving me with my legs and arms spread wide, bent over at the waist. "Good girl. You look so pretty splayed out for me, little one."

"Thank you, Sir." My voice trembles as I speak, the gravity of what's about to happen hanging in the air between us.

I hear various noises, but they're unfamiliar, making them difficult to place. It's not until he walks in front of me that my breath catches. He's holding a long, wooden cane.

"Safeword once again." He levels me with his stare.

"Lavender, Sir."

"Good girl. You will receive fifteen lashes. Remember to count, or you'll be forced to take an extra lash for each one you miss."

"Yes, Sir."

"This allows me to assess your tolerance and preference for pain. I require absolute honesty. If it's too much, you say your safeword." He starts to pace, letting the cane slap against his hand. "If you feel overwhelmed, you say your safeword. Certain rules are different in training. The main one is, if you have a question, you. Say. Your. Safe. Word. Understood?"

"Yes, Sir."

"Good, then we'll begin."

He walks behind me, my body jolting when his large, warm hand caresses my ass. I try to slow my breathing. This is the moment I've been dreaming of for years.

The anticipation is killing me, but I steel myself when his hand disappears and is replaced by the cane. I feel a gentle stroke across my cheeks on display in the thong he made me wear.

Crack!

The cane makes contact with my naked flesh, the sting making me flinch.

"One, Sir."

He brings it down a second time with more force, setting every nerve ending in my body on fire.

"Two, Sir."

Again, and again, and again.

"*Yes!* Five… Sir." It's everything I dreamed it would be, the pain straddling the thinly veiled line of pleasure.

I give myself over completely, lost in the moment, lost in *him.*

Crack!

"Six, Sir."

"You're doing so well, little one." His voice almost pushes me over the edge, so turned on I can feel my arousal start to wet my thighs. I want him more than my next breath, all inhibitions gone. Any inner turmoil eradicated with each strike of his cane.

"Yes… oh God… seven… *Daddy!*"

His rhythm falters, silence crawling over every inch of my skin as I lay prostrate and shackled.

What have I done?

Chapter 11

PIERCE

What did she just say?

My dick is hard as steel at her address.

"Keep counting," I force myself to say after a beat.

"Eight, Sir," she whispers with trepidation.

"No. Say it again." It comes out more clipped than I intended.

"Eight, Sir."

I bring the cane down on her ass once more. "I want to hear you call me Daddy."

Just the thought of it has me ready to shoot my load.

"Nine... *Daddy*."

The cane is heavy in my hand, my desperation to touch her skin to skin so overwhelming. It takes everything I have to focus on the task at hand.

Again.

"Ten, Daddy." Jesus Christ. I never indulge this kink. It's always a footnote in a submissive's training. A box I check off when I know if it's something she likes or dislikes. But the way it trips off her tongue as she lays wide open for me, her ass a pretty shade of red— it drives me wild.

My little one is doing so well with her first punishment. She's getting off on it, and it's a glorious sight to behold. This moment right here is why I do what I do. Teaching a submissive comes with great responsibility, and it's always been about assessing *their* needs and desires.

I rarely indulge my darkest kinks. It's for the best. Growing up the way I did, I know I can't lose control with a sub. It's my duty as her Master to focus on what she wants as she prepares herself to be someone's forever submissive.

With Freya—just the way her name sounds on my lips—it's different. I crave her submission. I want every moan of pleasure to be mine. She's breathtaking. Hearing her let go and call to me as she wishes might be the hottest thing I've ever heard.

The cane connects with her beautiful ass, reddening even further, my cock just as stiff, aching for release.

"Eleven... Daddy."

I have to actively pace myself as I deliver the final lashes. Fighting the urge to rush it is something that *never* happens to me. When she speaks that last count, I drop the cane to the floor.

"Fifteen, Daddy." My dick is the hardest it's ever been, enforced by the sight of the woman before me.

Sliding my hand between her legs and moving her thong to the side, my fingers are slick with her arousal. Then, I lean over, pressing gentle kisses to her crimson flesh. "You are so fucking resplendent when you submit, little one."

"Thank you..." She hesitates, her breathing labored. "Sir." She's unsure of herself now that her punishment is complete.

I round the table before slipping my hand under her chin, forcing her to look at me. "As I said, the rules are slightly different for a trainee sub. You may choose what you wish to call me. You will not be afforded that by any future Doms." Just the thought makes my chest tighten. She's mine.

"I..." Her shyness after what we just did is beyond adorable.

"Speak up for yourself, little one. You're safe with me. Do as you're told, and I'll let you suck my dick."

Her eyes light up, so I reach for my jeans, tugging the rest of the buttons open before reaching down and freeing my aching dick.

Fisting the base, I hold her gaze, watching as she licks her lips in anticipation.

"I wish to call you Daddy if you are comfortable. If not, I am happy to call you Sir."

"Say it with conviction, little one. There is no judgment in this room." The exact opposite. I want to drop to my knees and beg her to call me Daddy, but I can't. It wouldn't serve her well in her training.

"I want to call you Daddy."

"You're such a good girl for Daddy. Now, open your mouth." I run my hand through her hair, giving her some tenderness after she took her punishment without complaint. She does as I ask, opening those perfect lips.

I shove my jeans down to the floor before stepping out of them, standing naked before her in more ways than one.

Touching her lips with the head of my dick, I can't take my eyes off her as I wrap a fist in her hair. "Suck Daddy's dick, little one. And, be a good girl and swallow when I come in your glorious little mouth."

"Yes, Daddy."

As I slip my dick in, she wraps her warm lips around me, flicking her tongue over the tip. Fuck, I need to get myself under control before I come in three seconds flat.

"That's it, little one. Now, relax your throat so you can take more of me." She does as she's told, moaning against my dick. Her mouth is too goddamn good. It was made to be fucked by me.

I push further until I hit the back of her throat, her gag reflex kicking in.

"Don't fight it. Let me fuck your throat. It's normal to gag. Trust me, you look fucking magnificent, little one." She hums at the praise, and I feel the moment her body relaxes, taking more of me. It'll take some training for her to take all of me, but this feels so damn good. When I'm sure she can take it, I let go of her head, bracing my hands on the edge of the table as I thrust in and out, her tongue teasing the length of me as she sucks my dick like a lollipop, her mask still firmly in place. She is transcendent, but I long to see her face.

"*Christ!* You were made for me, little one." I set a punishing rhythm, chasing my release as the wet warmth of her mouth leaves me undone. I'm a man possessed. Obsessed. I want her more than my next breath.

As the first surge of my climax pulses through me, I try to stall even a few seconds, telling myself it's in the name of teaching her. "Remember to swallow my cum."

A few thrusts and I'm gone, an orgasm ripping through me as I continue to fuck her mouth, riding it out as hot spurts of cum spill down her throat. I ride the aftershocks before pulling out, almost collapsing to the floor it's so intense.

Freya splutters, my cum spilling out of her mouth with a gag. I take a moment to get my breath under control before smearing a finger through it and holding it up to her. "I said swallow, little one."

"I'm sorry, Daddy."

I push my finger into her mouth. "Lick it clean."

She does as she's told, tears pricking at the corners of her eyes. "Yes, Daddy."

"You did so well, little one. Your punishment. Your reward. Do you understand it's a reward to suck my dick?"

"Yes, Daddy." She slumps against the table, and I can imagine how tight her body must feel. I want nothing more than to fuck her and listen to her scream my name, but I said tonight was a lesson in punishment. Letting her come would show weakness.

Leaving her for a moment, I make my way to the door of the bathroom I had installed when I first bought my room. It's imperative to carry out proper aftercare with a submissive, especially a trainee. It is often overwhelming for them and doubly more so for Freya. Sex is new to her. As strong as she is, there's a softness I must allow her to lean into when it comes to submission.

For many, their real life is stressful and often high-powered. This room is a retreat. An oasis. After turning the faucet on to fill the tub, I grab a fresh washcloth and dip it in the water before heading back out.

"Such a pretty sight." As I approach the table, I can see that Freya is crying, and it makes my heart ache. "What's wrong, little one?"

I take the wet washcloth and clean her lips and chin of my cum. "Nothing, Daddy." Her voice is strained as her eyes flit closed beneath her mask. Dropping to my knees, I unbuckle the restraints around her ankles before moving behind her and freeing her wrists.

Her small body slumps back against me as I slip my arm under her legs and lift her into my arms. Pressing a soft kiss to her forehead, she trembles as I walk us into the bathroom. "I've got you, little one."

Setting her down on the tub's edge, I check the temperature before shutting off the faucet. I unlace her basque and tug her thong down her legs before I gently lower her into the tub, knowing how the hot water will sting her ass before it soothes her pain. Her legs and arms are limp as I slide in at her back before pulling her against my chest.

Soft cries escape her. "I'm sorry, Daddy."

"Don't apologize. Submission is emotional at the best of times. This is your first. I would be concerned if you weren't emotional."

I lift one wrist to my lips, pressing a kiss where the restraints held her in place. I repeat it with her other wrist. Then, I dunk a sponge in the water and start washing her from top to toe.

"Tell me how you feel, little one. What's going on in that beautiful head of yours?"

"I'm just... so... happy." I release a breath I didn't know I was holding.

"Was it as you expected?" I desperately want to remove her mask and mine. I want her to know who wrung such happiness from her.

"So much more. I feel... powerful. That doesn't even come close to explaining it. The perception of submission is that women are nothing more than an unpaid whore."

"People who think that are so wrong. You're not a whore, Freya. You are a rare diamond to be cherished. You're exquisite in your submission."

"Thank you… Daddy."

"You are very welcome, little one. I am so proud of you."

"Really?" She rests her head against my chest.

"Yes. You did exceptionally well for your first punishment. Are you sore? I have lotion to help with the sting after I'm done washing every inch of your delectable body."

"It hurts, but in the best way. I almost came just from the cane. Is that normal? Am I strange?"

"No, you're not strange, little one. I think we can safely say that you have a kink for pain, and it is more than possible to come during a punishment. For future reference, if you come before I allow it, you'll be severely punished."

"Is that a promise?" Her laughter tinkles through the air, delighting my senses.

"It's a certainty. Now, let's talk about the other kink we uncovered tonight."

She visibly shrinks at the mention. "I was out of order. You commanded that I call you Sir. I got carried away."

I grip her chin and tilt her head back to see me. "Stop apologizing for indulging a kink. If you didn't notice, I have the corresponding kink."

"I thought…"

"That I was placating you?"

"Yes."

"No. I will never do that. My job as your Dominant is to help you discover your soft and hard limits. Your wants and *needs*. Hear that again. You have *needs*, little one. It is brave to explore. In truth…" Now, I'm the one who hesitates. "I've never had a submissive call me that outside of a single lesson on the kink. *Sir* ensures that I keep a healthy distance from the subs I train."

"Why? If you don't mind me asking, Daddy."

"Because I train submissives so they can live the lifestyle with the knowledge of their particular kinks. I help them realize what they want in a partner. Short-term, long-term, or forever."

"So you don't keep submissives? Is that the right word?"

"I've never kept a submissive. I'm…" I trail my fingers down her arms before wrapping mine around her, holding her close.

"Just because I'm the submissive doesn't mean you can't talk to me, Daddy."

"I'm fucked up, little one. I am not fit to be anyone's forever Dom."

"We're all messed up in our own ways. I'm still wearing a mask after letting you do all kinds of wicked things to me. Tell me I'm not messed up."

"You'll be comfortable enough in time. What's wrong with me can't be fixed. It won't go away. I'll never be a man worthy of your… affection. It's better this way." The truth of my words is a physical pain in my chest. Honestly, I've never wanted to be that man until now.

"I think you're a better man than you believe yourself to be."

"I appreciate that, little one. For your next lesson, we will explore your Daddy kink further."

"Is that what you want? You said you don't let submissives call you that."

"I enjoyed you calling me Daddy. It seems only fitting that you're my *little one*. It seems I uncovered a kink myself. With you."

"I'm honored."

"Time to get out. The water is getting cold." I extricate myself from the tub and grab a towel, holding it for her. Her ass is crimson from the cane, and it's a beautiful sight. Once we've dried off, I grab the aloe vera and lead her back into the playroom and over to the bed. "Lie face down."

She is so elegant as she lowers herself onto the plush covers. I climb on the bed, straddling her as I squeeze a generous amount of aloe into my hand. She flinches as the cool lotion makes contact with her sensitive skin.

I smooth it out, careful not to rub too hard. "Your ass suits this shade of red."

"Thank you, Daddy."

"Are you frustrated, little one?" I already know the answer. How could she not be?

"Yes, but I understand why I'm not allowed to come."

"Why haven't you asked my name? I am eager to know more about you, and yet you desire nothing more than my dick and my ability to make your ass crimson. I'm not asking to make you uncomfortable. I want to understand so I know how best to teach you in our six months together." It's bullshit, and I know it. I want her to *want* to know more about me.

"It's easier to be free with you. Not knowing who you are, I don't have to carry the guilt of what pleases me. I don't have to be ashamed of what I want."

I still my hands before twisting her onto her back, making sure she's looking at me as I say this. "Whether you know my name or not or if you show your face, and I show mine, it won't change how you should behave in this room. I will *never* make you feel guilty for knowing what you want. You shouldn't feel ashamed of yourself, Freya. I will look at you with the same adoration as I do now, do you understand?"

"Yes." She chews on her bottom lip.

"Yes, who?"

"Yes, Daddy."

"Good girl." I lower my lips to hers, darting my tongue out to lick the seam, begging for entrance she freely gives. I could lose myself in this woman.

When I'm done with Freya's aftercare, I watch enraptured as she slips into her clothes. She makes jeans and a simple white T-shirt look so elegant.

"My driver will take you home. He'll be waiting out front."

"Thank you, Daddy."

"Come here, little one." I shrug on my pants and shirt, then hold out my arms to her. She gladly accepts my embrace, resting her head against my chest and listening to my heart beat wildly. "I am so proud of you. It was a pleasure to teach you this evening."

"Thank you, Daddy. Does that mean there will be a next time?" She cranes her neck back to look up at me expectantly.

"Yes, little one. I am helpless to refuse you, even if you will not show me your face." I lean in, pressing my lips to hers in a fervent kiss. "Mark the calendar when you get home."

"I will. I have a lot going on at work this week, but I'll find the time. A week and a half was far too long."

"I'm glad we're in agreement." I hold her tight, my stomach unsettled at having to relinquish her to the real world. There, she doesn't know me, crave me, or submit to my commands. In reality, I am nothing to her outside of this room.

"Until next time, Daddy." She pushes up onto her tiptoes, kissing me with the tenderness of familiar lovers, and it's all I can do not to tie her to the bed and never let her leave. I am the one who craves to know more about her. To make her mine long past our six-month agreement.

I can't think this way, losing sight of my raison d'être. She is not mine to keep.

"Goodnight, little one."

"Goodnight, Daddy." I watch as she heads for the door, leaving me bereft as I stand in my private room, the gravity of the situation hitting me like a wrecking ball. I'm getting into dangerous territory with Freya—a position I've never allowed myself to inhabit.

"I will be at your side the entire time, Perrington. You're ready to fly solo. You've watched, assisted, and committed this procedure to memory. Take a deep breath." We go through the rituals of scrubbing in for surgery—something we've done multiple times.

"Thank you, Dr. Harrison. I appreciate the opportunity." Perrington transferred from Vanderbilt this year, blowing my other residents out of the water. I'm not sure why, but the teacher in me is eager to bestow as much surgical skill as possible.

When we're scrubbed and ready, we enter the operating room, the nurses gowning and gloving us, the patient already sedated and properly draped for the procedure. I do find it difficult to relinquish control in my OR, but I required the same opportunities when I was a resident. If my mentor had not afforded me the chance to hone my skills, I wouldn't be the youngest attending this hospital has ever had. You've got to pay it forward to create the next wave of talented surgeons.

I stand on Perrington's left side, watching the initial cut of the scalpel and every move thereafter. The air in the operating room is tangible as everyone holds their breath.

"That's it. You're doing well."

Just when I think it's plain sailing, the monitors start beeping that obnoxious noise that tells me something isn't right. Perrington hasn't made a single wrong move, but every patient is different.

I kick into high gear, starting compressions and requesting the nurses to administer the necessary drugs. I can see the concern in Perrington's eyes.

"It's nothing you did. The procedure was flawless."

"I... what did I do?"

She's not listening to me. The first time operating solo is terrifying, even when everything goes to plan. When it doesn't, most surgeons will have a moment of panic, though they'd never admit it. This can make or break a surgeon.

"Listen to me, Perrington. You did *everything* right. Take a beat and tell me what needs to happen next." I don't falter, continuing to do what's needed for our patient.

"You should take over. I'm not sure I can do this."

"Stop. Look at me."

She meets my gaze, her eyes the only part of her face I can see behind the surgical mask. I speak just loud enough for her ears only.

"Breathe, little one."

Chapter 12

FREYA

"I'm right here. Quiet your mind and decide what we do next, little one."

No. No. No.

It can't be him.

This can't be happening.

What do I do?

"Look at me," he commands, his voice booming through the operating room as he continues compressions.

"I need to make more room for the brain swelling."

"Good. Do it quickly. We're running out of time to save this man."

My breathing is too fast, my pulse hammering in my ears, drowning out everything but the sound of his voice.

I get to work, the bone saw in my hand as I cut away more of this man's skull. It's the only thing that could save him. Did I do something wrong? Dr. Harrison is saying I did everything right. Dr. Harrison. *Daddy.*

There's no time to care about that right now. I have a patient's life in my hands. "Mannitol." I practically bark the dosage at the nurses, but they are cool, calm, and collected.

Just as I'm about to lose hope, Dr. Harrison says the words I'm desperate to hear.

"We've got a heartbeat. Sinus rhythm."

"Thank God." I take a gasping breath.

"No. Thank *you*, Dr. Perrington. Let's continue, close him up and get him to the ICU." He turns his attention to the rest of the room. "Great work, everyone."

He's always generous with his praise for nurses but rarely with residents.

I hold it together and take my time, giving my very best until the patient has been wheeled out of the operating room. I make short work of degloving and washing my hands. Dr. Harrison enters the scrub room, pulling his scrub cap and mask off. "We need to talk, Freya."

"I can't. Not here. Not now." I reach for the doorhandle when he stops me dead in my tracks.

"Stop, little one."

I look around as if other colleagues will appear out of thin air to witness my shame. "No. Goodnight, Dr. Harrison." My heart is pounding so hard *I'm* about to go into cardiac arrest.

"*Freya.*"

I spin to meet his gaze. "No. Do not talk to me right now. How long have you known?"

He crosses his arms over his chest, the corded muscles sending a jolt of electricity straight to my core.

"You either want an answer, or you want me to shut up. Which is it?"

"This…" I gesture between us, "… is done."

"Like hell it is. You're mine, little one." He closes in on me, bracing his hands on either side of me as my back hits the door.

"Not anymore. Let me go."

"Not until you address me properly."

"Let me go, Sir." I practically spit the words at him, disgusted by my traitorous body.

He leans in, his lips brushing the shell of my ear. "Wrong answer."

A shiver runs down my spine, my eyes on the floor. "Let me go… Daddy."

"Good girl."

He moves aside, letting me open the door, all the air sucked out of this room by his imposing figure. I walk out with my head held high, forcing myself not to look back, knowing his eyes are boring into me. It's not until I reach the residents' lounge that I collapse, dropping to my knees in defeat.

I almost lost my patient today. It took *Daddy* to stop me from spiraling. Tears fall unbidden down my cheeks as I hang my head. This wasn't supposed to happen. I wanted no strings attached. To be anonymous. Somehow, I managed to find my way into my boss's bed. His playroom, no less.

"*Fuck.*"

Calming myself, I shove what's going on with him down, knowing I need to get through the rest of my shift. I have notes to write up on the surgery and a patient to watch over. He deserves my very best and not this pathetic excuse for a woman I find myself to be at this moment.

Breathing deeply, I compose myself and get to my feet. I've fought too goddamn hard to get where I am. No man will stand in my way. I can find another Dom to train me. I can't find another neurosurgeon of *Daddy's*—Dr. Harrison's—caliber. I value his surgical skills over his cock, no matter how much I reveled in his dominance.

All I need to do is get through the night, then I can go home and fall apart at how badly I've messed up.

I find sanctuary in the ICU, sitting at my patient's bedside, monitoring him while I chart. Thankfully, Dr. Harrison only stops by once to check his vitals before heading home for the night. He doesn't try to engage me in conversation, and I don't even lift my eyes to meet his gaze.

My heart cracks at the gaping wound that festers in the air around us, and I breathe a sigh of relief when he leaves me to do my job.

~

The moment I see Celest sitting on the park bench at Strawberry Fields, I burst into tears, and she comes running.

"Oh my God, Frey, what's wrong?" She pulls me into her arms, my whole body sagging against her.

"It's over. It's him. He's Daddy."

She pulls back, pushing the hair off my face, cupping my cheeks with such tenderness. "Slow down. I thought you didn't know your Dad."

"No. *Him*. My Dom. He's my boss. Dr. Harrison."

She takes my hand and drags me to the bench, entreating me to sit and catch my breath.

"Start from the beginning."

"The Dom who has been teaching me is my boss, Dr. Harrison. Pierce Harrison."

"*Master Harrison* is your Dom?"

"Yes."

"Okay, but you've been training with him for weeks. Why is it a problem now?"

"We kept the masks on. I wanted to keep it simple, and the exact opposite is now my reality."

"Jesus, Frey."

"I let him eat me out with spectators, Cel. I gave him my virginity. I've been calling him Daddy. He's my attending. My new mentor I've been waxing lyrical about."

"Shit." Then, the penny drops. "You were a virgin? How is that even possible? You are smoking hot."

I wipe my eyes, chuckling at her observation. Of course, that's what she chooses to focus on. "I've always known I'm not vanilla. The longer I left it, the more it magnified. I dated guys who slut shamed me for asking for what I wanted when we started fooling around. In the end, I threw myself willingly into work. That's what's so hard about this. My mentor in the playroom is my mentor in the operating room."

"Fuck. He's a ten. I'd let him do all kinds of shit in the playroom."

My heart grinds to a halt. "Have you and he…"

"No. I didn't need training when I became a member at Venom. He doesn't sleep with established subs."

"Yeah." I can't help the pang of sadness that takes root in the pit of my stomach. "Six months is all I was going to get."

"He offered you a six-month contract?"

"Yes."

She rests her hand on my leg. "He doesn't do that, Frey. I can see you have feelings for him."

"It doesn't matter. I'm not going to be his submissive anymore."

"Why the hell not? He is a respected Dominant, Freya. You're lucky to be training with him."

"The things I've let him do to me, Cel. *My boss.*"

"You have a daddy kink? That's hot."

I shove her shoulder. "Stop."

"You're overreacting."

"Am I?" I say with indignation. She can't be serious.

"Yes. Venom is as discreet as they come. You can still separate work and the playroom. That's the point of a playroom, Frey."

"I don't want to get surgeries because I'm sleeping with my attending. It's tacky."

"Why are you so adverse to taking what you want in the bedroom?"

"What?" I'm taken aback.

"You heard me."

"Because I'm not normal, Cel. I want… pain. To be tied up and punished. I get off on it. I almost came when Daddy was caning me. Dr. Harrison. Pierce. Fuck. I'm so confused. This was supposed to be easy."

"Since when have relationships been easy? Nothing worth having ever is."

"*This* was supposed to be separate. I didn't want to know his name. I wanted pleasure and pain. Nothing more, nothing less."

"Then why the fuck are you sitting here crying to me about it? Tell him. So, you ditch the masks and know each other's names. Big deal. Sex is empowering, Frey. Being a submissive is *power*. You have the upper hand here. He will fall at your feet and beg to be your Daddy if that's what you want." I could never see him doing that. He's too masculine and dominant to beg for anything.

"Six months. That's all we agreed to. No feelings. Maybe it could work. We'll just go our separate ways after my training."

"Exactly. Fuck 'em and chuck 'em. Training is about *you*. What you like and want from a Dom. Master Harrison is never going to be a forever Dom, Frey. Be his sub and enjoy the crap out of it. You get to walk away and still have your mentor at work. Don't let yourself be reduced to getting surgeries for pussy. You're better than that, and Master Harrison knows it. From what I've heard, he's not the kind of guy to put someone's life in danger to impress you. I'm sure you're a fantastic lay, but he's a strong-willed Dominant. He doesn't do anything on a whim."

"I don't know if I can separate the two. I'd always wonder. Last night, I flew solo in the OR. I thought I earned it before I knew he was my Dom. I was terrified. The patient flatlined, and I just froze. Only when he called me *little one* did I kick into gear and do what was necessary to keep my patient alive."

"He called you little one in the OR? Fuck me, Frey, I think my ovaries just imploded. How are you not riding his face right now? I would be." The thought makes me angry. I told him we're done. I have no right to feel anything about who rides his gorgeous, impossibly handsome face. Who fists their hands in his dirty blond hair for purchase as they come on his lips.

Shit.

"Earth to Freya."

"Sorry. What?"

"You've got it bad. You're blushing, girl."

"Shut up."

"I can't believe you're a daddy's girl."

"Is that weird or just so cliché it's pathetic?"

"Who cares? If that's what you want, and he's cool with it,

everyone else can fuck off, Frey. You worry way too much about everyone else and not enough about yourself." I know she's right, and I'm self-aware enough to know why, but that doesn't make it any easier.

"Let's just go and drink. I want to drown my sorrows."

"No. We can celebrate your accomplishments. You flew solo, and your patient is alive. That's something to be proud of. The rest will take care of itself."

"Where shall we go?"

"Venom." She's a pain in the ass.

"What if he's there? I don't want to see him." I'm not ready.

"If he's there, we can go to a private room or up to the voyeur floor. We have as much right to be there as him."

"There are a million bars in Manhattan, Cel. Pick somewhere else."

"The only place that even comes close to Venom is Viper. The owner is also a co-owner of Venom, so Master Harrison would find out if we were there. Doms are very territorial, Frey. You may as well get used to it. Sometimes, it's easier to hide in plain sight. At Venom, your choices are respected above all else. If you don't want to talk to Master Harrison, he won't come near you."

"This is a bad idea."

"All the best memories start with a questionable idea and a couple of drinks. You only live once."

I'm going to regret this in the morning. "Fine. Venom it is."

Arm in arm, we head out of the park and hail a cab to take us to the club. On the ride there, I sneak a look at the phone Sir—Dr. Harrison—gave me and pull up the calendar. I breathe a sigh of relief, knowing he's working tonight.

There's a sadness that creeps over me with its frozen tendrils as we pull up outside Venom. Every time I come here, I still marvel at how innocuous it seems. How do they keep such a well-hidden secret in a city like Manhattan?

"You ready?" Celest says as we shuffle out of the back seat.

"He's not here. I'll be fine."

"How do you know?"

"We have a calendar we both keep our schedules on. He's working tonight."

"Wow. You guys are very involved in each other's lives for people who wear masks to have sex."

"Shut up, Cel. You love me for my quirks."

As we enter, we smile at the security guard now that he knows my face.

"That's not a quirk, girl. I'm just surprised."

"Why?"

"Because Doms who train are notorious. They all act the same way, and Master Harrison was no exception before he met you."

"In what way?" I'm suddenly worried that I'm not a proper submissive if things aren't playing out the way it does for everyone else.

"It's not a bad thing, Frey. Trainers don't interact outside of the club. They keep it short and sweet. You're trained to be someone else's submissive, not theirs. You learn the ropes... literally," she says with a smirk. "His kinks don't matter. He'll craft you into a good submissive. But the calendar and calling you by your pet name in a public setting... that's not Master Harrison's MO."

"What about the phone?"

"What about your phone?"

"He gave me this." I reach into my purse and hold out the cell he gave me as we take the elevator to the club lobby.

She snatches it from my hand. "You have a Dom phone? It's like the bat signal but for kink! Holy shit."

"Not normal?" I say with trepidation.

"No. How often do you talk or message?"

"Every day. He has me call him after his driver drops me off at night."

"You have a driver?" she exclaims.

I grab the phone back and toss it in my purse. "Can I even call myself a submissive? Why isn't he training me properly?"

"He is, Frey, but he's not training you to be someone else's submissive. He wants to make you *his* submissive."

"You're wrong. You just said a minute ago that training is all he'll ever see me as."

She stares me down as the doors ping open. "Fuck what I said. Masters don't call or text unless it's an instruction. They don't send drivers for a three-month sub. Heck, he's already contracted you for *six*. You have all the power here, Frey. Whatever you want from him, he'll do. You must've been one amazing virgin."

"That's not funny."

"It wasn't supposed to be. Frey, I know you're new to the lifestyle, and I am so thrilled that you and I share this now, so I would never make fun of you for your lack of experience. I learned the hard way that vanilla wasn't for me. I tried to shove that square peg into a round hole for years. You knew what you wanted and didn't settle for anything less. I admire that about you, and I'm sure Master Harrison does too."

"I need a drink."

Celest takes my hand in hers, drags me into the dark, decadent bar, and sits me down on a stool.

"What can I get you ladies?" Even the bartenders here are hot. It's insane. This guy could be a Calvin Klein underwear model.

"Hey, Eli. My friend here needs a celebratory drink. Give us two of your fanciest cocktails."

He looks at me. "What are you celebrating? A birthday? New job?"

"I saved a patient's life in surgery this week."

"Wow!" He looks dumbstruck. I forget sometimes that it's not part of most people's job to save a life. "Two cocktails coming up."

He busies himself behind the bar, and I turn my attention to the amazing décor surrounding us. "I haven't been back in this part of the club since the night of the masquerade."

"Why not? It's awesome."

"I was trying to remain anonymous, and I wasn't about to come and sit in here with my mask on."

"You worry way too much what other people think of you, Frey. You could walk in here wearing a flashing neon sign that says, 'I love cock' and you'd get nothing but high-fives. Honestly, let your hair down for once in your life."

"You forget that the last time I did that, my boss was licking me out with I don't know how many strangers watching."

"Exactly! Only good things can come from letting your hair down and your legs spread." Her timing is impeccable as always, the bartender serving our drinks as she references my spread legs.

"Cel. We don't need to be talking about that in front of poor Eli here."

A broad, panty-melting smile meets my gaze. "Trust me, I've heard worse in here."

"I'm..." I turn to Celest. "I've got nothing. Help me out."

"She's a newbie. People openly discussing kinks gets her panties in a wad."

"I get it. I think I spent my entire first shift blushing when I started here." He gives me a conspiratorial wink.

I take a sip of my drink, then chug the rest down and request another.

"Pace yourself, Frey. We have all night to get up to all kinds of mischief."

"Can we go up to the voyeur level?"

"There's my bestie! You don't have to ask me twice."

Eli supplies us with another round before we head upstairs to where it all began. As we ascend the staircase and the room comes into view, it's like a physical blow to my chest—the memory of seeing Dr. Harrison across the room. He made my knees weak as we danced and his lips felt as they pressed to mine in that first, soul-destroying kiss.

There are many couples, throuples, and more scattered throughout the space in various stages of undress, and my breath catches when I see a woman writhing on top of a table as one man feasts between her thighs and another is fucking her mouth.

"You okay, Frey?" Celest nudges my elbow, a little minx smile playing on her delicate features.

"They're all so... free." Excitement blooms in my chest as I take in the beauty of all I see around me. *It truly is beautiful to me.*

"That's because they are. Free to embrace their sexual appetites and revel in the ecstasy of connecting with other souls." Celest isn't usually so insightful. She's an amazing friend, and I love her to death, but this is new territory for us. She's the only person—other than Daddy—I've shared my wants and desires with.

"Have you done this before?"

"Yes," she says with a shy grin. Something I've never seen from her.

"How did it feel?"

"How did *you* feel when Master Harrison ate you out?"

"Dangerous. Thrilling. It was…"

"Powerful?"

"Yeah. But afterward, I felt an oppressive guilt settle over me."

"That's why you need to keep doing your training, Frey. There's nothing for you to feel guilty about. Everyone in here consents to anything that happens." She takes my hand in hers and walks us slowly around the room, moving between naked bodies in the throes of passion.

"She loves to have your eyes on her as she pleasures her Dom." I follow her line of sight to a beautiful brunette on her knees, her legs spread as she takes her Dom's cock in her mouth, moaning in delight as her eyes find mine. Holy shit. A jolt of desire strikes my core. "Beautiful, isn't she?" Celest's voice brings me back to the room.

"Gorgeous."

"Does it turn you on?"

"I… well…"

"It's safe to voice your desires here, with me. It doesn't leave this club. I would never betray your trust. No one you meet here would ever divulge your secrets. That's why this place exists."

"Yes, it turns me on. It makes me want to try it, but I don't know if Daddy would like it."

"Master Harrison will give you a lesson in voyeurism, participation, and observation."

A thrill courses through me. "Why do you refer to him as

Master? He's not your Dom." The words come out cattier than I intended.

"Because I command respect from *all* submissives, little one."

His voice douses the flame of my arousal like an ice bucket. He's not supposed to be here.

"Daddy?" I turn to face him, looking impossibly handsome. It's the first time I've seen him in this setting without a mask, and he is a thing of beauty. A Greek god.

"On your knees, eyes to the floor."

Chapter 13

PIERCE

"Do I have to spank you in front of everyone in this room? Get in the position." I'm hard as a fucking rock already. Seeing her watch other submissives embracing their kink on this floor is hot as hell. I'm not particularly fond of her observing other Doms, but it comes with the territory. Eventually, six months from now, she'll go off and find a forever Dom who can give her what she wants for the future. Until then, I will make her mine in every way I can.

She drops to her knees, resting on her heels as she gazes at the floor. It's not ideal since I have no ropes to restrain her arms, but she looks hot as fuck right now. Everyone in this room can see her submit to me, and I want to rip her clothes off and claim her as mine.

I didn't realize she was friends with Celest. She stands, mouth agape, as Freya sits in the position. Celest dips her head in acknowledgment. "Good evening, Master Harrison."

"Are you the reason my little one is engaging in voyeurism without permission?"

Her cheeks flush. "Yes, Master Harrison. I'm sorry. I meant no disrespect."

"Where is your Dom?"

"I... don't have one. I recently ended my contract." There's something in her eyes—a sadness—but she quickly schools her expression.

"Fine, then you won't have a problem kneeling beside your friend as punishment for leading her astray." She doesn't even attempt to fight me on it, instead falling to her knees beside Freya.

I derive no sexual gratification from Celest's submission, but I'm a teacher at heart, and she needs to learn that my little one is not permitted to engage in any behaviors at this club without me. If she wants to watch people fuck, I'll be on my knees licking her cunt while she does it. If she wants to participate, then I'm happy to have her drop to her knees and suck my dick while the whole goddamn club watches her greedily swallow my erection.

I pace around them, coming to a stop in front of Freya. "Did I give you permission to look at another man's dick?"

Her chest's rapid rise and fall betray her attempt at playing this aloof. "I'm not your submissive anymore." There's no conviction in her voice, but it smarts just the same.

"Like hell, you aren't. If you want out of our contract, then we will sit down and discuss it. Understood?"

"No." Her gaze lifts to mine. "I told you I'm done."

"And yet here you are on your knees at my command. I know you want me, little one. Your body doesn't lie. Tell me, if I slipped my hand into your panties right now, would you be wet?"

She doesn't answer.

I wait her out, knowing the answer all too well.

"Yes... Daddy."

I reach down, ghosting the back of my hand down her cheek, her skin like velvet. "You are not permitted to enter this floor without my say-so. Do you want to be punished in front of everyone?" My dick twitches at the thought, but who am I kidding? It would be for my pleasure rather than her punishment.

"Yes, Daddy." *Fuck me.*

"Stand up, little one." She does as she's told, her friend remaining on her knees. "You, too, Celest." She obeys.

Freya suddenly looks concerned, her brash dismissal of

moments ago lost on her lips as her eyes flit between her friend and me. Does she think I'm going to fuck another submissive?

"Celest, you will undress my little one. I want her completely naked."

"*Daddy!*" Freya tries to protest, but her cheeks are flush with arousal, and I know her panties will be soaking wet when her friend removes them. If she wants to be on the voyeur floor, then I'll teach her a lesson.

"Do you have something to say, little one? I asked you if you wanted your punishment here. You said *yes*. Don't tell me that was all bravado. You will learn that I don't respond well to bratty behavior. Now, are you going to take your punishment like a good little girl or not?"

She lowers her head. "May I ask a question first? Please, Daddy."

"Only because you addressed me so nicely."

"Will I have to share you this evening?" I already know she's a smart woman. Training to be a neurosurgeon isn't for the dimwitted.

"Are you asking if I'm going to fuck your friend?"

"Yes, Daddy."

"The answer is no. But, I will have her undress you and keep count for me as I bend you over my knee and spank you for coming up here tonight."

I look to Celest. "Would you be so kind as to strip your friend and keep count of her spanking? She needs to understand that I *will* take her anywhere, anytime, and with whoever I please watching."

"Yes, Master Harrison." Her breaths are ragged as she looks to her friend for a sign that she consents to this. Freya gives a small nod, and I'm ready to shoot my load.

"Follow me." I walk to the center of the room, where an oversized wingback chair is unoccupied, and sit.

When they are both before me, Celest speaks up. "Where would you like me to begin, Master Harrison?"

"I want to feast my eyes on her ample breasts."

"Yes, Master Harrison."

As she moves to unbutton Freya's blouse, I hold my little one's gaze. "You can say your safeword at any time."

"Yes, Daddy." Her voice shakes as her friend slowly undresses her.

"Good girl." I watch, enthralled, as first her blouse is discarded on the floor, then Celest unclasps Freya's bra and pushes it off her shoulders, letting it fall. Her nipples are already tightly budded as the air kisses them, on display for all to see.

"What next, Master Harrison?"

"Lose the heels and strip her down to her panties." I'm transfixed by the look of unbridled arousal on her face as she lets her friend tug down her skirt until all that's left is a scrap of lace to maintain an ounce of modesty.

When I take in the sight of Freya in nothing but her panties, my dick aches to be inside her once more. Technically, I told her I wouldn't fuck her until I knew who she was. She didn't tell me, but the cat is out of the bag now.

Celest's hand trails up Freya's leg, but she stops dead in her tracks at my command. "Nobody touches what's mine. You've relieved her of her clothes, now you can stand back and watch as I spank her pretty little ass, or you can touch yourself as I make your friend scream in pleasure and pain."

Freya's gaze meets mine, trepidation and excitement at war in her expression.

"I wish only to do what Freya is comfortable with, Master Harrison."

"Then ask her. You may address her as *Master Harrison's little one.* In this room, at this moment, she is not your friend. Only a fellow submissive."

She turns to Freya. "Would you like me to watch your punishment, Master Harrison's little one, or would you like me to touch myself as you receive your spanking?"

I know what Celest wants to do. It's written all over her face and in the way she presses her thighs together.

Freya looks to me for permission, which I give with a curt nod. This has to be on her terms.

"I would like you to… touch yourself." This woman is going to wreck me. I can already feel it.

"Very well. Now, come here, little one." I beckon for her to stand right in front of my chair.

When she's mere inches from me, I look around her at Celest.

"Master Harrison, may I remove my clothes?"

"Yes." It doesn't matter to me if she's naked or not. My eyes will be fixed on my little one, but I think she'll get a kick out of seeing the full show from her friend. The fact that she asked her to touch herself is a big step forward for my girl. She's slowly learning to ask for what she wants.

"Thank you."

I turn my attention back to Freya. "Would you like to watch your friend strip before I put you over my knee?"

"Yes, Daddy," she whispers, her breaths shallow and rapid. She must be soaked.

"You can watch her if you hand me your panties. Otherwise, you can go over my knee now and miss the show she's about to give you."

She hesitates, staring me down. She's as pissed off as she is turned on right now. The spark in her eyes becomes a blazing inferno. Freya has avoided making contact for days. She came here without me and was planning to spend the night here on the voyeur floor. I'm the one who should be pissed.

Without another word, she slips her fingers under the sides of her panties and shimmies out of them, devastatingly beautiful as she gives herself over to the club. *To me.* Suddenly, the room is empty, everyone else fading away as I take in the sight before me.

This isn't how I imagined Freya submitting to me for the first time without her mask, but I'm so fucking proud of her right now. I know this isn't easy for her, and considering she hasn't spoken to me since I revealed myself as her attending, I'm aware of how much faith she's putting in me tonight.

"You are stunning, little one," I growl.

"Thank you, Daddy. May I watch Celest now?"

"Yes, but you can watch her as you lie across my knees. She has to count every spank." Her breath catches as she steps to my side. I offer my hand to steady her as she gets into position across my lap, her ass presented and ready to be spanked.

Running my hand over her cheeks, I delight in the way she trembles beneath my touch.

"May I look now, Daddy?"

"Yes, little one. Watch her strip down the way she did you."

She tilts her head, her breathing labored as she focuses on Celest. Her friend grips the hem of her dress, pulls it over her head, and casts it to the floor, her eyes on Freya. Standing in her bra and panties, she diverts her gaze to me. "Is this to your liking, Master Harrison?"

"It is not me who desires to see your body this evening. That is a question for my little one."

I give Freya's ass a short, sharp slap. "Answer her."

"Take off your underwear." My little one is bold tonight, though her voice wavers as she chokes out the words.

Celest meets her gaze, nodding in agreement. As my good little sub watches intently, I slide my hand between her legs, feeling how wet she is.

"Are you aroused at the thought of seeing your friend's pussy as wet as yours?"

"Yes, Daddy," she breathes out.

Celest slips her underwear off before taking a seat in the chair across from us, opening her legs wide for Freya to see her cunt, slick with arousal.

"You will receive ten spanks for coming to the voyeur floor without permission. Do you understand, little one?"

"Yes, Daddy." Fuck. Every time she calls me that, my dick is harder than steel.

I speak so only she can hear me. "You are fucking resplendent, little one, and so wet. Do you like seeing your friend's naked body?"

"Yes, Daddy." When we're done here, I'm going to fuck her so hard she won't be able to walk tomorrow.

"Now, watch as she pleasures herself, and take your punishment like a good little girl."

Celest caresses her breasts before letting her hand stray down between her legs, and my little one can't take her eyes off her. "Yes... Daddy."

I administer the first spank, delighting in the way Freya's body tenses and her legs part.

"Count, Celest." I bark the order.

"One, Master Harrison."

"You may address my little one as you count." I've never had a problem being addressed by multiple subs at one time. In fact, I've welcomed it. But with Freya, it feels different.

I land the second slap, her ass turning a light shade of pink.

"Two... little one." Celest continues to tease herself.

Freya squirms in my lap, trying to ease the ache I know is growing between her thighs.

Another spank and my girl starts to writhe against me.

"Spread your legs, little one." She does as I ask, and the next slap connects with her cunt. "Oh, you're so wet. So greedy for release. Do you want my dick? Or is it Celest's pussy you crave right now?"

She doesn't answer immediately, transfixed by her friend as she shouts, "Three, little one."

"Answer me."

"I... want your dick, Daddy."

"And yet you hesitate." Another spank. Celest continues to count as she presses two fingers into her pussy, writhing on the chair with her eyes fixed on Freya and me.

Another, and another, and another. "Seven, little one." I can see Celest is on the brink of orgasm, but I have other ideas.

"Celest, do not come until I grant you permission."

"Yes, Master Harrison." Her voice drips with desire while my little one grows wetter by the second.

Three slaps to go, and I know exactly where I'm going to focus my attention. Freya has been on the edge since she took off her underwear and bared herself to everyone in this room. We're drawing quite the crowd now, people forming a circle around the two chairs and two submissives currently answering to me.

If Freya so much as brushes my dick the wrong way right now, I'll come. It is so fucking hot watching her as she marvels at her friend's blatant, unapologetic pleasure.

"Eight, little one." Celest moans as her fingers pick up pace.

"That's it, little one, almost there. Are you ready to come for me?" Freya's soft mewls are all the confirmation I need. I bring my palm down on her cunt, the sting sending a shockwave of desire ricocheting through her into me.

"Nine, little one."

"Good girl. Now, are you ready to come when I give your friend the go-ahead?"

"Yes, Daddy. *Yes!*"

"Come for her, Celest. Let my little one see you come undone because of her."

I lean down, pressing my lips to the shell of Freya's ear, whispering so only she can hear. "Come for me, little one, but don't you dare take your eyes off Celest. See how beautiful she is as she falls apart. *You* did that to her. Come for *me*. Now."

As my hand connects with Freya's pussy one last time, Celest is screaming her release.

"Ten, little one. Oh fuck... yes..." She throws her head back, half the room watching intently.

Freya convulses over my lap as she finds release, but my name on her lips is what sends me over the edge. "Yes... Daddy. Oh God, yes, Daddy!"

I quickly maneuver her, limp in my arms, a soft sheen of sweat covering her entire body.

"Unzip my fly, little one. You're about to ride my dick for everyone in this room to see what you do to me." Without question, she unleashes my achingly hard dick and positions the tip at her entrance.

I slam her down onto my lap, impaling her with one harsh, mind-altering thrust. She's so fucking tight, and there's only one thought on my mind. *She's mine.*

"Good girl. Take every hard inch of my dick."

The building crowd is silent. If it weren't for the ambient

music in the background, you'd be able to hear a pin drop, everyone mesmerized by my girl, and I can't blame them. She's in her element, free as a bird and soaring high on the wings of release.

"Daddy…"

"You're okay, little one. Let go and show them what's mine."

She moans in reply.

So lost in Freya, it takes me a moment to realize Celest is naked at my side.

"May I kiss her, Master Harrison?"

"Her lips are mine," I groan as my girl continues to ride me like no one is watching.

I brush the hair from Freya's shoulder, burying my face in her neck. "Do you want Celest to kiss you? Not your lips. Those are for me."

"I… I want… want…"

"Get up, little one. Turn and face the other way and take my dick like a good little girl." She's quick to reposition herself, greedy for my dick once more. With her back to my chest, I spread her legs as wide as they'll go. "Chest out." She's so responsive and such a good little girl for Daddy.

"What do you want me to do, Master Harrison's little one?" Celest now stands before Freya, still unashamedly naked.

My little one tenses in my arms, and I know she's too shy to ask, even after everything we've done tonight.

"I will allow you to kiss her breasts while I bring her to orgasm. I want you to bite her nipples until she feels the sting as my dick splits her in two."

"Yes, Master Harrison."

"Her mouth and her cunt are off limits. She belongs to me."

"Yes, Daddy," Freya interjects, panting as she continues to circle her hips with my dick deep inside her, seated to the hilt.

Celest reaches forward, cupping Freya's ample breasts, heavy with arousal as her friend leans in, pressing her lips to my little one's wickedly sinful curves. Freya's head drops back against my chest, every thrust of her hips hitting the spot. It takes everything in me to delay my gratification. I'm hard as a rock and aching to come, but this isn't about me.

With the masks gone and the truth out, Freya is a vision of blissful sensuality as she gives herself over to the pleasure being wrung from her body by Celest and me.

I'd be lying if I said it didn't turn me on to see another woman sucking on my little one's breasts. I watch enraptured as Freya pushes her chest forward, leaning into her friend's caress. She reaches one arm behind my neck, anchoring herself as she continues to thrust. To take what she wants.

"Daddy… it's too much. I can't. I need. I want."

I wrap my arm around her waist as I meet her hips with mine, forcing her to take everything I have. "It's okay, little one. When you're ready, you can come."

Celest licks, kisses, and nibbles Freya's nipples, teasing her to the edge of madness. I feel the moment my girl lets everything else fall away, giving herself completely to the sensations hitting her from all angles. As her cunt tenses around my dick, I slam into her until she cascades over the edge, screaming for me as she comes *hard*. "Daddy… oh God… yes… Daddy. *Daddy!*"

She pulls me down with her, my dick pulsing as I spill myself inside her. We ride the aftershocks together, the crowd clapping for the show they just witnessed.

Every fiber of my being is buzzing with adrenaline, turned on, my dick still hard inside her.

I press a gentle kiss to Freya's shoulder as she slumps back against me. "How was that, little one?"

"A-mazing, Daddy. I never knew it could be this way."

"I believe we just uncovered a few more of your kinks." Her cheeks blush as she turns to meet my gaze.

"Was it… okay for you?"

"Yes, little one. But I've shared you enough for one night. My private room, now. You'll have to dress to go through the bar downstairs, but I expect you naked, in the right position in ten minutes."

"Yes, Daddy." I can't take my eyes off her as she slips on her clothes on and stops to embrace Celest before disappearing down the stairs.

As I force my erection into my pants, Logan Fitzgerald comes to a stop in front of me, a slow clap echoing through the room. "That was quite the show. You finally decided to find a forever sub."

His words are jarring. He was a Master Dom, training submissives for over a decade before falling in love with his now wife. We're not the same. That's what I'm telling myself.

"No. She's a trainee."

"It didn't look that way. I've never seen you allow a sub in training to dictate what someone else, male or female, may do to them."

"She's new to, well, everything."

"Kink?"

"All of it." I pull him aside as the crowd disperses. "Do you have time for a drink?"

"Don't you have a sub to attend to?"

"Sitting in the position will build her anticipation."

"Then, sure. Let me just tell Vittoria. She was intrigued by your dynamic with the other sub. She better not be getting any ideas. I don't fucking share her with anyone, male or female."

We make our way over to the bar, people congratulating me on a successful fuck. I utilized the old voyeur room on occasion, but I've never fucked a woman with a room full of people right there, inches away. It was exhilarating seeing how Freya got off on it. I'd never let another man fuck her, but she enjoyed having the small introduction of another submissive. I hope she doesn't let her thoughts get the better of her now that the haze of the moment has passed.

Logan is a trusted friend and respected Master. I value his opinion. As we take a seat at the bar and order drinks, I ask the question I dare not ask anyone else. Not even Dalton.

"How did you know when you wanted more than a trainee to fuck? How did you know Vittoria was the one?"

He doesn't hesitate. "The moment I kissed her, I knew my life had changed. No one else mattered. Fuck, I risked my friendship with Carter for her. He wasn't exactly happy when he learned the nature of my relationship with his sister." Carter is one of the co-owners of Venom and a good guy. Protective as hell, so I can only imagine how that all went down.

"She's a twenty-four seven submissive, yes?"

"Yes, and I'm a twenty-four seven Dominant. With one comes the other. You can't forget about that if you're considering that dynamic."

"I'm not." *Am I?*

Fuck.

I wanted answers, not more questions, especially when I'm not ready to face the truth.

"Oh, shit. You're in love with her."

"Who said anything about love?"

He pins me with a smug grin on his stupid face. "You're so screwed, my friend. Come back and talk to me when you're ready to admit it."

"There's nothing to admit. I love her. *Shit.* I mean, I *don't* love her."

"Can you say Freudian slip?"

"Fuck you, Logan."

He throws his drink back before clapping me on the back. "I think we both know who's fucked here. That would be you, my lovesick friend. I'll be around when you want some pointers on the whole marriage, twenty-four seven situation."

"You're wrong," I exclaim as he walks away, laughing his ass off.

"Delusional," he tosses over his shoulder.

Shit. The problem is, I'm not delusional at all. I *know* I'm fucked.

Chapter 14

FREYA

What if Celest can never look me in the eye again? As I sit on my heels, my wrists above my head, secured in the ropes, I wait for Daddy to arrive. My heart is pounding, my pulse racing in my ears as I spiral out of control.

I let my best friend kiss my tits, and what's worse is that I loved every minute of watching her get herself off in a room full of strangers. It was such a rush. I've never come so hard. I couldn't take my eyes off her. She's so beautiful and self-assured. It didn't bother her that people were watching such an intimate moment. The way she fell apart as she shouted each of my spanks was just magnificent. I never considered myself to have any sexual attraction to women, but tonight has shown me that there's a spectrum.

I was turned on beyond belief when Daddy let her suck my tits while I rode his cock. One thing I know above all else is that I can't walk away from this relationship with Dr. Harrison. It might be the smart decision to cut ties now, but the way he brought my body to life tonight has me wanting to make bad decisions. He let me shed everyone's preconceived notions of sexuality and made me purr like a kitten.

I want more. I *need* more from him. He's everything I ever fantasized about, and I'm not ready to let go of that.

The soft click of the door alerts me to his arrival. "Such a good little girl. You were breathtaking up there. Everyone was enraptured by your pleasure. I know I was."

"Thank you, Dr. Harrison." The words leave my lips before I think better of them.

I hear him getting closer before his hand fists in my hair, yanking my head back until he can look into my eyes. "You forget where you are, little one. Apologize."

"Sorry, Daddy."

"There's my little one." He doesn't untie me as he normally would, leaving me vulnerable and at his mercy. "Now, let's talk about why you were punished. Care to explain yourself?"

Suddenly, my indignation bubbles to the surface. "You lied. You knew who I was and didn't tell me. When did you realize I was your resident?"

"I don't like your tone, little one. If you don't want a harsh punishment with no release, I'd be careful how you continue. Firstly, I didn't lie. You walked into the fundraiser in that fucking exquisite lavender dress. It's been burned into my brain since the masquerade ball."

"You've known that long? Fuck you."

He leans over, yanking the ropes up, forcing me up off my heels. "Fuck me? I've been *trying* to get to know you since the night we met. You're the one who didn't want to let me get closer. I didn't fucking lie."

"What are we going to do now?"

"Well, we start by discussing the fact that you came here tonight to watch Doms fucking their submissives all around you. My permission is needed for such things."

"I can do what I like."

"Is that right?" He tugs even tighter. "You signed the contract, little one. The one that says you will abide by my rules. Do you think you've trained enough? Are you ready to go back up there and offer yourself as a sub to a seasoned Dom who doesn't give a shit about your training or lack thereof? If you don't comply, they will exact punishments you couldn't even imagine."

It's not lost on me that I squeeze my thighs together at the mention of punishment. I have a major punishment kink.

"Then tell me, Daddy, what would they do to me?" I know I'm goading him, but I'm annoyed at myself for giving in so quickly. I came here tonight to prove I can live this lifestyle without his training, and the second he showed up, I called him Daddy and dropped willingly to my knees.

He twists me in the ropes, and they burn as he makes me face him—a wall of pissed-off, hot-as-hell muscle crowding me in the corner, my back now pressed against the cool, hard wall.

"They'll do nothing to you, little one. You're mine, and nobody touches what's mine unless I decide otherwise. Do you want other men to fuck you? Other Doms? Male submissives? Shall I parade them in here, and you can have your way with as many as you can manage before cum is dripping from your pussy, asshole, and your smart mouth?"

The rapid rise and fall of my chest betray my attempt at composure. "No."

"Right answer, little one. I own your cunt, and you only have yourself to blame. You gave your virginity to me without question, and I'll be damned if some other man takes what's mine. I want all your pleasure, pain, and everything in between."

"What if I don't want you anymore? Now that I can't be anonymous." I quiver as I speak, a thrill coursing through me as he drops to his knees and yanks one of my legs over his shoulder, opening me up to his ministrations.

He buries his face between my thighs, sucking on my clit as he thrusts two fingers inside me. I cry out from the intrusion, my arguments dying on my lips. "Daddy."

"Yes, little one? You were saying you don't want me anymore." He hums against my most sensitive skin, his tongue wicked and made for sin.

"I want you, Daddy." The second the words fall from my lips, he leaves me bereft.

"The next time you call me anything other than Daddy in this room, being denied release will be the least of your worries."

I tug against the ropes, frustrated beyond measure. "Maybe I'll just have Celest get me off. I'm sure she'd enjoy sucking more than my tits."

He jumps to his feet and grabs my face with one hand, his lips an inch from mine. "Don't let tonight go to your head, little one. I may have indulged you up there, but no one, not even your friend, is allowed to taste your arousal. If you want her to lick you out, go ahead." He unties the ropes and strides over to the chest of drawers as I massage my wrists. "But this…" he says, holding up our contract, "… will be null and void."

"I." I'm lost for words as panic sets in.

"Cat got your tongue, little one? Are you ready to apologize to Daddy and be my good little girl?"

I want to scream, shout, and push back, but I find myself dropping to my knees at his feet, my eyes on the floor. "I'm sorry, Daddy."

"Now, we can talk about the predicament we find ourselves in. This wasn't exactly what I had planned the night of the masquerade ball." He starts to pace the room while I remain in the position of complete submission. "If I'd known you were my protégé, I wouldn't have pursued you."

"And when you did find out, why did you continue to let me train with you, Daddy?" Holy Mother of all that is good and pure, I love calling him that. Psychology 101 isn't a requirement to understand why I have deep-seated Daddy issues.

"Because you were already under my skin. In my every waking thought and every blissful dream. I'm a selfish man, little one, and I want more of you. You're mine, and I will *ruin* you for any other man."

My breath catches at his honesty. The idea that I belong to him should send me running, but I find myself filled with delight. "They say a Dom who trains submissives, by definition, doesn't want a sub of his own. Why would you want to ruin me for my Dom?"

He grabs me under the arms and hoists me up until I wrap my

legs around his waist. "Because I'm your fucking Daddy. I don't want you to leave and find a Dom more deserving of your affection. I *need* you more than my next breath, and I…"

His lips crash down on mine as he walks us over to the bed, never breaking our kiss as he lowers me onto the comforter. Reaching between us, I make short work of his pants, fisting his impressive erection, guiding him to my entrance, begging for more.

He takes me in one painful, delicious thrust, seating himself to the hilt as our tongues twist and tangle in a frenzied fuck.

"You're mine, little one. Say it."

I moan as his cock fills me, owning me with every move of his hips. "I'm yours, Daddy."

"Fucking right. Your cunt is mine." He swallows my cries as he fucks me hard.

"Yes, Daddy." I rake my nails down his back, leaving my mark on him. If he wants to own me, then I stake the same claim to him. He's *my* Dominant. *My* Daddy.

I've heard the phrase 'fuck into submission' before, but at this moment, I understand. Daddy is fucking me into submission, and I take it willingly.

His dirty blond hair is sex-mussed, and his features are devastatingly handsome as he hovers above me, his cock driving into me time and time again. Even though we just had sex, I was facing away from him. This is more intimate, not due to the lack of other people watching, but because we are finally face to face, naked and unashamed, with no barriers to hide behind.

"Fuck, you feel too good, little one. I could spend the rest of my life buried inside you." His lips find mine once more, his tongue stroking mine in the most tantalizing of ways.

"Yes… yes… Daddy." It's like a red rag to a bull. He loses all control, setting a punishing rhythm as he circles his hips, owning me every time he seats himself to the hilt.

"That's right, little one. I'm your fucking Daddy. Don't ever forget it," he growls as he struggles to stave off the orgasm threatening to rip through us like a tidal wave. He is savage in his desire for me, and I've never felt so wanted in my life. I give myself over to him completely—body, mind, and soul.

"Oh God... I'm close."

"Come for Daddy." Now, I'm the savage, feral with the need for release, clawing at him as my lips find his. Nothing else matters. Only us, in this room, taking and giving as much pleasure as we can wring from each other's body.

My orgasm is a crack of thunder before the lightning storm as Daddy pulls me under, the roar of his release catapulting me into a second climax. I never want to leave this room or him.

"Jesus, little one, I'll never get enough of you." He presses gentle kisses to my neck, just below my ear, making me moan as his hand caresses my breast.

When he finally collapses at my side, I can't take my eyes off him. Everything that's happened between us thus far collides with the reality of work and the many conversations we've had over the past few months as resident and attending.

The night of the hospital fundraiser comes to mind. He told me to take off my panties, knowing who I was and that he was sitting right there.

"Why didn't you tell me sooner? I feel like I've been played this whole time. You knew I wanted the club to be no strings attached."

His jaw tightens, ticking as he considers his words. As with everything else, he is meticulous. "All rational thought goes out the window when it comes to you. I've broken every rule in the book for one more kiss, caress, or even a damn phone call."

"What rules?"

"I don't sleep with virgins. I don't train subs for more than three months because attachments are made... on their end. I've never crossed the line as a Master. I don't date at work. The list goes on."

"Why me?" He reaches over, tucking a loose tendril of hair behind my ear, his gaze soft and sensual.

"Because you're brilliant, beautiful, and there's a shyness to you that's endearing."

"Shy?" I chuckle. "We just had sex in front of a room full of people."

"And yet you're avoiding my gaze as you lie here with my cum dripping from your cunt. I've never met a submissive who can be bashful and brash at the same time."

"I've never done any of this before."

"Your inexperience isn't the issue. You proved that upstairs. What matters is *you*. Did you enjoy what we did?"

"Yes, but I'm already afraid that Celest won't be able to look me in the eye. She and I have never coexisted in a sexual scenario."

"*Coexisted?* Is that what we're calling it?" He gives me a panty-melting smile, and I melt.

"What would you call it then, oh wise Dom?"

"I'd say you got off on watching your friend come. You appreciated her beauty and the way her mouth felt as her lips kissed your breasts. You loved every second of it. I felt how wet you were while I spanked you, little one. You're an exhibitionist."

"Ugh." I cover my eyes, so embarrassed.

"Freya," he whispers, pulling my arm from my face. "You're allowed to enjoy all those things. Trust me, Celest is open-minded. She engages only in activities that she's comfortable with. She didn't strip, get off, and kiss you because she didn't want to say no. She did it because you're beautiful, and she wanted to help you learn what you like and dislike. I promise she will look you in the eye when you leave here."

"I'm usually such a confident person. I've always known what I want from my career, and even that is proving difficult right now."

"Why? Because of me?"

"Yes. And no. It complicates things, but not enough that I want to stop whatever it is we're doing here. I respect you as a doctor, and I'd be a fool to walk away from your mentorship."

"Simplify it then. I'm your mentor at work. I'm your mentor in this club. The two don't have to intersect unless you want them to."

"You mean we can keep us a secret at work?"

"If you want." A pang of disappointment hits me out of left field.

"That's what you want. I guess it wouldn't look good to be dating your protégé."

He grabs my chin, forcing me to meet his gaze. "I asked you a question. This isn't about me. I'm taking your lead here, little one. You use the word dating, yet you told me we were done just a few days ago. Until you decide what you want from me, I won't speak a word of it, mostly because it's nobody else's fucking business."

"I don't know what we are. We're not boyfriend and girlfriend, are we? What do people refer to each other as in the lifestyle? Sure, in here, I can call you my Dom or Daddy, but I'd be crucified for using those terms with normal people."

"*We* are normal people, Freya. And, yes, I'm using your name because wherever you are and whatever I call you or you call me, we're good people. We save lives every day. You have to get out of this close-minded thinking. The world is far more accepting than you think. More and more people are embracing their kinks and are unapologetic for it. As it should be."

"I'm scared."

"Of what," he whispers, softly caressing my cheek, his eyes in a haze as he stares at my lips.

"Needing you."

"I'm your Dom. You're supposed to need me."

"I'm your trainee. We have an agreement, not a relationship."

"And would it change things for you if what we have had a different definition?"

He trails his fingers down my chest, the lightest of touches kissing my nipples. His hands are beautiful, literally and physically —strong, manly, and yet I know they are capable of the closest humankind can come to magic.

"I love your hands." I blurt it out without thinking.

"Good to know," he says as it moves lower, cupping my pussy.

"I meant as a surgeon. You have such skilled hands."

He dips one finger inside me, making me squirm. "Only skilled for surgery?"

"I... yes. Your hands are amazing no matter what you're doing."

"You still haven't answered my question. Does the definition matter?"

"At work. Yes."

"That's an easy fix. At work, I'll be your boyfriend. In here, I'm your Daddy." I'm surprised he's so amenable to the idea. He's always been known as a lone wolf at the hospital. Sort of grumpy. Now, I see his confidence that so many call cocky is nothing sinister. He's self-assured and knows what he wants. He doesn't suffer fools gladly and invests his time in the most noble of careers. His life is about saving his patients.

In this room, he teaches women to feel empowered in their femininity and sexuality. It gets me to thinking.

"Have you ever trained male submissives?"

"Where is your head at, little one? You've gone from wanting a boyfriend, a Daddy, and now you're questioning my masculinity."

I stiffen at his words. "I don't think it changes your masculinity at all. I'm just curious about your status as a Master Dom."

"Good, because I don't equate sex with masculinity. I'm more than confident in how manly I am. You should know that by now, little one. To answer your question, yes, I have trained male submissives before. Two to be exact. However, I'm not sexually attracted to men. I trained them in all aspects outside of penetrative sex."

"Does that mean you've given a guy a blow job?" I should stop talking, but I'm so turned on at the thought of him teaching a man to submit.

"No. I'm all about burying my head in cunt, if you haven't figured that out. I have *received* a blow job from one of my male subs. He was in search of a same-sex Dom."

"Holy shit."

"How did you reward them if you didn't pleasure them?"

"I worked in tandem with a prospective Dom."

"If they had someone in mind, why not train with them?"

"Because Masters make it their goal to uncover the kinks of the submissive, not to mold a submissive to their particular preferences."

"I don't get it." If you like someone, and you want to be their submissive, why go to someone else?

"Take us, for instance. As your trainer, I perform different kinks to explore your likes and dislikes. You came to your own conclusions that you enjoy pain and have a Daddy kink."

"Which you said you like."

"I do. I really fucking do. But I never asked you to call me Daddy. Therein lies the difference. If I met you here in the club and were looking to make you my forever sub, you'd have come in here on day one, and I would've had you address me as Daddy, not Sir. As a Master, I keep my kinks out of the equation in order to help a sub uncover their kinks."

"So, you don't do anything you enjoy with me? Your kinks?"

"I shouldn't have used us as an example."

"Why?"

"Because it's different with you."

"Am I a terrible student?" I move to put some distance between us in the bed, but Daddy pulls me closer.

"You're perfect, little one. I do indulge in my kinks with you, but this is the first time I've ever *wanted* to share my kinks with someone."

"Really?"

He lifts my chin before leaning in and pressing his lips to mine. "Yes. I can't explain it, but I want you to know me, Freya... my flaws, my kinks, all of it. Here in the club and at work. Let me be your boyfriend in the hospital and your Dom in here."

"Doesn't that complicate things?"

"I'm trying here. What do you want from me? I'm trying to give you more."

"I didn't ask you for more." It comes out harsher than I expected.

"Fine. Do you want me to go back to wearing a mask so you don't have to remind yourself that I'm the guy fucking you?" He shrugs out from under my resting head and grabs his clothes.

"I didn't mean it the way it sounded."

"You kept the fact that you were a virgin from me. I shouldn't be surprised that you want to keep this clinical. I'll train you like I do all the others. We needn't bother with the trifling details of our lives."

"Stop," I say as I wrap the sheet around my naked body. "I just meant that I don't expect you to want the dating and all the stuff that comes with it. I've never been very good at it anyway."

"Bullshit. You've never had a man who *knew* you."

"And you do?" I can't stop myself. This is what I do. I run when I'm scared, and if I get a whiff of feelings for someone, I mess it up because eventually, everyone leaves. Better to be the one walking out the door than the one left crying in the corner.

Chapter 15
PIERCE

"I'm fucking trying to!" Freya is the most frustrating woman I've ever met.

"What?"

I stop in my tracks, naked as the day I was born, standing with my jeans in my hand.

"I'm trying to fucking know you, Freya. We tried it your way. Masks, distance, and nothing more than words in a contract. Where did it get us? Neither of us anticipated that we were already in each other's lives, but here we are. If you can't handle that, then walk away now because I can't."

"What do you mean you can't? You don't want to be the one to end it because you're the mighty Dom and world-renowned Dr. Harrison."

"Jesus Christ, woman. Are you even hearing me?" I drop my jeans to the floor and hold my arms out, vulnerable and completely out of my element. "Do I have to spell it out? This isn't about my reputation in or out of the playroom. *I have feelings for you,*" I exclaim.

She goes stock-still as if she'll become invisible if she doesn't move.

"I'm not a dinosaur, Freya. My vision isn't based on movement.

Do you have anything to say? I don't exactly go around professing…" I stop myself before I say something to really spook her.

"What if I want you to be both? What if I want you to be my Daddy all the time? And I want that to come with you being my boyfriend?" My heart is hammering in my chest.

"Don't fuck around, Freya."

"I'm not."

"To be your Daddy, you're asking for something outside of training. Just so I understand, you have to clarify, little one."

She takes a deep, steadying breath, her hand trembling as she rests it over my heart. "I still need training, but the thought of walking away after six months makes me feel sick to my stomach. I know I'm asking a lot. You don't date."

"It's a rule for a reason, Freya. New submissives may *think* they want me to be more, but I disappoint people. You're caught up in the excitement of exploring your kinks. I get it. But when the time comes, you'll want a Dom who's worthy of you." I couldn't even make my parents stay, and they were obliged to love me, though they never got the memo.

"Why do you think yourself unworthy?"

"We don't need to talk about my tortured soul, Freya."

"Will you stop for a minute? I didn't mean what I said earlier. If you want to know me better, then this is it. I say dumb shit all the time, especially around people who intimidate me."

"You're intimidated by me? That's not how this dynamic should work."

"I'm not talking about when we're in this room. I mean at the hospital. You are this amazing surgeon who I aspire to be like. You're the youngest neurosurgery attending in the country. The most skilled. You don't let your personal life interfere with work."

"Until now."

"I'm not *fucking around*, as you put it. I want you to be my Daddy, and when we're at work, I don't want to hide our relationship. I don't know what that looks like. I've never dated a coworker."

"Me either."

"So how do we do this?"

"We figure it out as we go along. I'll let the Chief of Surgery know that we're dating. It's best practice in this instance. Then, we just go about our lives. People might see us eating lunch together or a stolen kiss in a quiet hallway. If you're lucky, the on-call room might become your favorite place for me to bury my head between your legs."

Fuck, I'm hard just thinking about it. I quickly slip into my jeans and wrestle my dick under control.

"We can't do that at work."

I lean in, pressing my lips to the nape of her neck. "If I tell you to spread your legs so I can feast on you, you *will* obey. I'm your Daddy, and you'll be a good little girl and do as you're told."

"I can't call you *Daddy* at work. People would be shocked."

"You can still call me Dr. Harrison, but you and I both know I'm your Daddy no matter where we are or what's going on around us."

"Okay." My heart takes flight, a thousand bats leaving behind the darkness and shadows of a cave, seeing the light for the first time in years.

"Are you sure, little one?"

She pushes herself up onto her tiptoes and plants a kiss on my lips, still clinging to the bedsheet wrapped around her beautiful body. As I dart my tongue out to meet hers, I tug on the sheet until it puddles at her feet before sweeping her into my arms and taking her back to bed.

I'm terrified that I won't be enough, but a bigger part of me would die trying.

For her, I'll try.

The first thing I did when I got to work this morning was set up a time to meet with the Chief of Surgery, my mentor, Joseph Milligan. We've been friends for many years, and he knows I wouldn't haphazardly enter into a relationship with a resident. It's not prohibited, so there's not a damn thing the hospital could do about it anyway, but he wishes me well, and I go about my day.

Freya is on my service today, so I ask her to present during my patient rounds. I can already see the rumor mill churning in hushed whispers and sideways glances. It's already getting to Freya. Every muscle in her body tenses as I ask her to scrub in on my glioblastoma case.

"I guess it pays to sleep with your attending," I hear one of the residents mumble as we usher out into the hallway.

"Do you have something you'd like to share with the group, Dr. Kerr?" I've never liked this guy. He has the hands of a butcher, not a surgeon, and especially not neuro. It requires finesse and a level of skill he'll never possess.

"No, Dr. Harrison."

"That's what I thought. Maybe you should spend some time in the skills lab. God knows you need it."

"Not all of us have private tutelage." He grumbles.

"You're off my service. Who I date is none of your business, and Dr. Perrington doesn't get special treatment in this hospital. When you show me something other than surgical skills I wouldn't even trust in the morgue, then you can come back and speak your grievances to my face like a goddamn man. Get out of my sight."

He scurries off with his tail between his legs like the cowardly little prick he is.

When we finish up rounds, Dr. Perrington waits behind with my charts clutched to her chest. "You didn't have to do that."

"I know. This isn't about you, Freya. He disrespected me and suggested I would entrust you with surgery to get in your pants. I took an oath. What happens between you and me doesn't change my ethical responsibility to my patients."

"Are you sure? I froze in that first solo surgery. Was I truly ready for it, or were you looking at me through the eyes of the man I'm sleeping with? You knew who I was."

She has got to be kidding. I almost expect it from doctors like Kerr. All bluster, no muster. But to have Freya question my judgment makes me downright angry.

"Give me the charts."

"What?" Her brows rise, her eyes going wide.

"If I need to answer that question for you, then I'm not the person to be your mentor." I take the charts from her, barely able to meet her gaze. "You're off my service today. I don't have time for this immature shit. I have lives that hinge on me being focused on nothing but their well-being. If you really think I'd risk a patient's life to impress you, I..." I'm not sure how that sentence ends, but I know I need to calm myself before I step into the operating room today.

"I was just asking."

"And I'm *just* telling you, I don't need this bullshit in my day. When you realize how insulting your question was, then we can talk. Until then, you can take care of my post-ops. Don't ever question my decisions as your attending again, Dr. Perrington."

I turn on my heel and stride down the corridor, anger radiating off me in waves. This is why I've never mixed work with my personal life. Everything in me wants to take her to an on-call room right now, make her strip and get into position before spanking her.

That's exactly what I'll be doing the next time we're in my playroom. Any disagreements in our personal lives will stay that— outside of this hospital. But if she challenges me, resident to attending, that's where I have a problem.

I can't believe she could even *think* for a second that I would be so shallow and callous with another human being's life. It bothers me. I might not be a man worthy of her love, but I deserve her respect.

The rest of my day gets worse. The worst it can get. One of my patients didn't make it through surgery, and even though her chance of survival was heavily tipped toward a bad outcome, I really wanted to beat the reaper on this one. I always do. But this hit me harder. Gloria was a single mom, doing her best to raise her son alone. Now, he'll be raised by grieving grandparents, and my heart aches for all of them.

Surgeons are seen as cold and detached for the most part, and the job is easier when you don't let personal feelings get involved. But I'm not a heartless asshole. Sometimes, I find myself too invested in the patients I operate on, and I know what it is to lose a mother at a young age. It plagues me to this day.

Telling her parents that their daughter is gone and their grandson is now their responsibility was devastating. No one should know what it is to bury a child.

By the end of the day, I need a stiff drink, and I head straight for Venom.

∼

"Hey, brother. Haven't seen you in a while. Where have you been?" Dalton nurses a whiskey sour at the bar.

I slump onto the stool beside him, giving the bartender the nod. Eli knows what I want and promptly sets a glass in front of me.

"In my private room for the most part. Work and play."

"I heard you and your new sub put on quite the show last week."

"Yeah," I say with a wry smile. "She's fucking amazing."

"I don't know how you do it."

"What?"

"Let another man watch what's yours."

It makes me chuckle and heave a large sigh. "It's different for you. Nad is your wife. I'm just a Master. Freya isn't really mine, so who am I to deny what she wants to explore?"

"Are you asking or telling? You don't seem too chipper." He eyes me warily.

"Work was brutal today, and I'm sure you've heard about my new trainee."

"One of your residents."

"Gossip spreads like wildfire in here. Thank God everyone signs an NDA for outside these walls."

"Is it an issue? Naddie could have been disbarred for being with me."

"No. It's fine. I've just never navigated waters like this before. In so many ways."

He signals Eli. "Another round of drinks. I think Pierce needs a steady stream tonight."

"Coming up."

"Talk to me, Pierce. What's eating at you?"

"I lost a patient that I was too fond of. I threw Freya off the case this morning because she questioned my ethics as a doctor. You know I fucking pride myself on my work."

"What did she say?"

"The day I told her who I was, we were in surgery. Her first solo."

"Why would you tell her on a day like that?" he says as he sips his drink.

"She was choking in surgery when the patient's heart stopped. It just came out. I told her to breathe, and I called her *little one*. Was it the smartest move? Probably not. Would I do it again? Yes. She needed to center herself, and as a submissive, she responds to dominance."

"So, what did she say that got you riled up?"

"She questioned my motives for letting her fly solo in the OR. I would never jeopardize a patient's life for pussy. How shallow does she think I am?"

"Why *did* you choose her?"

"Because she's the best. Her hands are instruments, Dal. No other resident even comes close to her skill level. She has natural talent and a work ethic far beyond her peers."

"Then, why do you care what anyone else says about it? You know you did it for the right reason."

"I don't give a shit about anyone else in the hospital, but Freya's opinion matters to me. If she can't trust my judgment at work when lives are on the line, then how can she trust me in the playroom?"

"Why is this even an issue? It's a three-month contract."

"We have a six-month agreement."

"Hold the fucking phone," he exclaims before slinging back the rest of his drink. "You're falling for this woman."

He says what I've been thinking for weeks. If I'm honest, I started falling for Freya the night of the masquerade ball. "There's just something about her. It's not just her submission I crave. She's beautiful, but I'm attracted to more than her body. She's smart and sweet, and fuck me, she's a natural submissive. I've never wanted to keep a submissive until now."

"Then tell her."

"She spooks easily. Dalton, if I tell you something, it goes no further. Not even Flex."

"Of course."

I take a deep breath. "She was a virgin when we met."

Dalton's face reflects my reaction the night I found out I'd just deflowered Freya.

"What were you thinking?"

"I didn't know. I only found out *after* I tied her to the cross, called her a slut, and hammered her into submission. It wasn't until I pulled out with blood all over me that I realized."

"Fuck," he mumbles, rubbing his hand over the scruff of his jaw. "That's a trust issue, Pierce."

"I know. With anyone else, I'd send them packing for an omission of such epic proportion. Yet, I find myself so territorial over her. I fucking love that she's only been with me. Is that archaic?"

"Yeah, but we all feel that way. I can't tell you how much I hate that my wife slept with other guys in the fifteen years we were apart. It's irrational, but we were each other's first. We had the opportunity to be the only one for each other, and circumstances took that away. I get it, bro."

"I feel like such a dick for thinking it. I get her, innocent and begging for more. What do I have to offer? A string of hookups and trainee subs… too many to count. I'd be ashamed to share my body count with her. The fact that I don't know the exact number just enforces how inadequate I am when it comes to her. She deserves so much better."

"Let me enlighten you, Pierce. My wife could definitely do better, but I'm a selfish man, and I need her more than my next breath. The way I see it, a man worthy of her could never satisfy her desires. I'm a lucky son of a bitch, and I will strive every goddamn day of my life to become a better man. To be worthy of her. If you have genuine feelings for Freya, then do what needs to be done. *Earn your worth.*"

If I hadn't seen this happen before, I'd run with it, but there's a part of me—a niggling dread—that knows this could all be fake. Not that she's lying to me, but that her body is ruling her head right now. "You know as well as I do that subs in training can believe they're 'in love.' It's a rush when you enter the lifestyle. I'm the guy teaching her how to wring every drop of pleasure from her body in ways she never imagined. If I fall in love with her, she could get to the end of our contract and walk into another Dom's arms after she realizes I'm not the shiny forever guy."

"You're in denial, bro. You don't have an option anymore. It's not 'if you fall in love with her.' You're already there. Fuck the shiny dudes. We're dark, and that only makes our choice to love and trust a woman more impressive. Shiny won't raze the world to the ground for the woman they love. They won't push them to explore how fucking amazing pain and pleasure can be when wielded properly. Shiny is boring as fuck. You love her. Go tell her that and let the chips fall where they may."

That sounds terrifying. "And if she walks away?"

"Then she wasn't yours to begin with."

"Fuck."

"Yeah." He slaps me on the back. "Manning up sucks, but you might get the woman of your dreams. I'd say it's worth the risk."

I contemplate his advice for a moment. "Would you have walked away from Nad if she didn't feel the same?"

A wicked grin creeps at the corner of his lips. "That's the beauty of being the dark guy. Defeat isn't a word we accept. If Naddie had tried to walk away, I'd have done whatever it took to make her mine. I made my peace with that at the very beginning. Walking away was never an option. So, ask yourself the question... would you walk away?"

"No." It's that easy and that complicated.

"Welcome to the dark side, Pierce. Go get your girl."

I know Freya is still at the hospital, so I pull out my phone and type out a quick message.

> **Me:** Tomorrow morning. My apartment.

I nurse another drink while I await her reply, chatting with my friends as they come and go, retiring to their private rooms for some well-deserved kink after a long day. This is one of the problems dating a fellow surgeon. Our schedules will always be crazy and often conflicting. When she becomes an attending, it will only make it worse.

I realize as the thought crosses my mind—I *want* to be around when she reaches that stage in her career. I don't care if we only have one hour a week to spend together. I'd rather have an hour with Freya than unfettered access to any other submissive. *I love her.*

When my phone finally beeps, it's her.

> **Lavender:** I don't know where you live.
> Besides, I'm off your service, remember?

> **Me:** Don't pout. You deserved it at work.
> Don't ever question my judgment again.

> **Lavender:** Yes, Daddy.

> **Me:** Good girl. My driver will be outside your apartment building at seven. I want to administer your punishment before your shift.

> **Lavender:** Your wish is my command.

> **Lavender:** Daddy.

> **Me:** That's my good little girl. Goodnight, little one.

> **Lavender:** Goodnight, Daddy.

I stuff my phone back in my pocket, drop a tip on the table, and head home. I have a punishment to plan. Dalton is right—I may not be worthy of Freya's love, but I'll die trying to become the kind of man she deserves, and I'll quash any obstacle that gets in my way.

Chapter 16
FREYA

Butterflies swarm my stomach as the driver pulls up outside Dr. Harrison's—Daddy's—building.

"Take the elevator to the penthouse, Dr. Perrington."

"Thank you for the ride." Trepidation courses through every cell in my body as I step out of the town car onto the sidewalk. I don't know why I'm surprised that he lives on the Upper East Side, but I'm intimidated, nonetheless.

My heels click-clack on the lobby's vast marble floors, the sound echoing off the walls. I make my way over to the concierge. "Could you let Dr. Harrison know that Freya Perrington is here to visit?"

"He's expecting you, Dr. Perrington. He's just coming down to take you up to the penthouse."

"Oh, I don't need him to do that."

"You do. The Penthouse requires a key in the elevator."

"Oh."

"He'll be right with you."

"Thanks." I try to make as little noise as possible as my heels repeatedly hit the cold marble. This is not the place to be inconspicuous.

When the elevator doors open, my breath is knocked right out of me at the sight of Pierce. He looks effortlessly handsome in a plain white T-shirt that hugs his biceps and washed-out jeans. He's younger-looking than he is at work or in the playroom. I forget that he's only a few years older than me.

I took a few years after high school to work and save up some money before I started college. I wouldn't change it, but I do forget that my peers tend to be a little younger.

"Are you getting in, or are you just going to gawk at me like I'm a meal and you haven't eaten in a week?" he says with a wry grin. His voice is like gravel in the morning, that delicious rasp tantalizing my senses.

"I haven't decided yet." My attempt at playing hard to get is rather redundant, considering I came to his building.

He reaches out, grabs my hand, and tugs me into the elevator before pressing me up against the mirrored walls, his lips crashing down on mine. His hands slide up into my hair, holding me in place as his tongue licks the seam of my lips, begging entrance I freely give. He smells of fresh laundry and a subtle scent of cologne. He tastes of coffee, and I melt against the hard planes of his body.

"Morning, little one," he says as he twists the key for the penthouse.

"Morning, Daddy."

He presses his growing erection against my thigh. "Fuck, I love it when you call me that."

"*Daddy.*" As the doors ping open, Pierce breaks our kiss and tosses me over his shoulder in a fireman's lift, spanking my ass as we enter his apartment.

When he sets me down, I take in the palatial surroundings. It's everything I would expect. Minimal, ordered, and serving a purpose. There are no dirty dishes in the sink or signs that he regularly inhabits this space.

"Are you ready to apologize, little one?" He catches me off guard.

It's a good question, the answer I'm unsure of.

"Can't you just punish me, and we can move on?"

"No. You'll be punished but not before you acknowledge how disrespectful you were."

"I choked! I wasn't ready. It makes sense that you would give me preferential treatment."

He wrings his hands through his hair, pacing in front of me. "Jesus, woman, why are you so damn defensive? I would *never* put a patient in jeopardy. It's fucking insulting."

"I had to know."

He steps toward me, his imposing frame looming over me as I back up against the wall. "Is it so hard to believe I did it because you show more promise than any other resident?"

"I..." He braces his hands on either side of me, his lips mere inches from mine.

"Own how good you are, Freya. You can become an amazing surgeon but not as my little one."

My heart is hammering in my chest, and panic is setting in. "You don't want me anymore?" Ugh. I hate how much I want him.

"Of course I do. You're mine. But, when you set foot in the operating room, you can't be submissive. Not to me or anyone else. I need you to be certain that you're in there because you have the skill to save a life. There's no room for second-guessing. If I see you question yourself with a scalpel in your hand, I'll have you removed from the OR. Understood?"

"Yes." It's a breathy whisper. I can't take my eyes off his lips and the way his tongue darts out to wet them.

"Good. Now, you may apologize to me for questioning my judgment."

"I'm sorry, Daddy."

"Take off your clothes."

"But I have to get to work."

"Are you really questioning me right now? Take. Off. Your. Clothes. I want you naked and bent over my kitchen island so I can administer your punishment." A thrill courses through me, craving the pain.

"Yes, Daddy."

"Good girl. I'll be back in a moment. I expect to see your ass ready and waiting for me when I get back." He presses a gentle kiss to my lips before leaving me bereft. I watch as he strides out of sight with such a confident gait. He's sexy as hell, and he knows it.

I make my way over to the stunning granite island, running my hand over the cold, hard surface. The penthouse has floor-to-ceiling windows with a stunning view of the city. Kicking off my heels, I grab the hem of my dress and pull it over my head before folding it neatly and setting it on the countertop. Doing the same with my underwear, I stand naked and vulnerable. My breathing is labored as I lean over the granite, my nipples pebbling against the cool, unforgiving island. I keep my legs together, and I can already feel myself getting wet with anticipation.

"Aren't you a sight to behold, little one? Arms out in front of you."

His command is like velvet, caressing every inch of my body. I do as he asks, my stomach doing somersaults just knowing his eyes are on me.

"For questioning my judgment, you will count to six as I paddle you."

"Paddle?" I squeak.

He walks around until he's in my line of sight, smoothing his hand over a wooden implement. It looks like a pickleball racquet. A paddle. Fuck, it's going to hurt, and I can't wait.

"Remember your safeword, little one."

"Yes, Daddy. Lavender."

"And how many counts?"

"Six, Daddy." I'm practically panting.

"Before I start, I have a little something for this pretty little ass of yours." He sets the paddle down at my side and reaches into his front pocket. My breath hitches as he pulls out a small tube of lube and a silver butt plug with a lavender jewel on the end.

As he squeezes some lube onto his fingers, I clench my thighs together, trying to relieve the growing ache. I startle when he smears the cold lube between my cheeks before slipping one finger inside me, stretching my ass in preparation for the plug.

"So tight, little one. Relax." He presses a second finger inside me. "That's it. Be a good girl for Daddy."

I find myself pushing back, wanting more. "Oh God."

"Such a greedy little thing." When he pulls his fingers out, they are immediately replaced with the lubed tip of the plug. "Breathe through it."

"Yes, Daddy," I choke out. The fullness is overwhelming, and the anticipation of my punishment has my legs shaking.

When the plug is in, Pierce caresses my ass. "I'm going to enjoy turning these cheeks red, little one. Maybe you'll learn to trust my judgment."

"I trust you, Daddy."

He grabs the paddle off the counter and leans in, his lips caressing my ear. "Don't lie, little one. It will only hurt more."

I gasp as the hard wood of the paddle comes down on my ass, the metal plug vibrating, sending a torturous and delicious jolt of desire straight to my core.

"One, Daddy."

He smooths his palm over the spot the paddle connected. "Good girl."

Another strike.

"Two, Daddy." I'm soaking wet for him, and he knows it, this time sliding his hand between my legs. "My girl enjoys punishment."

Again, and again, and again.

When he lands the last bite of the paddle, I cry out in exhaustion and frustration. "Six, Daddy."

The paddle drops to the floor with a thud before he sinks to his knees and spreads my legs, devouring my pussy, swollen and drenched with arousal. His tongue feels so good it should be illegal.

With the butt plug still in place, he pushes two fingers inside my pussy as he sucks my clit into his mouth.

"Daddy."

He gives my ass a sharp slap, and I love the sting as I'm overwhelmed with pleasure. Sliding his fingers back inside me, he sets a punishing rhythm. "That's it. Be a good girl and come all over Daddy's face, little one."

Flicking his tongue over my clit, I lose all control, and he has to pin my legs to stop me from bucking wildly. "Yes... oh God, yes, Daddy." He lets me ride out the aftershocks before relinquishing his grip. I slump off the counter and into his arms, my breathing labored as I come down from the high. "That was..."

"You're so fucking beautiful when you behave yourself." He tightens his hold on me, kissing the top of my head. "Let's get you cleaned up and lotion on before work."

"Oh God. How am I going to make it through the day? I won't be able to sit down after the paddle."

"You will. I get the impression you'll rather enjoy the discomfort. It'll remind you to respect me in the hospital. Otherwise, I'll have no problem taking you into an on-call room and making your ass sting even more." A thrill courses through me at the thought. He knows me too well already.

"We can't do this stuff at work."

"Oh, little one, when are you going to get it through your pretty, amazing brain, that I'll do whatever I see fit, *wherever* I choose."

"I..."

"It's not up for discussion, so let's get showered, and you can put that smart mouth of yours to good use."

"Yes, Daddy," I say with a wicked smile.

Work is relentless in the best of ways. I'm back on Dr. Harrison's service, and he is blowing my mind. Every move he makes is poetry in motion. I'm in awe of his skill. I hate to admit he was right, but he's not wrong. Giving myself over to the freedom of people knowing about us at work, I'm able to embrace a level of submission that is euphoric.

I've always seen being a submissive as a bedroom-only aspect of my life. That was before I knew what it entailed. The freedom I would feel. I love that I have Celest to talk to, and she understands what I mean by it.

I am *free* to be every inch the strong, confident surgeon I strive to be every day. Pierce is able to separate our work and private life with ease. He knows what I need and gives me the space to do it. I wouldn't trade his tutelage for anything. He's patient when I ask questions. He takes the time to teach me and hone my skills as a surgeon. It means so much more to me than I can express because *he* means so much more to me than I ever thought possible.

Dr. Harrison sees me for my talent, and it doesn't intimidate him. Why should it? He accepts everything about me and doesn't try to make me feel small and fit whatever mold men have tried to shove me in in the past.

After a long shift and three surgeries, my ass is still stinging as I grab my coat and purse from my locker. My fellow residents are still talking in hushed whispers, but when it comes down to it, I've realized I don't really care.

The door to the residents' lounge opens, and there he stands in black jeans and a crisp white T-shirt, his hair tousled from wearing a scrub cap all day. "You ready to go, Freya?" He's tired. I can hear it in the rasp of his voice.

The whispers start again, and I'm just completely over it. "If any of you have something to say… don't bother. I don't want to hear it. If you were half the surgeon I am, it wouldn't even cross your mind to fuck an attending to get ahead. Pierce and I are in a relationship. You don't like it… I really don't give a shit."

I stride over to the doorway, push myself up onto my tiptoes, and plant a firm kiss on Pierce's lips. The scent of his cologne and his innate smell intoxicates my senses. He smiles against me, holding in a chuckle as he wraps his arm around my shoulder.

Before the door closes, he looks over his shoulder to my coworkers standing dumbstruck. "Yeah, what she said."

I lean into his touch as we walk the hallway to the elevator. "I'm sorry. I am just sick of their childish behavior."

"You don't have to explain yourself to me, little one. That was hot as fuck. I like this territorial, badass side of you. Everything you said was true. I know without a shadow of a doubt that you would never sleep with me to further your career."

"Thank you."

"You do it for the whips and chains." He laughs, so full of youthful exuberance. I sometimes forget that we're relatively close in age.

I shove his side, but he pulls me tight against him. "Don't deny it, little one."

"Yes, Daddy," I whisper so only he can hear.

"Oh, you're coming home with me tonight."

"What?"

"You heard me. You're staying at my place. I want you in my bed. As much as I enjoy us falling asleep in the club, I'd like you to start spending the night at my place."

I'm not sure what to say.

"Don't rush to say yes. I'm only the most eligible bachelor in this place."

"I love your humility." We step into the elevator.

"I love everything about you, Freya."

My entire body sparks to life, fireworks radiating through every cell, setting me on fire. My heart is about to beat out of my chest when the door closes, and I launch myself into his arms, our lips coming together in a cataclysmic, life-altering kiss.

Fisting my hands in his hair, I pull him closer, darting my tongue out to meet his, pouring everything I want to say into this one long, languorous kiss.

Pierce wraps his arms around me, lifting me as if I'm light as a feather, before pressing my back against the wall, his kiss ravenous as he takes the lead. By the time the doors reopen, I realize we didn't choose a floor. Now we're on the top floor of the hospital as people shuffle in beside us, my breathing ragged as I attempt to find some composure.

I can see myself in the mirrored walls. I look freshly fucked, just from a kiss, and Pierce—holy hell, he looks hot. His dirty blond hair is messy, just the way I like it, knowing it was my hands raking through it only seconds ago. He meets my gaze in our reflections, a dark, wry grin on his face. I know exactly what's going to happen when we get back to his place.

~

Startled, I awake, the serenity of sleep decimated by the thrashing next to me.

"No… stop." Pierce's voice is unfamiliar as he shouts so loud it makes me jump.

"Get out." His arms are flying everywhere as I attempt to wake him.

"Pierce, wake up. It's just a dream."

"Stop hitting her." I try to place my hand on his chest, but he fights against my touch.

"Pierce. It's me, Freya. Everything is okay. It's just a nightmare."

"No, Daddy. Please. No." And just like that, my heart shatters into a million pieces, broken by the pain of realization. It's not a dream. It's a memory.

I drag in a shaky breath, knowing that the splintered shards of my heart may be the only way to bring light into this moment. Reaching over, I cup his face with my hand. "Wake up, Daddy. I'm here. It's your little one. I need you to wake up for me. *I love you, Daddy!*"

His eyes fly open, wild and disorientated, his breathing erratic as he finds my gaze.

"Freya?"

"Yes, Daddy. It's me."

He pulls me into his arms, my head against his chest, listening to every thudding beat. "I'm sorry if I scared you, little one."

"Do you want to talk about it?"

"No." One word carries so much devastation. I've been keeping Pierce at arm's length since the moment we met, but now all I want to do is *know* him and help in whatever way I can. "I'm going to get a drink of water."

He starts to move, but I pull my head up as I reach for him.

"Talk to me." I lean in to kiss him, but he shirks away from me, out the bed, and through the door in seconds.

My body trembles as I grab the first piece of clothing I find—his T-shirt. It's hugely oversized, but I don't care. The scent of his cologne lingers, wrapping me in much-needed warmth. I pad down the hallway to the kitchen, the light from the refrigerator casting Pierce's shadow as he gulps a bottle of water.

"Are you okay?"

"I'm fine. Go back to bed." His words are clipped, cold, and devoid of anything close to the man I've grown to love.

"You're obviously not fine. I tried to wake you multiple times. You're shaking right now."

"Do as you're told, little one. This isn't the time for you to catch feelings. Either go back to bed or get in the position."

"What do you want to do to me?" I say with trepidation, my voice nothing more than a whisper.

"I'm your Dominant. Does it matter what I'm going to do? It ends with an orgasm. If you keep talking when I tell you to leave it alone, I'll be the only one coming."

"You're my Dominant? What happened to you being my Daddy?"

"For fuck's sake, Freya. What do you want me to say? You wanted me to take your virginity. *I did.* You wanted me to teach you. *I am.* You wanted to call me your Daddy. *I let you.* What more do you want from me? Go to fucking bed and leave me alone."

A pain I've never felt before slams me square in the chest—not for me, but for him.

I grab the bottom of his T-shirt and pull it over my head, discarding it on the floor as I walk toward him, every step feeling more vulnerable than the last.

"Go to bed, Freya."

Without a word, I drop to my knees at his feet, clasping my hands above my head. I'm at his mercy.

"I am yours to do with as you wish… Sir." If he doesn't want me to call him Daddy, then I'll stop. At this moment, I would do anything to ease his pain.

"Get up. We're not doing this."

"You gave me two options, Sir... go to bed or get in the position. I am here for your pleasure. Do with me as you wish."

He slams the refrigerator door, startling me as we're plunged into darkness. "Open your mouth." He doesn't sound like himself, but I'm not afraid. Pierce let me lean into my darkest desires. For him, I can willingly walk into the shadows.

I do as I'm told.

"Clasp your hands at the small of your back while I fuck your pretty little mouth."

"Yes, Sir."

The moment my hands are behind my back where I can't touch him, he grabs me by my hair and thrusts his cock into my mouth, swearing as I take every hard inch of him, "Fucking hell."

There's no question of my pleasure, and a part of me revels in it. I *want* him to use me to chase his demons away—to be his light in the darkness.

Chapter 17
PIERCE

The nightmares won't stop, no matter how hard I push back. I exhaust myself at work. Spend every spare hour at the club with Freya. Fall into my bed, alone, only to wake up in a cold sweat night after night.

Freya hasn't forced any further conversation, and it's exactly what I need. She relishes our lessons, and I'm going back to the list I had her complete at the beginning of her training. I want her to be sure of her choice when it comes to me. I *need* her to pick me because I'm what she wants rather than because she's never tried anything else.

She's such a good little girl for me, every night, on her knees or shackled to the St. Andrew's cross. She takes it hard and fast or torturously slow, lapping up every ounce of pleasure and pain I can give.

It kills me not to have her sleep at my place because watching her give in to sleep after a long night in the club is as close to heaven as I think I'll ever get. I'm enchanted by how angelic she is in slumber, but until I get these nightmares under control, I don't want to risk hurting her or letting her see how fucked up I truly am. I can't see her look at me the way she did that night. There was pity in her eyes and an understanding that terrified me to my core.

She *saw* me.

Today, I have Freya assisting with the surgery for one of my long-term patients, but we have an hour until we need to be in the OR. I paged her to the on-call room. We said—or she said—that we wouldn't fall into our Dom/sub roles at work, but she sashays down the hallways of this hospital, looking too good in scrubs, and all I want to do is bring her to her knees.

She's always had the confident swagger of a surgeon, but to see it translate to her role as my submissive is truly a thing of beauty.

The moment the door opens, I meet her hungry gaze, and before the door is locked, she's tugging her clothes off. I quickly twist the lock into place before she reaches beneath the waistband of my scrubs and massages my cock.

"Whoa, slow down, little one."

"I assume you called me here for sex, Sir." Fuck, I miss her calling me Daddy, but after what I think she heard the last time we slept in the same bed, I can't bring myself to ask for what I want.

"Have we dispelled with the pleasantries?"

"Yes." Her statement is matter-of-fact, and I find it jarring. I know I've been taking more than I give lately, but it wasn't my intention to turn Freya into a sex doll. She pushes up onto her tiptoes, capturing my lips with hers, pressing her warm, supple body against mine, reaching between us and back to my now rock-hard dick. "Where do you want to fuck me, Sir? My mouth or my pussy?" She's so detached as she offers her body to me. It doesn't sit well. I love that she and I have always shared more than just sex. Even that first night, I knew she was different, and we would mean more to each other.

"Freya, stop."

"What?" She drops to her knees and frees my erection from my pants, fisting her hand around the base and flicking her tongue over the crest of my dick. Jesus, it feels so good it should be illegal, which makes it so much harder to pull away.

"Seriously, Freya, can we talk for a minute?"

"You never want to talk, D… Sir."

My dick aches as I shove it back in my pants and hold out my hand to help her up.

She simply grabs her clothes and slips them back on without another word. She's hurt, and it's my fault.

"Are you prepared for surgery this afternoon?"

"I'm always ready, Dr. Harrison." The cool detachment with which she addresses me is like a dagger to my heart. I knew this would happen. I can't do relationships. I do sex and dominance. I excel. Right now, I feel like a failure as Freya refuses to meet my gaze.

"Are you still planning to meet me at the club tonight?"

"Of course."

"I've been thinking about your training."

"Okay." I wait for her to say more than two words, but they don't come. She chews on her bottom lip the way she always does when she's feeling vulnerable.

"Is there anything on your list you'd like to explore?" I'm trying to connect.

"I'd like to have another man watch us and possibly join in. I enjoyed Celest's involvement."

It's like a punch to the gut. I've shared submissives before while they explored their kinks, but the thought of sharing Freya with another man makes me feel physically sick.

"Do you have someone in mind?" I force through gritted teeth.

"Flex." Fuck. She's put some thought into this. Her body stiffens as she raises her chin, and her eyes find mine. "If you're okay with that. And if Flex would even be interested in me."

"You don't have to worry about Flex. You're beautiful, and I know he'll… relish the opportunity to share our bed."

"Have you and he shared women before?" I don't like where this is going, but I want to be honest with her. It's the least she deserves.

"Yes."

"And do you two have sex with each other or just me?"

"Freya."

"Yes or no."

"No, we don't have sex with each other."

"Just me getting railed by two of you then. Sounds good. Do you need me for anything else right now? I want to do some last-minute prep for surgery."

I reach for her hand, but she's reluctant as I pull her into my arms. "I'm sorry things have been so impersonal lately. It's nothing you've done."

"I know. Everything is fine. I am here to be your submissive and learn from you."

"Freya, stop, please. We need to talk about this. About us. Please look at me."

She lets herself melt into my arms for a fraction of a second before she thinks better of it. "Everything's fine. We set our boundaries, and that's a good thing. Am I not a good submissive? Am I doing something that displeases you, Sir?"

"You could never displease me, little one. Go and do whatever you need to before surgery. We'll talk at the club."

She turns on her heel without another word, leaving me with a sour taste in my mouth at the way things are unfolding. I thought we were past the point of her contemplating another man in my playroom. In *our* playroom.

I told her I love her.

A war stirs to life in the pit of my stomach. My father has taken enough from me in this life. I'll be damned if I'm going to let him take Freya. If she wants to bring someone else into our playroom, then I'll do it, but I make no apology for what I'm willing to do to ensure it never happens again.

"You're coming back to my place tonight, little one." Freya is breathless and boneless, shackled to the new four-poster bed I had Carter bring in.

"Sir…"

"I'm in no mood for your bratty behavior. It's not a request. You sleep with me in my bed. Just you and me."

"I wasn't going to argue. I wanted to ask if it would be okay to stop by my apartment to pick up some clothes and pajamas?"

"Yes to the clothes. No to the pajamas." I'm rewarded with a sly grin as I remove her restraints. She still wants to sleep with me. I heave a sigh of relief.

"As you wish, Sir." That's the first thing that we're sorting out tonight. I'm done with this *Sir* crap. She's tiptoeing around me like some fragile little bird about to break. I'm her fucking Dom. Her Daddy.

"In fact, why don't we just sleep at your apartment? Then you can't skip out on me in the middle of the night."

Her expression sobers. "But *you* can skip out on me. If you want to sleep at my place, I only have one rule."

"Name it."

"You *stay*. I don't want to wake up to an empty bed in the morning." There it is—the vulnerability I fell in love with that she's been hiding from me.

"Do you want to do your aftercare here or at your place?"

"My place," she says as she shrugs into her jeans and Converse.

"Okay. Let me grab a few things, and we'll go."

I quickly dress and pull a bag from the chest of drawers. Throwing in a few items for aftercare, I slip a little something fun in there too.

The car ride to her place is longer than I expected as my driver navigates his way to the address she gave him. I know he's driven her before, but I never thought much of it, having not been with her at the time.

Her neighborhood is a little sketchy as we pull up at her building. She opens the car door but stops to look back at me. "Are you coming?"

"Yeah." I give my driver instructions to come and pick us up in the morning. Early.

I slide out of the back seat and take her hand in mine.

"You already hate it. We should just go to your apartment." She chews on her bottom lip.

"I don't *hate* it. Let me get in the door first before you decide how *I* feel about it."

"I'm going to move soon."

"I know." As we head inside, it's marginally better, but that's not exactly an accolade.

"What?"

"You're definitely moving out of here ASAP."

"I know it's not exactly the Upper East Side, but I have two hundred grand in student loans, and I'm a few years away from making the kind of money you do." Fuck, I've offended her.

"You said you were moving. I'm just agreeing. I hate the thought of you walking alone at night in this part of town."

"I've survived all these years by myself before you came along."

"And I'm here now, and as your Dom, I want you safe and well cared for. I only agreed with your sentiment."

"And in this ASAP scenario, when do I start shitting money to rent in an approved area?"

"You don't. You move in with me."

She stops outside what I assume is her apartment door and fumbles with her keys, her hands shaking. "Don't be ridiculous. That's absurd." She hurries inside her tiny apartment, trying to put some distance between us. "I've slept at your place once, and you freaked out on me. My life isn't a plaything for your whims."

I grab her hands, standing in front of her, feeling more vulnerable than I have since I was that small little boy my dad tossed across the room like a ragdoll. "Look at me, Freya."

I wait her out until she lifts her chin, staring up at me through hooded lashes, her eyes filled with unshed tears. "I can't. I won't survive when you're done with me."

My heart aches. Is this how nonchalant I've been lately that she believes my feelings for her are fleeting? I release her hands, sliding mine into her hair, my lips a hair's breadth from hers. "I've been remiss if you think there will ever be a time I'll be *done* with you, little one." I dart my tongue out to lick the seam of her lips. "I am... unequivocally, madly in love with you. You're everything I thought

I'd never want and everything I now crave. I need you, little one. I can't imagine my life without you. I don't want to, and I'll spend until my dying breath trying to be a man worthy of your love in return."

Her breath hitches before she closes the gap, her lips crashing down on mine. I'm intoxicated by her scent, the needy caress of her lips, and the way her curves press tight to my chest. It's the first time I've truly melted into a kiss, not caring if it leads to sex. I just want to savor every second of this connection. I have *never* let anyone get this close to me—body, mind, and soul.

"Bedroom," she says with a breathless rasp, full of sultry desire. She takes my hand and leads me to the door across the room, her eyes never leaving mine.

"Freya… we need to talk." What the hell am I doing? My dick is screaming at me to ignore my pesky feelings and fuck her.

"What about, Sir?" she asks with a sly grin, reaching for the hem of her shirt.

"Stop!" She visibly startles at my command.

"What?"

"You know what. Stop calling me Sir."

"Oh, you want to talk about this now? I've been here, every day for weeks, doing whatever you want while you distance yourself from me. You shut me down that night at your apartment. You can't just come in here with your savior complex and tell me you're in love with me. That you want to whisk me away to your penthouse, but you don't want to indulge the very thing I came to you for in the first place."

"This is about kink? You want to fuck Flex? Sure, I'll set it up." My heart drops into the pit of my stomach.

"This has nothing to do with kink and everything to do with you saying all these amazing things to me and acting the opposite. How do you go from not letting me sleep with you to having me move in with you?"

"I can't win. What the hell do you want from me?"

"I want *you!* I want my Daddy back," she exclaims.

"I…"

"I know your nightmares are memories. You were shouting for your Daddy to stop. Did he hurt you?"

"I'm not doing this." I turn to leave, but she runs in front of the bedroom door, slamming it shut.

"If you love me, you won't walk out."

"And if you love me… oh wait, you don't."

The furrow of her brow tells me I'm about to get a tongue-lashing. "Are you *that* clueless?"

"Clueless? I confess my undying love for the second time, ask you to move in with me, and it's not enough."

"When have I ever said you're not enough? *Never!* Do you know why?"

"No. Enlighten me."

"Because I love you too. I've never *needed* anyone before, and it terrifies me! I love you… *Daddy.*" With her back against the door, I step toward her, caging her in. "Daddy, I love you… more than my next breath." Tears spill from her eyes. "So much it hurts."

I hesitate—a plea for permission—an apology. Brushing my lips over hers, I can hardly breathe. "You love me, little one?" My voice cracks, a strange sensation spreading through every fiber of my being.

"Yes, Daddy. I love you."

I ghost a kiss on her soft, pouty lips, my heart taking flight. "Move in with me, little one." I continue to pepper her with kisses, cupping her face with my hands.

"Yes." It's the single, sweetest word I've ever heard. The last time someone told me they loved me was my mom, the day she killed my father.

"Let's go home, little one."

"Yes, Daddy." I relinquish her lips long enough for her to pack a bag and get her out of this hellhole. If I'd known she lived in this rough neighborhood, I would've had her out after our first week together.

I wasn't exactly planning on moving her into my place, but nothing with Freya has happened at a 'normal' pace or under 'normal' circumstances. She's extraordinary, and together we are breaking all the rules. She's mine now.

Another thought flits in and out of my mind—the tendrils of darkness clawing at my happily ever after. I quash it, silencing the same voice that's been in my ear for as long as I can remember. The devil on my shoulder that refuses to leave, no matter what I do.

It's then that it dawns on me—the tightening in my chest—this neighborhood is all too familiar.

"Are you ready to go, little one? I'll have the rest of your stuff packed and sent to my place tomorrow."

"It'll only take me a few hours to do it. You don't have to go to any trouble."

"I don't want you coming back here. Grab your bag, and let's get out of here." My tone is more abrasive than I intended. Actually, it *was* harsh, and it's exactly what I intended. My skin is crawling, and I hate that Freya's present is bleeding into my past.

"You're being unreasonable. This is my home. It's not much, but it's all I've got right now." She pouts.

"Your *home* is with me. Get used to it. You've got a twenty-four-seven Daddy now, and I'm always going to act in your best interests, even if it pisses you off. Enough with the petulant hands on your hips. Get the bag and come home with me."

I can tell by the switch in her demeanor that she's annoyed, and I know why.

"I was born in this neighborhood, little one. Two blocks over. My memories aren't homemade cookies and fun with my family. Can that be enough information for you, for now?" I know she wants more, but I don't have it to give. This is more than I've ever told anyone in my life.

She drops her bag and rushes into my arms, wrapping them tight around my waist. "I'm sorry, Daddy. Thank you for telling me. I'm ready to go. The only thing I truly need is you."

My heart aches, bursting with joy. An emotion that has been sorely lacking in my life until Freya bulldozed her way into my fucking heart and soul. I close my eyes, shutting out everything but the woman in my arms. There's so much I want to say to her, but I'm terrified she'll run if she understands the real me.

"I love you, little one."

"I love you, too, Daddy."

I pick up her bag and take her hand. She hesitates at the threshold. I'm sure she has some nice memories here. She made the apartment homey, but I can't see past its location. Giving her a moment, I wait in the hallway, hearing her neighbors arguing so loud I now have intimate knowledge of the poor guy's shortcomings in the bedroom. Pencil dick isn't exactly a nickname you want getting out to the neighbors.

"I'm ready." Freya slips her hand into mine, interlacing our fingers as we head for the elevator. This is really happening, and as I gaze down at her smiling face, I know *I'm ready* too.

"Daddy, no. Please." Daddy grabs my favorite toy and throws it at the wall, making a dent. "I'll be a good boy."

"I told your mother to have an abortion. She should've listened." I don't know what that word means, but Daddy is so mad at me. I just wanted him to play cars with me. He doesn't like to be with me. He gets mad when Mommy goes to work, and he has to stay home.

"I'll be quiet, Daddy."

"Stay out of my fucking sight." He hits me hard, and my tummy hurts, knocking me to the floor.

"I'm sorry, Daddy." He hits me again. "I'll be good."

A woman's voice reaches me in the depths of my despair, offering this broken little boy a lifeline. "Wake up, Pierce. It's me, your little one. I'm here, Daddy."

I gasp a huge lungful of air as her touch anchors me to the present. "Fuck." My breaths are labored as I grab her face and bring her lips to mine.

"Are you okay?"

"No." I swallow her moaning reply, desperate to shut out my demons if only for tonight.

"Pierce."

"Let me make love to you, little one."

"You're not okay."

"No, I'm not, but I'll still be broken tomorrow. And the day after that. And the day after that. Right now, I need you." When I pull her in for another kiss, she softens, letting me roll her onto her back, her legs spreading as she whimpers against my lips.

"Yes..." She's giving herself to me in such a gentle expression of submission, and I've never seen her look more beautiful than she is right now.

Chapter 18
FREYA

Living with Pierce is overwhelming in the best possible ways. He's a different man in his own space. I've been given carte blanche to redecorate the space as I see fit, and I'm more than happy to make some changes. The night after I moved in, I explored my new home and quickly realized that it wasn't a home. It's been a place where Pierce sleeps and nothing more.

There are no pictures of family or friends adorning the walls. His closet is clinical. The kitchen is nothing more than a staged area to reheat whatever takeout he had for dinner the night before. I'm not sure if he's ever cooked a meal in it.

Don't get me wrong, the apartment is stunning. It's styled like it should be on the cover of a magazine. Every piece of furniture was clearly handpicked but not by Pierce. I'd bet my career he hired an interior designer. There's nothing of his personality in the décor.

Although Pierce is a force to be reckoned with in the operating room and a commanding presence at Venom, there's a lighter side to him at home, and I want to reflect that in the space. He's funny—still a little grumpy—he watches *Friends* when he's tired but doesn't want to sleep. That's rare, given *I'm* his bedtime distraction now, but when I'm exhausted and in need of some shuteye, I hear the television on low and his soft chuckles drifting in from the living room.

With every new tidbit of his personality, I find myself falling deeper in love with him. I thought the separation of work, personal life, and the club was necessary in the beginning, but now, I can't imagine my life any other way. The whispers soon died down at work. Not because we're any less of a topic of conversation but because Pierce read the riot act to some residents when they questioned his motives.

I'm focused on my training. I have access to the foremost neurosurgeon in the world, and I refuse to waste that on the off-chance one of my colleagues is butt hurt by it. I know my worth. I've earned my position on Pierce's service, and I'm certain in the knowledge that if I left him today, he'd still be my surgical mentor. Above all else—and even though he doesn't see it—Pierce is a man of honor. He's a good, honest man. He prides himself on his career, and although others believe him to be cold and harsh at work, they don't see what I do.

He cares for his patients. Their lives matter to him, and he will fight to the death for every one of them. He doesn't believe in the term 'inoperable.' If someone comes to him for a second opinion, he will always put the decision in their hands. They know he's their last chance at a meaningful life, and if they want to stand in front of the dragon that is their tumor and stay steadfast as he draws his sword, then he will try. There are no words to describe the victory that permeates from every fiber of my being when we manage to save one.

That's what I want for my career. I want to slay the dragon and give someone back the life they thought was lost. It makes the losses more bearable, but they still take a piece of you. Char it. Claw it from your soul. But, to save a life is the greatest single feeling in life.

"What's on your mind, little one?" Pierce asks as we scrub in for surgery.

"You're a dragon slayer."

"Come again?" He raises his eyebrows in question.

"You truly care about your patients. All of them. No matter how hopeless their odds. You stand and face the dragon."

"And a lot of the time, I get burned. You know that."

"And sometimes you slay the fucking dragon." He's surprised by my cussing. I rarely do it, but as I stare at him in his scrubs, he may as well be wearing knight's armor. He's badass, and together we stand united.

The smile on his face is *everything*.

"You're cute when you're inspired, little one." I love that he still calls me his little one when we're alone at the hospital.

"And you're hot when you operate... *Daddy*. I'm seriously in love with you."

He grabs my face with his hands, his lips crashing down on mine as he backs me against the wall, deepening the kiss as my arms wrap around his waist. When we come up gasping for air, my body is on fire.

"We'll have to rescrub," I whisper.

"Totally worth it." He smiles against my lips. "We're going to the club tonight."

"Yes, Daddy."

A nurse appears at the door, a frown marring her otherwise pretty face. "They're ready for you, Dr. Harrison."

"Thanks, Annette. We're about to scrub in."

"Very good, Doctor."

I let my head drop against the wall as she leaves. "Great. One more person to hate me."

"She doesn't hate you. She's just a stickler for time. It's my fault for making us scrub again."

I push up and plant a kiss on his lips.

"Totally worth it."

We rescrub in silence, getting into the right mindset for surgery. The second we set foot inside the operating room, we are colleagues working together with the nursing staff and anesthesiologist to do our best for the patient and give our absolute focus.

When we're all in place, Pierce gives the order, and silence befalls the room. "Ten blade, please. Making the first incision."

No matter how many times I join him in the OR, I'm always in awe of his skill. Our patient today has been turned away by three doctors already, and I'd venture to say Pierce may be the only surgeon in the country willing to operate.

"Annette, please hand the bone saw to Dr. Perrington."

She does as she's told, and all eyes are on me.

"Are you sure, Dr. Harrison?" I can't help but ask.

"You've done this before. It's my job to get you ready to be the lead surgeon on your own cases. Don't question my methods, Dr. Perrington, or you can leave my OR."

"Sorry, Dr. Harrison. I didn't mean to question you. I'm eager for this patient to get our very best."

"Good. That's the goal of everyone in this room. Now, take the saw. We need the flap to be about eight centimeters in diameter."

The moment I step up to make the cut, a calm washes over me. It's like coming home. This is where I'm meant to be.

Pierce is meticulous as he navigates the various parts of the brain that create who we are as people—what makes us unique. It's one of the reasons neurosurgery is so elite. There aren't many who want to give themselves zero room for error. As surgeons in every field, our failures aren't just a bad day at work. They are literally life and death. When it comes to the brain, a millimeter can be the difference between a meaningful life and a vegetative state.

I know his reputation, but even I am stunned when he says the words this patient's family is waiting to hear but not expecting. "We got it all. Good work, everyone."

Just as he's about to start closing, one of the first-year residents appears at the entrance to the operating room. "Dr. Harrison, there's an urgent case in the ER. A four-year-old boy with massive head trauma. Dr. Wilder has requested your consult."

"Dr. Perrington, can you close for me?" He looks at me as I steel myself.

"Yes, Dr. Harrison."

"Thank you." He turns his attention to his scrub nurse. "Annette, can you get the OR prepped for a possible pediatric head trauma?"

"Yes, Doctor."

Pierce pulls off his gown and gloves and disappears through the door.

"Annette, 4-0, please."

I take my time, making sure every stitch is textbook, aware that this is going to be a scar this patient will have for the rest of his now *long* life. It's an honor, and I remind myself with every move of my hand. Everything I've worked for—every late-night cramming session and side job I've done to put myself through school. It's for moments like this. We saved a life today. We didn't just mend what was broken. This tumor thoght it had claimed its victim, and now it sits lifeless in medical waste, unable to leech off its host any longer.

With the last stitch, I thank the staff and take my leave, but Annette follows me into the scrub room. "He's different since he met you."

I turn to face her. "What?"

"There's… life in his eyes that wasn't there before. He's a good man."

"I know."

"He's not like the other attendings. He cares more than anyone, as much as he tries to hide it."

"Did you two…"

"No." She cuts me off, and I heave a sigh of relief. "He's never been in a relationship with a coworker. But I see how he is with you, and he's my friend. Don't hurt him."

It never crossed my mind that he has friends here at the hospital. Of course he does. He's a great man, and I shouldn't be surprised that he's not one of those assholes who only speak to other attendings. He would never look down his nose at someone because they aren't at his level.

"I don't plan to. I love him." It's the first time I've said it out loud to someone other than Pierce.

"I see that." She gives me a warm smile before leaving me to scrub out.

When I'm done, I head up to the waiting room to give the good news to our patient's family. With Pierce down in the ER, it falls on me to let them know how the surgery went. So often, it's a difficult conversation to have. The first time I told a patient's family that they didn't make it through surgery, I ran to the closest bathroom and puked my guts out the second I left the room.

Today, I get to deliver the best news.

Adrenaline courses through my veins as I open the door to the waiting room, and I'm met with somber faces, fear evident as they collectively stand to greet me.

"Where's Dr. Harrison?"

"He has been called to consult on another patient. I'm Dr. Perrington. I work with Dr. Harrison and was in your…"

"Brother. John is my brother."

"I was part of John's surgical team."

"Is he… dead?"

"No. He's recovering up in the ICU right now. Surgery went well. Dr. Harrison was able to get the whole tumor."

The hulk of a man in front of me drops to his knees. "You got it all?"

"Yes, sir. We won't know more until he wakes up, but he is in recovery and tumor-free right now. I will come back when he wakes up and get you up to see him."

"Thank you so much. You saved his life. I can't believe it. We've been sitting here all day, waiting to hear the worst. Bracing for it. Expecting it." When he stands up, I reach out my hand to shake his, but he pulls me into his embrace. "Thank you."

"Dr. Harrison is the best surgeon you'll find. Your brother was in good hands today."

"No one else would take a chance on John. They gave him six months to live."

"He's got a long road to recovery, but we'll keep you posted every step of the way."

"I… thank you."

"You're very welcome. I'm going to go and check on him now." I acknowledge the rest of the family with a nod and a smile before leaving them with the news and making my way up to the ICU. It's not long before my pager starts beeping for the ER. Pierce must be in surgery already with the boy he went to consult on. They always page him unless he's already tied up elsewhere. I've become his proxy for consultations these days.

When you get paged by the ER, you don't take your time getting there. As a resident, everywhere I'm paged is at a run, but when it's the ER, you'll see me sprinting down the hallway.

I come to a halt at the nurses' station when I take in the sight before me. My brain doesn't even know what I'm looking at.

It can't be.

Pierce is in handcuffs, his knuckles bloody, being led out of the hospital by a police officer.

I rush to his side. "Pierce, what's going on?"

"Call Dalton. His number is in my phone. His wife is a lawyer. Call him now, Freya."

"I will."

Shit. Shit. Shit.

The moment he's out of sight, I turn back to the nurses. "What happened?" My pulse is racing so hard it's whooshing in my ears. "Why is he in handcuffs?"

"A kid was brought in by his mother. He had major head wounds and was badly beaten. Dr. Harrison took one look at his films and confirmed what we feared. The kid has been abused for years. Old breaks showed up on his X-rays. The father turned up with bruises all over his knuckles, shouting that 'the bitch can't keep him away.' Dr. Harrison told him to leave, but he started shouting all kinds of terrible things at both the mother and boy. Dr. Harrison just lost it. They started fighting, and he took the father down right here in the hallway."

That's not the Pierce I know. He doesn't hurt people. He heals them. My hands are shaking as I cover my mouth to stop the sobs fighting to break free. Then, his words kick in. I need to get his phone *now*.

I quickly make my way to the attendings' lounge, grab his bag, and rummage for his phone. My heart sinks at the sight of the pass-code lock. I don't know the number to open his phone. With my mind racing a million miles a minute, I rush to my locker in the residents' lounge and dial Celest. I'm out of breath when she answers.

"Hey, Freya. Long time no see." Shit. I forgot about the last time we saw each other. I've been putting off talking to her for weeks, and I'm a bad friend for avoiding her.

"Celest. I'm sorry, but I can't talk right now."

"What's wrong? You sound weird."

"I'll explain later. I need to get in touch with Dalton Callaghan. It's urgent."

"What's going on, Frey?"

"Please. I promise I'll fill you in later, but I really need to speak with him. Can you help me?"

"Genevieve will have his number. I'll call her right now and forward the number as soon as I get it."

"Thank you so much, Cel."

"Sure. Is everything okay with Master Harrison?" I can hear the concern in her voice, but I have to hold it together right now.

"I hope so. Thanks for doing this for me. I need to go. I'll call you later."

"You know you can talk to me about anything, right? We're still friends."

"Yes."

"Okay. I'll text you soon."

I hang up the call and head for the Chief of Surgery's office. I need to get out of here and down to the police station. I've got five hours left on my shift, but I'll be more of a hindrance in my current state of mind.

I hurry through the hospital, everyone gaping at me as I pass. Gossip spreads like wildfire around here, so I would expect nothing less. When I reach Dr. Milligan's office, he's already up and throwing the door open to meet me.

"What the hell is going on, Dr. Perrington? Why am I hearing that my Chief of Neuro just got escorted out of the ER in handcuffs?"

"It's his story to tell. I came to ask if I can leave to go to the police station."

"Fine. Go. But you tell Pierce I want him in my office the second he gets out."

"Yes, Sir. Thank you." I don't wait around for him to change his mind.

Celest is true to her word, and by the time I reach my car in the parking lot, I have Dalton's number.

It only rings twice before he answers. "Dalton Callaghan." He has the same commanding tone as Pierce.

"Hello, Mr. Callaghan. You don't know me, but my name is Freya Perrington. I'm Pierce's… I work with Dr. Harrison."

"I know who you are. Why are you calling me?" *He knows who I am.*

"There was an incident at the hospital tonight. He asked me to call you."

"Is he okay? Is he hurt?"

"Physically, he's fine. I think. He got into an altercation with a patient's father. I didn't see it happen, but when I got down to the ER, Pierce was in handcuffs, and the police took him to the station. I'm on my way there now."

"Okay, I'm going to get Naddie, and we'll meet you there."

"Thank you." I start the car and peel out of the parking lot way too fast, but the need to get to Pierce is a physical pain in my chest.

When I arrive, they won't tell me anything, and I feel so helpless as I sit and wait. The moment Dalton comes barreling through the door, I let out a breath I didn't know I was holding. His wife is at his side, and they look every inch the power couple.

She steps up to the front desk.

"I want to speak with my client. Now. Dr. Pierce Harrison."

Dalton takes a seat next to me, resting his elbows on his thighs. "What the fuck happened? Pierce wouldn't throw down with *anyone*, let alone a patient's parent."

"I think the boy was being abused."

"Fuck." His response only gives credence to what I've suspected from Pierce's ramblings during his nightmares. Something triggered him tonight.

"I don't know if he threw the first punch."

"There's surveillance in the hospital, right?" he asks with such cold precision.

"Yes, Sir."

"Who do I need to talk to to get it?"

"The Chief of Surgery is your best bet. He's a good friend of Daddy's. I mean Pierce. I'm sorry."

"Don't ever apologize to me for showing your love for Pierce. I'm elated that he's happy with you."

"I can contact Dr. Milligan. I'll go back to the hospital."

"No. You wait here. Pierce is going to want to see your face when Naddie gets him out of here. I'll go and speak with Dr. Milligan."

"Do you think your wife will be able to get him out tonight? The thought of him in there makes me sick to my stomach. I don't know what provoked the fight, but I know *him*, and the guy must really have deserved it."

"Has Pierce ever talked to you about his childhood?"

"Not really, but I have suspicions. He has nightmares." I won't say more than that. It's not my place.

"He'll open up eventually. Just hang in there. He's a good man."

"You don't have to sell me on him, Mr. Callaghan. He's the love of my life."

"Call me, Dalton. Now, I'm going to go and get us that surveillance footage and see about getting Pierce out in the next few hours."

"Thank you so much... Dalton."

"You're welcome. If Naddie comes out, tell her where I went."

"I will."

The moment he's out the door, a silent sob racks my entire body as I drop my head in my hands. How did we get here? And how are we going to get out of this?

Whatever happens, I'll be by Daddy's side. He's mine, and nothing he could ever do would change that fact. A calmness washes over me at the realization. *He's mine.*

Chapter 19
PIERCE

"Are you going to tell me what happened so I can get you out of here?" Dalton's wife, Nadia, sits across from me, her eyes flitting to the handcuffs that chain me to the desk.

"He got a fraction of what he deserved," I say with cold detachment. If only I'd separated my personal feelings from my patient today, I wouldn't be in this predicament.

"Start talking, Pierce."

"What do you want me to say? I hit the guy. He deserved it. If he'd picked on someone his own size, we wouldn't be having this conversation."

"But we are. So start at the beginning."

"One of the residents came to the operating room to tell me they needed me in the ER for a patient. A young boy with major head trauma."

"Okay. What happened next?"

"I assessed him. His mom was screaming and begging us to help him. She had some bruises on her cheek… a perfect handprint. The boy needed surgery for a suspected brain bleed. The resident brought me his films, and there was more than enough evidence of old injuries and breaks to confirm he was being severely abused."

"Oh God, that's awful." How nice it must be to have sympathy without empathy for a fellow survivor. The moment I saw that boy, I *became* him all over again.

"The boy's father came in, shoving past my nurses, whooping and hollering that she couldn't keep him away. That he'd hunt them down if she tried to run. His knuckles were swollen and bloody... from beating his four-year-old son half to death. Without surgery, that boy wouldn't make it. What kind of man does that?" I choke out past the lump forming in my throat.

"Who threw the first punch, Pierce?"

"I don't know. It was all a blur. I just saw fucking red. I could see it in that mother's eyes. She was going to go back to him and let this happen again and again until that little boy ended up in the morgue rather than the ER."

"I need you to think. If he landed the first blow, then this is open and shut."

I move to wring my hands through my hair, but I'm shackled to the desk. "Fuck. I could lose my license to practice medicine for this." *Fuck!*

"It won't come to that. I'll find you the best defense attorney in the state if it comes to that. For now, I'm going to get you out on bail."

"Thank you. Is Freya here?"

"Yes. Dalton is with her in the waiting room."

"Is she okay?"

"She's fine. Worried about you, but she's holding it together. Dalton's got her. You need to focus on yourself right now."

"She's my submissive. She shouldn't have to deal with this."

"You don't get to pick and choose with people you love. It's about the good *and* the bad. This is a minor setback."

"You think so?"

Nadia reaches out her hand to cover mine. "You need to let her be here for you right now. Just because we are submissives does not mean we expect our Doms to shoulder every burden alone. Don't shut her out, Pierce. It's plain for anyone with eyes to see that she's madly in love with you."

"She wanted uncomplicated. You don't think this…" I say, clinking my wrists together, "… is complicated?"

"I'll get you out of here tonight. Just hang tight, okay?"

"I've got nowhere else to be." With a curt smile, she leaves me to ponder my life choices in the twelve-by-nine room. I'd be remiss as a Dom if I didn't notice how anchored to the table I am in these handcuffs. The things I could do to my little one with a setup like this. It's not dissimilar to the one I have in the playroom, but my rings are on either side of the desk instead of the middle.

I can't believe I let this happen. Everything I've worked for could be gone in one fell swoop. How will I face Freya? She loves my control above all else, and I lost it today. It wasn't a slipup, it was a catastrophic error in judgment. Seeing that little boy, knowing the look of resignation on his mother's face, it wasn't going to stop. She wasn't going to leave.

I lashed out. I had to save him. To save the boy I once was. The boy who couldn't fight back.

It's a few hours before the police officer comes back for me.

"You have friends in high places. Bail has been posted," he says as he unlocks the cuffs. "Good luck to you, Dr. Harrison."

"Thanks."

Still in my scrubs, he leads me out to the waiting area. Freya launches herself off the chair and into my arms. "Oh my God, Pierce, are you okay?"

"I'm fine, little one," I whisper as I wrap my arms around her, drinking in her scent. I'm not sure how long we stand in this embrace, but it makes me realize everything I could lose. My career. My girl. Life means nothing without Freya.

"Bro, do I need to have security on you twenty-four seven?" Dalton jests. I reluctantly relinquish my hold on Freya to shake Dalton's hand.

"Thanks for coming."

"That's what friends are for, man. I expect it with Flex, but I was surprised to get a call about you."

"Flex is too smart to get caught." I quip.

"Well, your lady put me in touch with Dr. Milligan. They are pulling footage from every angle in the ER to piece together what happened."

"Fuck. I just lost it."

"Don't beat yourself up. You were trying to protect the kid. No one can fault you for that."

"The police can absolutely fault me for it. Even if I get off on the charges, it doesn't guarantee I have a job to return to. I'm supposed to set the tone for my department."

"And sometimes the tone is to protect those weaker than ourselves. You're a good man, and you understand what that little boy faced day in and day out for years."

"There are better ways to deal with it." I cut him off. I'm sure I've confirmed what Freya has likely suspected for a while now. Putting off telling her my damage seems a little dumb right now, but I didn't want her to look at me with pity in her eyes.

"Let's get you a drink."

"That sounds good."

"Come on, I've got the town car waiting outside. We'll go to Venom, and Naddie can walk us through your next steps."

"I need to go back to the hospital and speak with Joseph."

"I spoke with him in person. He's expecting you tomorrow morning at eight."

"What did I do to deserve a friend like you?"

"You're not a total dick." He laughs.

"I guess. Flex lowered your standards years ago." We both have a chuckle as we head outside. I slide into the back of the car next to Freya, and she slips her hand into mine, squeezing tight.

"Are you okay, Daddy?"

I wrap my arm around her shoulder, pulling her tight to my side. "I'm okay, little one. Would you rather go home?"

"No. I want to hear what Nadia has to tell us about your case... what happens next."

"Okay."

We ride the rest of the way in comfortable silence, Freya giving me strength just by being here with me.

When we get to the club, Flex is there to point out the obvious.

"Aren't you supposed to be in an orange jumpsuit?" he says as I stand at the bar, still in my scrubs. I have extra clothes here for Freya and me, so I send her to get changed first, taking the opportunity to have a quiet word with him.

"Very funny. I hope Armani does a good prison pinstripe." If I don't laugh, I'll fucking cry. How to lose your career in twenty seconds.

"Seriously, bro, are you okay? What the fuck happened?"

"How did you know?"

"Celest called me in a panic, not knowing what happened. I called Genevieve, who had already spoken to Dalton, and I called him. Chinese whispers."

"So, my reputation is well and truly fucked. Great."

"You're a fucking hero. Any man who takes a hand to his kid deserves everything he gets."

"Look, I don't know what's going to happen moving forward. My job is on the line. I could go down for this if it doesn't go my way. I'm still training Freya right now, and there are a few things she wanted to try. Do you have a sub right now?"

"Not technically."

"She wants to try a threesome."

"Didn't you guys have a public moment with Celest?"

"She kissed her tits. That was it. On her list, she said maybe to a threesome with another guy. I don't want her to miss out because I don't want to share."

"You're asking *me* to fuck your sub while telling me you don't want to share her? Fuck no. I value our friendship and my cock."

"I might not get the chance to finish her training, Flex. I need to know that she can walk this journey without me if it comes to it."

"You're not asking for a threesome. You're asking me to take over training her if you go to fucking prison."

"Yeah, I am. I love her enough to know she needs the lifestyle. It brought her to life, Flex. It's been so fucking beautiful to watch. She's a great sub."

"This is not the time to be discussing this. You've had the day from hell, and you're not thinking clearly. If you still want to let her try it out in a few weeks when everything has calmed down, then come and talk to me. I'm not a Master. I don't train. A threesome I can do. The rest… it's too much responsibility for me, bro. I'm not that guy."

I start pacing the floor, running my hands through my hair, wondering why the fuck I just asked him to train her. The thought of it kills me. *Shreds my insides.*

He claps me on the back and pulls me into a man hug. "It's going to be fine."

Flex, Dalton, and the other Doms here at Venom are the closest thing I've ever had to a family. Meeting Freya—she made me realize I really fucking want someone in my life who *is* my family and won't run away when the darkness threatens to pull me under. Knowing that I've put that in jeopardy is soul-destroying.

We sit down with Dalton and Nadia, letting her fill me in on what happens now. She's already called her best friend, who is apparently some kind of computer genius, 1950s gumshoe private investigator to find out everything about the deadbeat dad whose nose I definitely broke earlier today.

"Leave it with us, Pierce. This time next month, this will all be a distant memory. If this guy has been abusing his family for years, it's only a matter of time before we unearth the other skeletons in his closet. You're a world-renowned surgeon who was defending an abused four-year-old. There's no jury who would put you behind bars for that, even if it goes to trial."

I notice Freya's absence. She never came back from our private room. "Thanks, Nadia. I really appreciate you helping me out. I'm not sure what I'll face at work tomorrow, but I'll sleep easier knowing you guys have my back."

"Always," Dalton interjects.

"Excuse me, I'm going to check on my little one."

"Of course," they say in unison.

Dalton levels me with a knowing grin. "She's a keeper, bro. Don't let her slip through your fingers because you don't want to face up to shit. Trust me, I know whereof I speak."

"He does," Nadia confirms with a conspiratorial wink.

"Thanks, guys."

I take my leave, needing to set eyes on Freya. I can only imagine what she must think of me. When I reach the playroom, a smile splits my face as I open the door to the sight of Freya nestled under the covers.

"Little one…"

No reply. She's sound asleep, and I don't blame her. It's been a long day.

I shrug out of my clothes and climb in beside her, draping an arm over her waist, pulling her tight to my chest.

"Daddy?" she whispers, stirring from her slumber.

"Yes, little one. It's me. Go back to sleep."

She wriggles in my grasp, shuffling around until we're face to face. "Are you okay?"

"Don't worry about me. I'll be fine." I say it as much for her as I do for myself.

"I know. But I'm here if you want to talk." The softness in her voice is my undoing.

Nothing else in the world matters when we're together. The darkness is chased away, leaving only the overwhelming love I feel for this woman.

"Marry me, Freya."

She stiffens in my arms. "Don't say things like that."

"I mean it, little one. I love you. Today just proved to me that you're my family now. You don't run when things get difficult."

"And I don't plan on going anywhere, but until you're comfortable telling me what happened in your past, I'm not saying yes. I love you, but I want all of you. I *deserve* all of you."

"Freya."

She silences me with a kiss. "Ask me again when all of this is over. I'll still be here, loving you and standing by your side."

"I know what I want. You're everything to me."

"I feel the same way, but there's still so much we don't know about each other. I won't look back years from now and wonder if you asked me to marry you because of today's circumstances and emotional turmoil or whether you did it because you want to spend the rest of your life with me."

"I've known the answer to that question for a while."

"Then a little while longer won't hurt." Her lips find mine in a silencing kiss, and I let her quiet the storm raging inside me. I can do this for her. I know she's my forever if I'm lucky enough to have it, but it's not fair to her to ask the same of her right now.

I could be behind bars.

I could lose my medical license, and I would no longer be the great Dr. Harrison she fell in love with.

"As you wish, little one."

I turn her so her back is against my chest once more, holding her close, breathing in the soft scent of her perfume. Tomorrow could end my career and any hope of a future with my little one.

"No matter how noble your actions may have been, Pierce, I have to suspend you until more is known. What the hell were you thinking?" It pains me to hear my mentor so disappointed. "As Chief of Neuro, you set the tone for the department. As an attending, the residents look to you for guidance. I can't have you go unpunished for this. You can't go around getting in fistfights."

"I wasn't thinking. He was spitting his poison at his poor wife and child. That boy had old breaks in his films, Joseph. We've seen it time and time again, and these guys just get away with it."

"And we call the police and child protective services. We don't take matters into our own hands, especially when the hands in question are the most valuable in this hospital."

"My hand is fine. How is the boy?"

"I did the operation myself. He's going to be fine. His mother is filing charges against her husband, and there is already a restraining order in place. Security guards are positioned outside his room."

"Can I speak to the mother?" He looks at me like I just grew a second head.

"Are you out of your mind? *No.* You are to go nowhere near them. Understood?"

"I just…"

"You've done enough. Go and brush up on your golf or whatever else you do. You are not to lift a scalpel in this hospital until further notice."

"And what of Dr. Perrington? I am her mentor. She needs guidance, Joseph."

"Are you *trying* to piss me off, Pierce?" I don't care what he thinks of me at this point. I'm always going to put Freya's needs before my own.

"She's gifted. Don't punish her for my misdeeds. She is the best resident I've seen in years."

He heaves a sigh, resigned to my judgment. "I'll ensure she has adequate tutelage. I will be operating on your patients until you return. She can work with me."

"Thank you, Joseph. I'm sorry I let you down."

"I hate to admit it, but I understand. It can be difficult to see patients being mistreated with no one to advocate for them. Leave it with me, and we'll see what happens. You know I'll go to bat for you with the board, but some things are out of my control."

"I appreciate it, Joseph." Shaking his hand, I turn to leave and find Freya lurking in the hallway.

"What happened? Are you okay?" She rushes toward me, any past trepidation at being seen with me at work gone.

"Don't freak out. Everything is going to be fine."

"Nothing good is ever prefaced with 'don't freak out.' "

"I've been suspended."

"For how long?" She steps into me, wrapping her arms around my waist. "I'm sorry."

"What for? This was my stupidity. I knew better, and I let my personal feelings get the better of me. I'm not sure how long it'll be. The hospital's legal department will be in touch. There may be nothing they can do for me. I'm going to meet with Dalton, Nadia, and her recommendation for a defense lawyer. I think their private investigator will be there too."

"Do you want me to come?" I can't believe this woman loves me. She'd drop everything for me, so I have to be strict with her.

"No. I've taken enough of your time. Dr. Milligan will be performing my surgeries for now. Your teaching in neuro won't be affected. You'll shadow him and assist when asked."

"I don't care about that. It's ridiculous that he's suspending you. You did nothing wrong."

"You should care. This is your career we're talking about."

"And what about yours?" she says with indignation.

"That's for me to worry about. I did everything wrong. I should have walked away and let the authorities deal with that guy. I took matters into my own hands. I'm ashamed as a doctor at this hospital and as a man for letting this happen."

"I should come with you to see the lawyer."

"No, Freya. I need you here, learning, operating. I can't handle compromising your teaching on top of everything else. Dr. Milligan is excellent. He was my mentor, and as soon as he sees you in action, he'll be happy to take you under his wing."

"I want to help."

I tuck a wayward strand of hair behind her ear before leaning down to kiss her. "You are. Just keep loving me, and everything will be fine."

"Promise?" I can't lie to her, as much as I want to shield her from all of this, so I capture her lips to anchor myself to this one port in my life. She's the calm in the storm that's coming my way, threatening to rip apart everything I've built for myself.

He took everything from me. I won't let him take Freya.

Chapter 20

FREYA

"Thanks for meeting me, Cel. I know I've been a shit friend lately." I embrace my best friend, holding tightly as she wraps her arms around me.

"Are you okay? You're shaking." We take a seat in the back corner of the coffee shop.

"I don't even know where to start. Everything is going to shit, and I have no idea what to do. I'm useless."

Celest reaches across the table, taking my hands in hers. "Let's start with why you called me in a frenzy looking for Dalton."

"Ugh." I heave an exhausted sigh. "Pierce is in trouble."

"Is it serious?"

"It could end his career. Shit... it could send him to prison, Cel." Saying it out loud is too much for me, and I finally break down. I explain everything to Celest—what I suspect, what we know happened, and what the lawyers are telling us right now.

She hands me a napkin to wipe my mascara-soaked eyes. I can only imagine what a mess I look. "How's he holding up?"

"He's busying himself at the club. He's decided to revamp his playroom so it's more tailored to *our* needs."

"Wow. So your six-month contract?" She leaves the rest of that question hanging in the air between us.

"I'm so far gone with him, Cel. A contract means nothing at this point."

"I don't know if that's wise, Frey. There's a reason we have contracts. It's really easy to fall for the Dom who trains you. Add in the fact that he was your first sexual experience, it only compounds those feelings."

"I understand the difference between infatuation and love, Cel. Being a virgin didn't make me completely incapable of identifying my emotions."

"I'm not trying to belittle your feelings. I'm just worried about you. Having all this legal stuff added in is just another level of commitment. What are you going to do if Pierce goes to prison?"

"I'll stand by him."

"Are you listening to yourself? You won't have a mentor anymore. There will be no 'Daddy' waiting for you at the club. No Pierce to warm your bed at night. Is that really what you want for yourself? You've only known each other for a few months."

"I don't care how hard it is for me, Cel. He's the one."

"Are you sure?"

"One hundred percent."

"Then I'm here for you. I worry for you as my friend, but if you're all in with Master Harrison, then I'll support you."

"Thank you." We order some coffee and cake. Calories don't matter today. I'm eating the biggest slice of carrot cake they have and a large cappuccino.

With a weight lifted off my shoulders, I relax back into the leather booth.

"How have you been, Cel?"

"That depends."

"On what?"

She hesitates just long enough to make me uncomfortable. "Are we still friends?"

"What? Of course we are."

"Other than getting Dalton's number, we haven't spoken since the voyeur floor. Since I… got naked for you and touched myself. Since I kissed your breasts."

"I…" I don't know what to say, but the memory of that night makes me squirm in my seat.

"Did you not like it?"

"No. I *did* like it. I've just been too embarrassed to mention it. I didn't know what to say."

"How about, 'Hey, Cel, you're hot when you get yourself off.' Or maybe, 'Cel, the way you flicked your tongue over my nipples really turned me on.' I'd even take, 'That was weird, let's never do that again.' I would take any kind of acknowledgment at this point."

I hang my head, knowing I'm a shit friend right now. "I'm so sorry, Cel. I know you were just doing it because I wanted to experiment. It was amazing, and I loved every second of it. You were so beautiful and free and open. I really did enjoy everything that happened."

"I didn't do it just because of you. I wanted it to happen too. You looked so stunning over your Daddy's knee. Watching you being punished. Counting for you. That was hot, Frey. Trust me, I was into it for purely selfish reasons, and I'd do it again." She takes me by surprise.

"You would?"

"If you wanted to. Yes." It's the first time I've seen Celest look anything other than one hundred percent confident.

"I don't know how to feel about it. I can't lose you as a friend, Cel. I know I'm not gay, and I've never really considered being attracted to a woman. But I can't deny that watching you and feeling your lips on me felt good."

"You're overthinking it. The beauty of Venom is that there are no strict labels. Just because you watched me get off and liked it doesn't mean your whole sexual identity is in question. You don't have to define every little thing. We had some fun. It was hot. End of story. If you want to do it again and it happens, I'm not expecting the three of us to become a throuple. You and Master Harrison have something special. If I occasionally get off or watch you getting off, it's fight club. What happens at V, stays at V. We're still best friends regardless of any of that, okay?"

"Okay." I'm so relieved. I've been carrying this around for weeks for no good reason. If I'd just called Celest the next day, she'd have been fine. "I'm sorry for not calling sooner."

"It's fine. Let's just get back to normal. You have enough on your plate right now."

"I wish I could do more to help Pierce. I'm doing anything and everything he wants at the club, but we haven't really spoken about the real reason behind this whole thing."

"Woe is you. Having to submit every night to one of the hottest Doms at Venom." That makes me laugh. She's not wrong. Submitting to him in the playroom isn't exactly difficult. I relish every moment, falling into bed each night completely exhausted. We don't talk about work, or rather, *I* don't bring it up. It would feel like I'm rubbing it in his face.

"If he keeps this pace up much longer, I'm going to need a vaginal repair. I'm in a permanent state of being saddle sore."

"Bitch," she jests.

"It's a tough job, but someone has to do it."

"I volunteer as tribute!" I burst out laughing as she waves her hand in the air.

"Do you have a new Dom yet?"

"No. It's hard to find a Dom who's going to get excited about a single mom."

"Don't sell yourself short, Cel. You're a catch, and Belle is the cutest munchkin on the planet. The right guy is out there."

"Is he? Her father sure as hell wasn't it."

"Does he know you're in the lifestyle?"

"No. He's not around, and I need it to stay that way. He'd try to take Belle if he knew. Not because he wants to be a father to her. He'd do it out of spite."

"Could he really gain custody, though if he's been absent this whole time?"

"I don't think so, but it doesn't stop me being terrified he's going to show up and cause problems for us."

"I'm so sorry, Cel. I hate that for you. For both of you."

"Thanks. It's what I get for always picking the bad boy."

"What happened with your last Dom, if you don't mind me asking?"

"He found out I have a kid."

"Seriously?"

"I can't blame him. He wanted low maintenance, not a ready-made family."

"So, are you casually seeing anyone at the club?"

"Not really. I'm not in the mood for friends with benefits right now. It wouldn't be fair to a Dom for me to get involved. My head's all over the place."

"Why have you let me prattle on about my crap when you're going through so much?"

"We all have problems, Frey. I'd say you've got more than a little 'crap' going on."

"Promise me you'll talk to me, and if there is anything I can do, you'll let me know."

"Yes, and the same goes for you. Master Harrison is a good man."

"I promise. No more burying our heads in the sand. We're friends who sometimes watch each other get off, and that's… kinda awesome."

Celest throws back her head and laughs. "I'll take it. Some girls braid each other's hair. We trade orgasms. I'm good with that."

We sit for a while longer, moving on to lighter topics and making plans to have drinks at the club later this week. I lose all track of time, only realizing when my phone rings that I'm late to meet Pierce.

"Hey, little one. Is everything okay?"

"I'm so sorry, Daddy." Celest makes a love heart sign with her hands. "I'm with Celest. I didn't realize the time. I'll be at the club in ten minutes."

"Don't rush. It's fine. We're not staying at the club tonight anyway. I have other plans for you. I'll just grab a drink and wait at the bar. Come find me when you're done."

"Okay. Only if you're sure."

"Of course. See you soon, little one."

When I hang up the phone, Celest gives me that wicked smile of hers.

"God, every time I hear you call him Daddy, it makes me all hot and bothered."

"It just sort of slipped out one night. I had been calling him Sir, but I got caught up in a spine-tingling orgasm and blurted out, 'Yes, Daddy.' He loved it. Part of me feels like it's weird, and don't even get me started on my clear daddy issues, having never had one."

"Who cares why we like what we do? So you get wet for Daddy. That's no one's business but yours and his."

"We spend all this time talking about my kinks, but what about yours?"

"Don't you have to go meet Daddy?"

"He told me to take my time. So, what are you into?"

She sits back, considering her answer. "Obviously, I like getting myself off in front of other people." I know that all too well, and she looks hot doing it. "I enjoy a little girl-on-girl action, but I could never go without cock. I love giving head while others watch. It makes me feel... powerful. With the right Dom, you can feel his pride as you take him deep, moaning while he shoots his load down your throat."

"Holy shit, girl. That does sound hot."

"I love that you understand what I mean when I say being submissive is empowering."

"Me too."

"I love wax play. Have you and Master Harrison done that yet?"

"No, but I want to try."

"Go straight for the nipples. It stings like a bitch, but when he tears the hardened wax off and sucks your nipple into his mouth... you can come just from how fucking good it feels."

I'm officially bumping it up the list.

"You're making me wet right now, Cel."

"Then what are you waiting for? Go tell your Daddy what you want."

"Are you sure?"

"Yes. I need to get going. My mom has Belle. I need to get her home, bathed, and ready for a bedtime story."

"Thank you for today. I really needed this," I say as I slide out of the booth.

"Me too. I'll catch up with you at Venom later in the week."

"Love you, Cel," I say as I lean over and hug her.

"Back at you, Frey."

I walk the three blocks to the club, knowing that Pierce will probably be annoyed that I didn't call for his town car or hail a cab. By the time I arrive, I'm more than a little worked up after my conversation with Celest. There are so many things I still don't know if I like. It's exciting. I want to try giving Pierce a blow job in the voyeur lounge, but I also want to test out wax play. Maybe Pierce could drip wax on me while I give him head. The thought makes me laugh. If I could have everything at once, I would, and then I'd probably die of sensory overload. At least I'd die with a smile on my face.

As soon as I set foot in the bar, he turns to meet my gaze, leaving Flex hanging as he strides toward me with that effortless swagger of his. Wrapping his arm around my waist, he pulls me in for a kiss, leaving me breathless. "I missed you today, little one."

God, I'm so turned on already, and we haven't even done anything. "I missed you, too, Daddy. Do you want me to go and get in the position?"

"Fuck," he growls, pressing the length of his erection against me. "I want that so bad it's not even funny, *but* I made plans outside the club. I'm taking you out on a proper date."

My pussy clenches with the need to be sated at the same time as my heart skips a beat. We live together, and yet this will be our first non-playroom date. "Really? Where are we going?"

He offers his hand which I gladly take. "You'll see. Trust me."

"I do."

When we step outside, Pierce's town car is waiting. He ushers me in before sliding in beside me and pulling a blindfold out of his pocket. "I think you've seen enough for now."

I love when he takes my sight. All of my other senses heighten. This is the first time he's done it outside the playroom, so I'm a little nervous as the car pulls into traffic. He doesn't speak as he caresses my skin—my cheek, my neck, across my collarbone, along my arm, sending a shiver down my spine. He leaves a trail of kisses where his fingers were, leaving me panting as the car comes to a standstill.

"We're here."

"I... please tell me we're back at the club," I whisper breathlessly.

"Not tonight." He gently helps me out of the car and leads me to wherever we're going. I feel a blast of air conditioning as we enter a building and the familiar lunge of an elevator.

"When do I get to see where we are?"

"Patience, little one. We're almost there." He leads me from the elevator and out into the night air. Positioning me, he runs his fingers up my arms, leaving me breathless and crying out for his touch elsewhere.

I'm giddy as he loosens the blindfold, but I'm not prepared for the scene before me. We're on a gorgeous rooftop, with twinkling lights creating an ethereal canopy above us and a single table set for two sitting in the center of the space. A bottle of champagne is waiting in an ice bucket and two glass flutes.

"Oh my, God, Daddy. It's... so beautiful. You did this all for me?" Tears well in my eyes. No one has ever done something this romantic for me. I've never let anyone close enough.

"I wanted to show you how much I appreciate your love and support. I know life isn't exactly all moonlight and roses right now."

"I like the whips and floggers," I quip.

"Oh, I know, but you didn't sign up for prison handcuffs and the suspension of your mentor. It means so much to me that you're by my side through all of this. I just wanted you to know how special you are."

I push up onto my tiptoes and plant a soft kiss on his lips. "Thank you, Daddy."

"You're welcome, little one."

He pulls my seat out like the gentleman he is and pours us both a glass of champagne, lifting them in a toast. "Here's to a long and happy future together. I hope."

I clink my glass to his and take a sip. "That *is* going to happen. I have faith in your lawyer. Nad wouldn't steer you wrong."

"Her friend, Jenna, the private investigator, has pieced together the footage from that night. I'm hopeful this will work in my favor. One of the security cameras has a decent angle of the altercation. It looks like he threw the first punch."

"That's amazing."

"Yeah, I just hate that it's all a little fuzzy in my mind. I remember putting myself between the boy and his father. He was shouting all kinds of obscenities, and then one of the security guards was pulling me off him."

I reach across the table, resting my hand on his—so large compared to mine. "We know that can be a trauma response. Something he said clearly triggered you."

"Yeah," he mumbles, pulling back his hand and taking a long swig of champagne. "It could still cost me my career. There's no excuse to act that way as a doctor."

"We're all human, Pierce. You never give yourself grace."

He shifts uncomfortably in his seat. "Do you want to take a look at the menu?"

He hands it to me. We're on the rooftop of the Four Seasons. Holy crap. I don't even want to know what it must have cost him to rent this place out for the evening.

"What would you recommend?"

"I'm not sure. I've never brought anyone here before."

"But you've dated other women?"

He casts his eyes to a mundane spot on the table. "I'm ashamed to say no. I've treated women like my own personal playthings. I never made any room for dates or feelings. Certainly not for love."

"Don't be ashamed. You've never professed to offer more than a consensual trainer/trainee, Dom/sub relationship. Every woman you've been with knew what she was getting."

"Except you." He picks at a piece of lint on the table linen. "I blindsided you with so much. Too much." There's a pain in his eyes that crushes me.

"You've given me a love I never knew was possible. Acceptance of anything I ask to explore. A life I want. We'll get through this."

"What if I never operate again?"

"That won't happen," I reassure him.

"But if it does?"

"Then you'll find another way to fulfill your life and use your talent. We'll talk about it over dinners in *our* home."

"This isn't what you signed up for."

"Pierce. Daddy. I love you. I'm *in love* with you. It's not contingent on how many surgeries you perform or your accolades."

"I'm supposed to be your mentor. I can't bear the thought of taking that away from you."

"What I can't bear is the thought of losing you. The man, *not* the surgeon. My Daddy. My Dom. My lover and friend. And one day… my husband."

His eyes shoot up to meet mine. "What?"

"You heard me. I want to be your wife. I want you to be my husband. There's no one else I want to explore and experience this life with."

"You're saying yes?"

"I'm saying yes." Within seconds, he has me out of the chair and in his arms, twirling me around under a twinkling fairy tale in the heart of Manhattan.

"I love you so much, Freya. You're making me the happiest man in the world."

"I love you too. No matter what comes our way, we'll face it together."

Pierce kisses me with a passion so fierce it overwhelms me. I never thought I was capable of a love like this. I always felt out of my element. That I didn't fit in with the 'norm' when it came to dating. Now, at this moment, I know I was holding out for something that's so much more than 'normal.' I found the other half of my soul. He sees me and accepts me—my flaws, my kinks—everything that I've been holding in for so long, fearful I'd be judged and never believing I'd be loved.

"If I'd have known this was where tonight was going, I'd have brought your ring with me," he says between kisses.

"What? You have a ring? But when you asked me, it was so spur of the moment."

"I've had the ring since the day after we met." My heart takes flight, a swarm of butterflies filling my chest as his lips crash down on mine.

I was so worried that he proposed in a knee-jerk reaction to everything that's going on. The thought he knew long before I did that we were meant to be—it's more than I could ever hope for. "Really? You didn't even know my name or if I'd ever come back to the club."

He sets me on my feet, cupping my face in his strong hands with a smile that could melt a glacier. "The second I laid eyes on you across the room, your soul called to mine, little one. I knew I had to know you, love you, and make you mine. You've always been the one, Freya, even before I saw your face. I fell in love with your vulnerability and willingness to take the leap and let me worship your body. I'm hook, line, and sinker in love with you, Dr. Freya Perrington."

"That'll be Dr. Freya Harrison to you."

"Are you kidding me?" His eyes become glassy, his demeanor so serious I worry he doesn't want me to change my name.

"No. You're my home, Pierce. We're family now."

"I don't remember what it's like to have a family. Are you sure you want to take my name?"

"Yes. I'm proud to be yours, and I always will be. It's you and me from here on out, okay?"

"Okay? I'm... I don't deserve..." His lips press so tight against mine it hurts, pouring every ounce of overwhelming emotion into this one kiss.

Sealing our forever, no matter what comes our way. *I am his, and he is mine.*

Chapter 21

PIERCE

She said yes.

My career hangs in the balance, my freedom uncertain, and Freya said yes. I feel like the luckiest son of a bitch on the planet. We're engaged. *Me* of all people. Tonight is our engagement party at Venom, and I have an unconventional gift for my little one.

As we get ready at our apartment, I walk in to see her fastening a delicate diamond necklace around her neck. I told her to splurge with whatever she wanted to wear for the night, but not my girl. She bought a simple silver chain with a single small diamond dangling from the center. And her dress—the one she was wearing the night we met. My lavender queen.

"Look at you, little one. So beautiful, but there's something missing."

She turns to face me with a shy smile. She knows what's coming. She insisted I wait until the party to give her the ring that's been burning a hole in my pocket. Dropping down on one knee, I open the box and present it to her. "Freya, I didn't know what love was until the day you came into my life and silently stole my heart. I love you more than words could ever adequately convey. You're my family. One I didn't know I was longing for. Will you marry me, little one?"

"Yes, Daddy." She launches herself at me, knocking us both to the floor as she kisses me with wild abandon. She barely even looks at the ring, more eager to seal the moment with a kiss. I'm good with that. I know Freya has never been interested in the money I bring to our relationship.

"Don't start something you can't finish, little one," I say as I roll her onto her back, straddling her. "We have a party to get to."

"No one will notice if we're a little late." She's a minx, knowing I can't say no to her.

I tug at her dress, pulling it up as I slide down her body and bury my head between her thighs. "Fuck me." She's wearing lavender lace panties from La Perla, the signature string of pearls highlighting her perfectly rounded ass. I want to forget about the party and worship her body all night long.

"Yes... Daddy." Those two words are my undoing. Pushing the lace aside, I thrust two fingers insider her already wet cunt, my lips capturing her clit as she moans, writhing on the floor of our closet.

We're an hour late to our engagement party, and my friends don't let us get away with it. Flex is the first to speak up. "Couldn't keep it in your pants until the party? Seriously, bro."

"You shouldn't spend so much time thinking about my dick, Flex. I've got plenty of stamina for later." He gives me a wry smile, and a pang of jealousy courses through me.

When I told Freya that I have a gift for her tonight, I wasn't kidding. A gift I'm not that keen on giving her, to be honest, but she's basically given up on me 'training' her at this point, and I don't want her coming into this marriage with unanswered questions when it comes to possible kinks she may have. Of course, we'll always be exploring and learning new ways to connect, but she expressed her desire to try having Flex in the equation, and tonight, that's what I'm going to give her, no matter how much it pains me.

If I don't let her do it now, I never will. The moment she becomes Freya Harrison, I won't be able to share her unless it's something she discovers she *needs* as my submissive.

I'm playing a dangerous game, betting everything I've got on the fact that I can be enough for her. The more I think about it, the less sure of myself I become. I've never been enough for anyone. Not my parents. Not my foster families. Not even as a Dom. Why should this be any different?

As always, the club looks stunning. Dalton and Carter went all out on the decorations up in the voyeur lounge. It's a ballroom tonight, just as it was the night Freya and I met. I'm still mesmerized by her—a vision in lavender—as she talks and laughs with friends. Celest is by her side, excited to celebrate with her best friend. I love that Freya has someone to talk to about the lifestyle. It's not an easy road when you have no one to confide in. It took me a long time to trust the men I've come to know here at Venom.

Flex appears at my side, offering me a whiskey. "Hey, brother. Thought you might need this."

I welcome the liquid courage. "Thanks."

"Are you sure you want to do this?"

"It's nothing we haven't done before, Flex."

"You've never been in love with the subs we've shared. This is your fiancée."

"You don't think I'm painfully aware of that?"

He holds up his hands, "Don't shoot the messenger. I value our friendship, Pierce. I don't want to do anything to fuck that up."

"You're the only person I trust with her, man. And if I end up going to prison…"

"Don't even think about finishing that sentence."

"I'm serious. This…" I gesture to the frivolity happening all around us, everyone celebrating the future I hope I get to experience with Freya. "If it doesn't go my way, she needs to finish training. Promise me you'll help her." It pains me to choke out the words.

"Why me?"

"Because I know you won't fall in love with her. She needs this lifestyle, Flex. She's become such a force to be reckoned with. Please, I can't live with myself if I'm the reason she leaves it behind."

"What makes you think she would even accept me as a Master for however many months she has left?"

"She requested you for trying a scene with another man. She trusts you… and so do I."

"I need to think about it, Pierce. I don't want to promise something I can't deliver on. Let's just see how tonight goes."

"Hopefully, none of this will matter, and I'll get my happily ever after, but life doesn't often surprise me with the best-case scenario."

"Well, I'd say your luck is changing." He points to Freya across the room, her eyes locked on mine. "I'd say she's a pretty fucking amazing surprise in your life."

"You got that right. I'm going to go tell her the plans we have for tonight. I'll meet you down in my playroom in fifteen."

"Sure thing."

I weave my way through the crowd of well-wishers, my focus solely on my little one. As I approach her, I can't help but want to recapture the moment when my life changed forever.

"Dance with me." I'm rewarded with a smile so sweet it makes my heart ache for her. I don't know how I'm going to get through tonight, but I'll do it for Freya. I want her to have everything her heart desires, even if that's another man in our bed.

I spin her around the floor, the only difference from the night we met being that I can see her stunningly beautiful face. There are no masks tonight, and her face is a sight to behold. She's breathtaking, and I don't think there will ever be a day in my life that I wake up next to her and don't feel complete and utter adoration for the woman she is.

"I have a gift for you down in our playroom." She visibly twitches in my hold.

"Are we allowed to leave our own party? We already arrived late."

"We can do as we please, little one. You haven't finished your training yet, and I have something to tick off your list of potential kinks."

A broad grin kisses her delicate features, her eyes sparkling with excitement. "Ooo… is it wax? Or shibari? Or a clitoral clamp?"

"You'll see when we get there." She practically drags me across the floor and down the stairs to the private rooms. She's an eager little thing tonight. I take note of the types of play she mentioned, sure to make them happen in the next few weeks.

When we reach the door to the playroom, my determination falters, only for a moment. "Remember your safeword, little one."

"Yes, Daddy."

"You are in the driver's seat tonight. Whatever you want is what will happen." I stumble over the words.

"O-kay. You're freaking me out. Are we going inside?"

"Yes." I swipe the card and open the door to show Flex sitting in the chair at the other side of the room, his hands steepled under his chin, his eyes fixed on Freya.

"What's going on?" She turns to search my gaze for answers.

"You expressed a desire to explore having another man in a scene. Specifically Flex. He and I have done this before, so I trust him to treat you with the respect you deserve, little one."

She's trembling as she steps inside the room, jumping as the door clicks shut behind us.

"I… what do you mean, I'm in the driver's seat?"

"Exactly that. This will play out as you choose, little one."

"Daddy… I want you to decide what happens." Fuck. I was afraid of this. How can I tell Flex to touch and caress what's mine? "Daddy?" She's looking to me for guidance. She wants to learn, and I promised to teach her.

"Take your dress off and get in the position, little one."

I can see a change in Flex's demeanor from previous times we've shared a submissive. He knows she's mine and what that means to me. His jaw is tight as he forces himself to watch her step out of her dress. With only her pearl thong still on, she makes her way to the corner, slipping her wrists through the ropes and letting them tighten as she takes up her position. Fuck, she looks stunning.

"Flex, isn't my little one beautiful?"

"Yes. She's exquisite." He can't even look me in the eye, transfixed by the sight of her submission.

"Tell me, little one, have you imagined what it's like to be taken by two Doms?"

"Yes, Daddy."

"And how did we fuck you?"

"You fucked my pussy, Daddy." She hesitates.

"And how does Flex fuck you?" I know she wants this, but it doesn't make it hurt any less. I'm the only man who's ever fucked Freya. After tonight, that will no longer be the case, and I never thought of myself as a jealous man until her. Now, at this moment, I don't want the answer to my question.

"He fucks my mouth, Daddy." Her voice quivers as she allows herself to ask for what she needs.

"Very well. Flex, take your dick out and show my little one what she does to you." He's hard as a rock. Who wouldn't be? She's gorgeous, submissive, and she's asking to be fucked.

I position myself over her, loosening the restraints before helping her stand and turning her to face Flex.

He slowly unzips his fly, pushing his pants down just enough for his dick to spring free, hard and ready for her.

"Where should we fuck you, little one? The bed? The table?" I run my fingers down her arms, lacing her hands with mine. "Shall I spread you on my table and let Flex see how wet your pretty little cunt is?"

"Yes, Daddy." Her breaths are shallow, her breasts heavy as she watches Flex fist the base of his dick.

I walk her over to the table. "Spread your legs, little one." She does as I ask, and I secure her in the leather cuffs. "Arms too."

When I have her completely at my mercy—our mercy—I stand at her back, caressing her ass.

"She's a good little girl, Master Harrison. A credit to your training." Flex continues to stroke his dick as he moves closer to the other side of the table toward Freya's mouth. "Tell me, little one, has he taught you how to deep throat a cock properly?"

I fucking bristle at his use of my pet name. He's just doing what we've always done, but this is different. *She's mine.*

He takes another step toward her. "Open your mouth." She

doesn't comply, and a surge of adrenaline courses through me. "Open your mouth, little one."

"Don't fucking call her that. She's mine," I roar. Flex doesn't even look phased as if he were expecting this reaction.

"Lavender," Freya exclaims, and my heart skips a beat.

"What is it, little one?"

"I'm done. I don't want to do this. I'm sorry, Daddy, but I want the only man I've slept with to be you."

Flex steps back with a smug grin on his face. He knew this was going to happen. I'm the only idiot who thought Freya needed this.

"Close your eyes, little one." She does as I ask without question. I round the table and gesture to Flex to sit back in the corner. My little one will enjoy performing for him, but the only hands that will be touching her are mine.

"Open your mouth."

"Daddy…"

"Trust me, Freya." She opens her mouth, waiting like the good little girl I know her to be.

I reach for my dick, working the base before stepping forward and brushing her lips with the tip.

"Keep it open, little one." I ease inside the wet warmth of her mouth. "That's it, take Daddy's dick like a good girl." She moans around my dick, the vibration of her humming with delight sends a shiver down my spine.

"She takes you well," Flex interjects from across the room, startling Freya, but she keeps working my dick.

"You hear that, little one? You take my dick so well. Do you want Flex to stay and watch me come all over your face?

"Yes, Daddy."

Flex sits back in the chair, his fist wrapped around the base of his dick, working it in long, strong strokes as Freya takes every last inch of me, still shackled to the table.

"Fuck, little one, you're so fucking good at that." She swallows around my dick as she takes it even deeper, her throat muscles clenching around the tip, making me struggle to keep a modicum of self-restraint.

She opens her eyes, looking up at me with such trust and unashamed pride. She's mine, and nothing and no one will ever get in the way of that.

"Would you like to watch Flex pleasure himself while you suck my dick?"

She nods, never giving up an inch of her Daddy.

"Flex, come closer. Let my little one see you work your dick at the sight of how fucking beautiful she is when she's giving Daddy head."

He's always been laid back, going with the flow during a scene unless it's his to command. He strolls over to us, his dick swinging hard as a rock as he takes himself in his hand. "Your Daddy isn't wrong. You're a greedy little sub, and your mouth is even more beautiful with a cock in it."

He comes close enough to be in Freya's line of sight, where she can watch him jack off as he takes in the sight of me fucking her mouth without apology.

Fisting my hand in her hair, I hold her steady as I begin to set a punishing rhythm, her tongue flicking the crest of my dick, driving me wild.

"That's it, little one, fucking gag on me." I continue to thrust, her eyes fixed on Flex as he watches her sucking my dick like a goddamn lollipop.

"Oh, she loves being watched while you fuck her mouth, Harrison."

"Yeah, she does. But no one touches what's mine. Isn't that right, little one?" She hums her approval. "Only Daddy's dick."

She gags as I thrust further down her throat, relishing the moment, knowing she is completely at *my* mercy.

"Fuck, I'm close. You guys are too fucking hot together." Flex strains as he tries to keep control. His eyes are fixed on where Freya's lips swallow my dick.

"Good. I want her to see what she does to you. To Celest. To everyone who watches her suck for Daddy."

I pull out of her mouth just long enough to ask her a question.

"Tell me, little one, do you want Master Navarro to come on your face while you swallow Daddy's cum like a good little girl?"

"Yes, Daddy."

Fuck, she's a dirty little minx. I fucking love this side of her. She wants just enough to color outside the lines but won't sully the special bond we share—the one she chose to only share with me.

"Then, open up for Daddy, and remember to swallow every last drop, little one."

She smiles up at me with such trust and adoration. It's so beautiful. I'll never get enough of her. As I pick up the pace, Flex pumps his dick to the same rhythm, stepping closer as he chases his release.

Freya looks fucking resplendent as she takes me deeper, tears pricking at her eyes as she gags me down. Jesus, I can't hold on much longer. She feels too damn good. As my orgasm takes hold, pulsing down the length of me, I can't contain the roar that escapes me. "Fuck... little one.. fuck, yes..."

Flex continues to stroke himself to climax, his cum spilling all over my little one's face as she continues to suck my dick, milking me for every last drop. "Fuck me," he curses as he rides the aftershocks, his head thrown back and cock still hard.

When we're both spent, I run my hand down Freya's cheek, cum running down her chin. "You are so fucking beautiful, little one. You were such a good girl for Daddy. I think it's time you get your reward. Do you want Master Navarro to watch me fuck you?"

"If he'd like to."

Flex leaves his dick out but walks over to the wingback chair in the corner, sitting and unbuttoning his black shirt to showcase his abs. He already knows my girl will be too hot not to jack himself off again and come all up his chest.

"I'd very much like to see your submissive come. She took your cock so well with that pretty little mouth. I can't wait to see how greedy her pussy is for you."

I leave Freya's face covered in cum and walk around to the other side of the table, her legs still spread wide for me. Sliding my hand up her leg to the apex of her thighs, she's already soaked. "My girl is so turned on, she's positively drenched." I lift a finger to my lips. "She tastes so fucking good."

I give her ass a sharp slap. "Who do you belong to, little one?"

"You, Daddy."

"That's right." I thrust two fingers inside her. "This pretty little cunt is mine and mine alone."

"Yes…"

I pull my fingers out, covered in her arousal, and move to her ass, pressing them slowly inside. "And this?"

"Yours, Daddy. Everything is yours."

"Did you hear that, Flex? Even her ass is mine and mine alone."

"You're a lucky man. Now, fuck her, and let me watch her scream and cream."

"Would you like that, little one?"

"Yes, Daddy," she pants. My girl loves an audience.

I slide her thong to the side and position myself at her entrance, slamming into her in one hard thrust. "Fucking hell, little one. You're so damn tight."

"Oh God… yes, Daddy."

I hammer into her over and over again, her muscles clenching around my dick as the beginning of her orgasm takes hold. I make her take every hard inch until I'm seated balls deep inside her.

"You feel that, little one? That's your cunt fucking loving my dick."

"Yes, Daddy. I need it."

"Look at Master Navarro as you come with my dick claiming you."

I follow her gaze to where he sits, jacking off with his eyes fixed on her, bound and pinned down to the table. It makes her whimper as I hold her on the edge of orgasm.

"Good girl. Now, come for me." I slam into her, sending her spiraling out of control as I find release with her, and a guttural roar rips from Flex's chest as he comes with us, his gaze never leaving us.

When she can't take anymore, I pull out, my breath ragged as I tame my dick into my pants and grab a towel to clean her up. I get one for Flex, too, and toss it to him as I clean off my little one's face.

She's completely spent, her eyelids fighting to stay open as I unbuckle the restraints. Freya slumps against the table, unable to hold her weight, her legs shaking in the aftermath of orgasm.

I gently lift her into my arms, and she rests her head on my chest as I carry her over to the bed. Flex gives me a nod and takes his leave. He knows I need privacy for aftercare. Hell, he knew his role in tonight's activities before I did. I'll thank him later. For now, I'm going to fill the tub and get my fiancée cleaned up.

She's almost sound asleep by the time I get her to the edge of the tub. "Shouldn't we be getting back to our party?"

"You're in no fit state to go out there. They can wait. Knowing our friends, they're already amusing themselves in the playrooms."

I help her into the water before stepping in at her back and grabbing a washcloth to clean her face. I love her, but I'm not kissing Flex's jizz off her face.

"I'm sorry, Daddy."

"For what?"

"I couldn't do what you wanted tonight. I don't want to sleep with another man, even with your consent." Is she for real right now?

I gently twist her chin to meet my gaze. "I did that for you. I didn't want to share you with Flex or any other man."

"What? But you had him waiting in here."

"Because…" I'm ashamed to admit this, but I don't want any secrets between us moving forward, "I'm worried that if I go to prison, you won't finish your training. I was trying to go through your list of possibilities. You mentioned adding another man, and after you enjoyed Celest, I thought…"

"Stop there. You are *not* going to prison."

"You can't say that for sure, and you've come alive as a submissive. I won't have you waste away waiting for me."

"That's why you brought Flex in? To train me if you're not around?"

"Yes."

"Oh my God. Daddy. *No.* You're my Dom. I don't care what

happens, I won't take another Dom, so get that idea out of your head right now."

"I can't stand the thought of you being alone."

"But you're okay with me sleeping with someone else?"

"No," I growl. "It was fucking devastating to contemplate. But I would do it if it's the best thing for you."

"*You're* the best thing for me, Pierce. Only you. I'm happy to watch or be watched. I love it. But I don't want another man to fuck me. I never will. It's you, and as old-fashioned as I sound, that's the way I want it to stay."

My heart almost bursts out of my chest, my pulse racing. "Are you certain I'm enough for you?"

"Pierce Harrison, I love you more than life itself. You are enough. You always have been and always will be. I love you."

"How soon can we get married?"

"The faster, the better for me."

I capture her mouth with a kiss, unwilling to relinquish her love, whether I deserve it or not. "Let's go home, little one."

"Yes, Daddy. Take me home."

Chapter 22

FREYA

Pierce has been thrashing around in his sleep for the past few nights. Always the same nightmare from what I can tell, but tonight is different. The words he's calling out—this is a new dream. My attempts to wake him aren't working, and with a court appearance tomorrow, I'm afraid he's locked in his past, and there's nothing I can do for him.

"Pierce, it's me, Freya. You're having a bad dream. Wake up, Daddy. I'm here." He continues to plead for forgiveness, and it breaks my heart.

"No, Daddy. Please. I'll be good." Tears fall from the corners of his eyes, and I can't hold back my own. It's painful to watch. With tears streaming down my face, I beg him to wake up.

"Please, Pierce. Come back to me. Wake up."

"I won't let you hurt her anymore." He curls into the fetal position. "I won't let you hurt us, Daddy. You broke me. You broke Mommy."

I wrap my arms around him, pressing my front to his back, giving him whatever strength I can at this moment.

"No one loves me, Daddy. Not you, not Mommy. I'm alone."

I brush his sweat-soaked blond hair off his forehead, pressing my lips to his cheek. "I love you. Wake up, Pierce."

"I'm alone. You've hurt me enough, Daddy. Enough," he whispers, and it makes my soul ache for him.

"Wake up," I plead through my tears. I want so desperately to help him, but he won't let me.

He startles in my embrace, fighting against my touch. "Freya?"

"Yes," I say, stroking his arm. "It's me. I'm here. You're not alone." I can feel his rapid pulse like the wings of a hummingbird.

He turns in my arms, facing me as tears spill from his darkened gaze. *Haunted.*

"The last thing my father did on this earth was throw me across the room so hard I needed brain surgery for a bleed."

I stay stock-still. Pierce has never opened up to me about his past.

"I was four years old, and he hated me with such vitriol that I knew it was because of me. Something I did. I was unlovable."

"You are very loveable, Pierce." I press my lips to his shoulder.

"What dad hates his own kid? I had this little ambulance truck that made the coolest sound. I loved it. I knew I wanted to be a doctor even back then. He smashed it to pieces before he kicked me in the stomach and lifted me above his head. Threw me so hard against the wall everything went black."

I want to be strong for him, but I can't contain my silent tears. The thought of anyone hurting him is devastating.

"My mom walked in and killed him. He died right there in my bedroom, and I was glad. I was glad that my father was dead." His voice becomes hollow. "I thought it would be better, just me and my mom, but it broke her. She loved my dad, even though he beat the crap out of both of us. She loved him and blamed me for what happened. She drank herself to death, and I went into the system. I've been alone ever since. No one stays, little one. I wanted so badly to have that with you, and then I let my father win one last time, and it could cost me everything."

I gently lift his chin, forcing him to see the love in my eyes. A love so overwhelming I still have to pinch myself to know it's real.

"We're going to get through this. Together. I'm not going anywhere, Pierce. I love you with every fiber of my being. I love the man you are, the little boy who endured so much more than any one person should. I love you as a surgeon, a Dom, and a man who stood up to a bully to save another little boy from the same fate.

"The dream was different tonight. I was standing in the ER between that little boy and his father, except it was my father, and when I turned around to see the little boy lying broken in the bed… it was me. I had to save him. To save myself. I couldn't let it happen again. I know I should've walked away, but I couldn't, Freya. I couldn't let that boy continue to be abused. The next blow could've been fatal."

I press my lips to his, the saltiness of his tears so bittersweet. I'm so happy that he's ready to open up to me, but knowing what he endured is heartbreaking. It's why he struggles at times when I call him Daddy.

"You did the right thing, Pierce. You saved that little boy. He and his mom are safe now because of you. Is this why you feel unsure when I call you Daddy?"

"I love it, but I wonder if it's because I'm fucked up."

"Yes, it probably is. Just like I love it, knowing full well that it's because my dad was never in the picture. It never upset me because I didn't know any different. I have a lovely mom who did her best to put food on the table. What I've realized is that all of our experiences make us who we are, and if that translates to a kink we share in a committed and loving relationship, who cares! Do you enjoy being my Daddy?"

"More than I can express," he admits, tucking an errant strand of hair off my face.

"And I love being your little one. Does it really matter what brought us to this place? We're together, and that's what's important. You're not alone anymore, Daddy. We're family, and I will spend every day of the rest of our lives together showing you how much I love you."

"That sounds like a plan." His lips find mine in a soul-shattering kiss, and, for now, nothing can touch us. It's just us, here, at this moment together until death do us part.

~

"Your honor, I have provided video evidence that my client was simply reacting to Mr. Lee's attack. Dr. Harrison is a respected member of the community and is at the forefront of his field of neurosurgery. He placed himself in danger between an abusive husband and father. If not for his intervention, the next blow to the boy could very well have been fatal. We have heard from numerous character witnesses who speak to Dr. Harrison's impeccable, professional behavior. We have also provided more than enough evidence of Mr. Lee's violent nature to conclude that my client was in no way to blame for the altercation that night."

The lawyer Nad suggested is the best defense lawyer in the state, and he doesn't disappoint. I can't even believe the case got this far. I thought the second they had the security footage, it would disappear. Instead, we're here, and I'm hoping the judge and jury see sense and do the right thing.

"Does the prosecution have anything to add?"

They were trying to strike a deal last night. They know they have no chance of winning. They've seen the footage but thought they could leverage this case to lessen the one that will be brought against Mr. Lee by his wife.

Nad advised us not to make a deal with them, confident that the charges against Pierce wouldn't hold up. I hope she's right.

"We have nothing further, your honor."

"Then the jury will adjourn to discuss the evidence provided and come to a verdict."

Pierce's jaw is tight as he sits at his lawyer's side. Celest, Nad, Dalton, and Flex came to support him, and they've all been hovering around me all day. I'm pretty sure Pierce told them to look after me, never worrying for one second about himself.

Flex rests his hand on my shoulder, pulling me back to the room.

"It's going to be fine. The jury knows what happened. It's open and shut."

"Do you really think so, or did Pierce tell you that's the party line?"

"Both. I do think he'll walk out of here with a clean record today. I really do."

"I hope so. Whatever happens here will have a direct effect on his career. He's unbelievable in the operating room, Flex. He's the best there is. Truly."

"I believe you. He's not exactly shy about bigging up his skills," he jests, trying to lighten the mood. "Come on, pull up your La Perla panties, and let's go give him some support."

"Are you really going to lord it over me that you've seen my panties?" I say with a sly grin.

"Only until the next time you watch me jerk off for you. I'd say you have the upper hand here. Although, my cock is very impressive."

"What makes you think there'll be a next time?"

"Your penchant for fucking on the voyeur floor. I hear you put on quite the show with Celest. What are the chances that's how you want to celebrate Pierce's freedom?" He wiggles his eyebrows at me.

"I'm sure Celest would put on a show for you, Flex."

She turns at the mention of her name. "What would I do?"

"Flex is sad he missed our little show on the voyeur floor."

"Oh, I could definitely do a repeat performance." Her eyes heat under Flex's feral gaze.

"I'll hold you to that one, pet."

I leave everyone else to filter out to the hallway and wait for Pierce. He looks tired today. Exhausted. "How are you holding up, little one?" He always puts my needs ahead of his own.

"Don't worry about me, Daddy. I'm fine. How are you? I think your lawyer sealed the deal with the closing statement."

"I'm okay. I just want this to be done. I miss operating. The thought that I might never get the chance again is more than I can fathom. These past few months have felt like a lifetime."

"You'll be operating by this time next week."

"I'm sure you're right. And you'll be at my side. Joseph agrees that you're the new me."

"High praise indeed."

"It is. He hates teaching these days. The fact that he has a smile on his face when he talks about you is a damn miracle. That's how good you are, and don't you forget it."

"I won't. Dalton has had lunch catered at the restaurant across the street. Come and have something to eat."

"Sure. Trust him to put on a fucking buffet at my court hearing. It could be days before the jury reach a verdict."

"We'll eat, hang out for a little while, and go home. He knows you need to keep your strength up."

"I didn't realize I needed a parent."

"They are our family, Daddy. Just get used to it. All four of them are family. You and I are family. Forever. End of discussion."

"You're a bossy little submissive today."

"Yep. Get used to that too. I'm the one who's looking out for you. This relationship isn't a one-way street. Just because you're a Dom doesn't mean you don't get looked after too. That's my job, and I take it very seriously."

"If we were anywhere else right now, I'd put you over my knee for the sass in your tone."

"Promises, promises. When we walk out of here victorious today, you can put me over your knee at the club tonight. Flex wants to see what all the fuss is about with you, me, and Celest."

"Does he? He can look, but he can't touch. You're mine, little one."

"Always."

We walk hand-in-hand out to where the others are waiting for us, Flex inhaling his lunch. You'd think the man was starved.

Pierce is obviously nervous about the verdict, but no one acknowledges it, aware that he wouldn't thank any of us for bringing it to his attention. I'm so glad they came to support him today. I believe the outcome will be in our favor, but I think he needs to see that more people care about him than he realizes. He matters to every person in this room. He is *loved*.

I'm so proud of him for standing up for that mother and son. So proud that he finally stood up to the demons that have been haunting him all these years.

We laugh and joke, distracting each other as much as we do Pierce. We're all on tenterhooks for the next few hours, trying to relax, knowing this is going to be a waiting game. What we're not prepared for is Nad getting a call two hours later saying the verdict is in.

I've got to believe that it's quick because it is so clear that Pierce isn't at fault here. He didn't initiate the skirmish, and even if he did, he was doing the right thing. I steel my nerves, stuffing them as far down inside me as I can and painting a smile on my face.

Taking Pierce's hand in mine, I lift it to my lips, savoring his scent. "Let's go and get your not guilty verdict."

He pulls me aside as everyone starts making their way out. "Promise me you'll finish your training."

"I will. With you."

"Of course. But…"

"No 'buts,' Daddy. It's me and you against the world. This is going to go our way. I can feel it. Now, kiss me like you mean it, and let's go."

Dropping my hand, he cups my face, his lips crushing hard against mine, his tongue begging entrance which I freely give. Keeping my eyes tightly shut, I force myself not to cry. This isn't a goodbye kiss. It's a deep, primal expression of the love we're going to share for the rest of our lives, which starts today after Pierce walks out of the courtroom a free man.

The walk across the street is quiet. Dalton and Flex flank us on either side, and Nad and Celest are at our back. I'm so nervous my hand is shaking as I cling to Pierce. If he notices, he doesn't mention it, his demeanor somber and silent.

I swallow past the lump in my throat as he kisses my cheek and releases his hold on me, going to take his place at the front of the courtroom next to his lawyer.

You could hear a pin drop as we eagerly await the judge.

"All rise."

A wave of nausea washes over me as I stand, Flex and Celest steadying me on either side. "Take a breath, Frey." Celest links her hand with mine, giving me whatever strength she can at this moment.

As we sit back down, I fight to keep down what little I had for lunch.

"Have the jury come to a verdict?"

"Yes, your honor." A gentle-spoken woman addresses the judge.

"And what say you?"

"We, the jury, find the defendant..." Time is endless as I wait to hear two words that give Pierce and me a lifetime, "... not guilty."

I collapse against Flex, incoherent, babbling joy escaping my throat. "It's okay, Frey. Everything's okay."

Before I know what's happening, Pierce has jumped the barrier and is pulling me into his arms. "I've got you, little one."

"Daddy," I sob into his chest. I've been holding it all in, telling him everything will be fine, but there was a small kernel of fear deep in my gut, telling me we wouldn't get our happily ever after. I didn't realize until now just how gripping that fear really was.

"I'll always have you, little one."

Our friends usher us into the hallway before whooping and hollering, wrapping their arms around us. "It's time to celebrate."

"Not at the club. You two will just disappear the second we get there. We're having a bonafide celebration tonight. I'm calling Carter. We're going to Viper." Flex knows us too well, and as much as I'd like to take Pierce home to our apartment and let him fuck me on every surface, in every room, I want to revel in this victory with the people who've been by our side through all of this.

"The man of the hour," Dalton proclaims as he lifts a glass. There are so many of our friends from the club. Carter went all out in Viper's VIP lounge. I've been taking it all in as I watch Pierce navigate the room, a genuine, heartfelt smile on his face, surrounded by friends—those who have quietly supported us and those who have been very vocal. "Pierce, you're a good man, and I think I can speak for everyone in the room when I say what you did was noble. You stood up for those not strong enough to stand up for themselves. You've conducted yourself with your head held high, and we're all so thrilled that the jury saw what we've always seen in you. So, let's raise a glass to Pierce and to good winning out in the end. It couldn't happen to a more deserving guy."

"Cheers," the room answers collectively.

Pierce gives a solemn nod before lifting his glass to take a sip. I move to his side, wrapping my arm around his waist and resting my head against his shoulder. "He's right, you know. What you did was noble, and I love you even more for it." He faced his past and slew the dragon.

"Thanks, little one. I couldn't have gotten through any of this without you."

"Lucky that I'm not planning on going anywhere then. You're stuck with me for life."

"Promise?" he asks as he pulls me against his chest, his index finger slipping under my chin, forcing me to gaze up into his striking green eyes. I could get lost in them forever and be completely content.

"Yes, Daddy."

His phone rings just as I'm about to drag him on the dance floor. "It's Joseph."

"Dr. Milligan?"

"Yeah. I'm going to go outside. I can't hear anything in here."

I'm surprised Dr. Milligan wasn't at court today. Pierce quickly makes his way toward the exit, leaving the merriment with a serious expression on his face.

I follow him out, too nervous to wait for his return. There's a line around the block outside Viper, people eager to get into the hottest club in Manhattan. The night breeze almost catches the bottom of my dress as I scurry over to where Pierce paces the sidewalk.

"Don't you think I know that already, Joseph? Hindsight is twenty-twenty."

I only get one side of the conversation, unable to hear what Dr. Milligan is saying. By Pierce's demeanor, I'd say he's giving a lecture.

"I understand."

Shit! What does he understand? That the hospital can't be associated with violence, even though Pierce was found innocent of any wrongdoing today? The firm set of his jaw gives me cause for concern.

"I know what you're saying, and I appreciate you going to bat for me. My behavior was inexcusable."

Now, I start pacing in the opposite direction, my heels stomping the sidewalk as I chew on my bottom lip. I can't imagine a world where Pierce Harrison isn't a neurosurgeon. He's too talented, and he's saved too many lives for it to be taken away by a child-abusing father, and I use the term 'father' loosely.

As I try to read Pierce's expression, my heart lurches into my throat.

"Thank you, Dr. Milligan. I appreciate it." He ends the call and shoves his phone in his pocket, his eyes meeting mine.

"What did he say?" My hands are shaking as I approach.

"I have bad news, little one." Tears well in my eyes.

"No. They can't do this to you."

"It's not me they've done it to. The bad news is for you. You're stuck with me. I'm going to be riding your ass hard in the operating room on Monday. Can you deal with having me as your mentor again?" A sexy, heartfelt smile spreads across his chiseled, flawless features.

I rush into his arms, squeezing him as tight as possible. "Oh my God, why would you do that to me?" I laugh through tears of joy. "I can't wait to be ridden by you, Dr. Harrison."

"Jesus, little one, you're going to make me hard as a rock in public."

I bury my head in his neck, the scent of his cologne intoxicating my senses. "Since when has that bothered you, Daddy?"

He lifts me off my feet, spinning me around. "Thank you so much for sticking by me, little one. I was so worried that I'd taken your career mentor from you in one fell swoop."

When he sets me down, I cup his face in my hands. "As much as I'm ecstatic to have you back in the operating room, it's not for me. It is for all the lives you're going to save. I have you in all the ways that matter to me. I have your heart, and you'll always have mine. From now until forever. You're my Daddy, and you are *mine*."

"Always." As his lips find mine, that one word holds the key to my life's happiness. I've found the love of my life, and he'll never let me go. I will love him with everything I have and relish the submission he commands. He's my forever, and as we walk hand in hand back into the club and our friends, I know that I'm safe in his arms, and he will always be safe in mine.

Chapter 23
PIERCE

The familiar scents and sounds of the operating room seep into my very bones as I'm gowned and gloved, ready to reclaim my career with an understanding and reverence I'd long since forgotten over the years. My heart blooms with a contentment that extends outside the walls of this room.

"Annette, could you put on my playlist, please?"

"With pleasure, Dr. Harrison, and can I say on behalf of everyone here that we are thrilled to have you back."

"The feeling is mutual. I appreciate all the support in my absence. Dr. Perrington passed on your well-wishes and encouragement. They meant so much to me during a difficult time. Now, let's get down to the business of saving lives."

"Sounds good to me." Freya smiles as she steps up to my side.

"Good morning, Dr. Perrington. So glad you could join us."

"It's nighttime for me, Dr. Harrison. Some of us still work the night shift." Masked for surgery, my little one can't hide that feisty spark in her eyes.

"Rest assured, I paid my dues. Isn't that right, Annette?"

"Yes, Doctor. Your fiancée is also mainlining coffee at an incredible rate. She reminds me of a young you."

"That's quite the compliment," I jibe.

"Indeed it is, Dr. Harrison." My girl's voice is like velvet.

"Keep talking to me in that tone, and I'll drag you right down to the hospital chapel and make you my wife tonight."

"I don't think our patient would welcome having their surgery pushed back." Even with a mask covering the bottom half of her face, I *know* she's biting that delicious bottom lip of hers.

"Very well. I guess it'll have to wait."

"I'd say so. We've just sent out the save-the-date announcements."

"Stationery is king. Who am I to meddle?"

"Exactly, Dr. Harrison."

"With that agreed upon, future Mrs. Harrison, let's save this man's life."

The second we're ready to begin, Freya and I fall into step with each other. Our relationship outside of the operating room has gone from strength to strength, and it translates in here. I can already see how much she's developed under Dr. Milligan's tutelage these past few months, and it thrills me. She's going to be an incredible surgeon—she *is* an incredible surgeon.

Six hours of painstakingly intricate surgery, and I'm in awe of my future wife. She's like a sponge—anything I tell her, she applies immediately. The thought has my mind going to other places as our patient is wheeled out to the ICU.

Freya is the most responsive submissive I've ever trained. I say that not because I'm madly in love with her but because it's true— the way her body responds to every touch, kiss, and lash of a flogger.

It's all I can do not to march her out of this hospital and straight to the club, but tonight, I have the biggest hurdle to jump in my quest to marry the love of my life. I'm meeting Freya's mother. Ms. Perrington is the only parent between the two of us who is alive or present, so I feel the pressure of the evening more than most. Freya heads home after her shift, hoping to get a few hours of sleep before I get back.

The rest of my shift drags on even though I spend the entire day in and out of the operating room. I'd hate to admit it to my little one, but I'm afraid for the first time in my adult life.

I spent so many years wishing for a family to love and who'd love me back. To be a son again. By the time I reached fifteen, I gave up hope and hardened myself to the world and to the prospect of being important to anyone. I've never had to impress a woman's family and win over a mother. What if she hates me? It could change how Freya sees me.

If I ever had a daughter, I wouldn't want her shackling herself to some fucked-up guy with a Daddy Dom kink who's never had to consider anyone other than himself. I know I'm a selfish man. I had to be. It was the only way to survive growing up in the system. I gave myself focus. I made a decision to pursue an elite career that required my undivided attention. That way, I didn't have to admit to myself that I was alone. I convinced myself it was by choice and gave myself over to a higher calling.

In truth, there was no sacrifice. That would require family and friends. The only thing I had to give up was the past, yet it clung to me in the darkest recesses of my soul, the longing for more—the long-forgotten desire to have a family of my own and a partner who could love me.

By the time I make it back to our apartment, Freya is sound asleep, sprawled across the bed in nothing but a damp towel. She must have passed out after she showered. I could stare at her for hours, committing every inch of her body to memory.

I sit on the edge of the bed before leaning over and kissing the top of her head. She stirs, instinctively reaching for me. "Daddy?" she murmurs, the soft, gravelly tone of her voice so enticing as she straddles the place between wakefulness and slumber.

"Yes, little one."

"Mmm..." She shifts to get closer to me, her towel slipping, exposing her naked body, and it's all I can do not to forget about dinner and ravish her all night long.

"Time to get up. We're meeting your mom in an hour."

Her eyes peek open. "Can't we cancel? I'm naked, and you look edible right now. I've missed you today. The bed is lonely without you."

My cock twitches at her request, but I'm resolute. Canceling an hour beforehand would paint me in the worst light, especially if she ever found out *why*. "As much as I would love to worship your body for the rest of the night, we can't cancel. I want to make a good first impression. I've never met a woman's parent before."

Her eyes soften, her expression so endearing as she pulls herself up and crawls into my lap. "Really? Never? Not even in high school?"

"No. Girls weren't exactly falling over themselves to date the loner, group-home kid." At this moment, I feel just as vulnerable as I did back then—always so eager to be included and matter to someone—*anyone*.

Her arms slink around my waist, holding me close. "Well, I'm happy I get to be your first. Don't worry. My mom is going to love you."

"You think?" I say as I kiss the top of her head.

"You save lives for a living. I'd say that makes you rather impressive." She pulls back to look up at me with so much love in her eyes. "You're a good and honest man. You stand up for those who need it. You love fiercely, and you make me feel so safe and cherished. I love everything about you, and my mom will see that. I promise."

"I hope so, little one. I'd hate to let you down."

She leans in, pressing her lips to mine in a soft, heartfelt kiss. "I'm so proud to call you my fiancé. Never doubt that."

"What did I do to deserve you, little one?"

"Something really, really good," she says with a cheeky grin.

"I'm sure." I capture her mouth with mine, unhurried but with a promise of what's to come when we get home tonight. "Now, let's get ready for dinner before I lose what little self-control I'm holding onto."

∿

Dulip is packed tonight. It always is. The hottest restaurant in town and almost impossible to get a reservation unless you know the owner, who frequents Venom. The second I called Ryder and told him about meeting Freya's mom tonight, he ensured we'd have the best table in the house. I'm sure whoever he bumped from the reservation they had for the last six months will be pissed as hell, but my need is greater than theirs.

My jaw is so tight it starts to tick as we await Ms. Perrington's arrival. Freya glances toward the entrance every few minutes, her hand resting on my thigh. "Stop holding your breath. It's going to be fine. I promise."

I hate that she knows how tense I am. I never want to look weak. As a Dom, it goes against everything I stand for. Since the day I realized I wasn't going to get my happily-ever-after family, I've gone to great lengths to become the stoic man I am today.

From the moment Freya danced into my life, she's been tapping my harsh armor, slowly chipping away at it. The second she broke through the façade, she's held my fragile heart in the palm of her hand, and I didn't realize I've been holding my breath, waiting for her to make a fist and obliterate me.

Tonight may not seem like a big step when we're already engaged and in a Dom/sub relationship, but I can't help thinking this could make or break our relationship.

"There she is!" Freya jumps from her seat with glee, and my chest swells, knowing she has a parent who inspires such joy and love in her. I hate to admit that my happiness for her is tinged with sadness for the boy I once was. That I still am in moments like this.

They embrace like no one is watching, the woman I love recognizable in the features of the older woman whose eyes find mine. Nerves take flight in the pit of my stomach. I don't think I've been this on edge since the day I sat my MCATS.

When Freya finally relinquishes her tight hold on her mom, she grabs her hand and drags her toward our table. I adjust my suit jacket as I stand to greet her. I swallow past the lump in my throat in an attempt to quell my nerves.

Holding out my hand, I channel my inner Dom. "Ms. Perrington, it's a pleasure to meet you. I'm Pierce."

She ignores my hand and pulls me into a hug. "I've heard such good things about you, Pierce. Call me Daphne." I wrap my arms around her, lost for words as realization dawns—Freya is the only person who has hugged me since my mother died. I fight back tears, quickly trying to regain composure.

When she pulls back, I take in her features—a warm smile, eyes that resemble my soon-to-be wife, and the same raven black hair, but with a little gray woven through. She's elegant like Freya. But what gets me most is the way she looks at her daughter. There is awe and adoration in her gaze.

I wait until both Perrington women are seated before taking mine. "Can I order you a drink, Daphne?"

"A glass of red wine would be lovely. Thank you."

"Of course."

I signal for the waiter and order a bottle of Châteaux Lafite, then I think better of it. I want to make sure she likes it, but I'm going to seem like a pretentious asshole for ordering the best bottle in the restaurant.

"So, Pierce, my daughter says you're the best neurosurgeon in the country. How do you find dating your student?"

"I…" *Shit.* I can remove a complex tumor from a patient's brain, and yet my own is failing me at this moment. Freya squeezes my thigh under the table, centering me before I make a complete fool of myself. "It's not without its challenges. I've broken every rule when it comes to your daughter."

"Really?" Her eyes soften, giving me a degree of comfort.

"I never date co-workers, especially not my residents. Your daughter and I came across each other at a masquerade ball." Freya's grip tightens, and it makes me chuckle. Does she really think I would divulge *all* the details of how we met?

"How fun."

"It was. Freya was a vision in lilac. At first, I didn't realize who she was, and by the time I did, she had already enthralled me. I've been a goner ever since."

"Love at first sight," Freya says wistfully as my eyes meet hers. "Yes, it was."

"Oh, I like him already, Freya. The way to a woman's heart is through loving her daughter the way she deserves to be loved."

"As I've told Freya, I will spend every day of the rest of my life trying to be worthy of her... with your blessing?" It's a question rather than a statement.

"I'm sure you know I raised Freya as a single mother. I always wanted her to know that you shouldn't settle for anything less than true love. I was the mom and the dad."

"You were everything I ever needed, Mom," Freya interjects. "I never felt like I lost out on anything. My father didn't care to know me, and I have never wanted to know him."

"Your daughter is a credit to your hard work, Ms. Perrington."

"Please, call me Daphne."

"Sorry, *Daphne*. You raised a remarkable woman... self-assured, skilled, and fiercely intelligent. Your parenting has a big part to play in that."

"And what of your family? Will I get a chance to meet them before the wedding?" Freya stiffens at my side, but I take her hand in mine, assuring her I'm okay.

"Freya is the only family I have. Both of my parents died when I was young, a few years apart. I grew up in the foster system."

"Then your success is even more impressive. I've watched my daughter give everything she has to becoming a surgeon. The fact that you achieved such success in the face of adversity speaks to your character."

Pride blooms in my chest. "Thank you."

"I do have to correct you, though. Freya is not your only family. You are going to be part of *my* family. I always wanted a son. If you're comfortable with it, maybe one day you'll call me Mom."

I don't know what to say, overwhelmed by her generosity of spirit. I planned to be the picture of strength and dependability this evening, yet I find myself completely disarmed in the presence of a true, maternal figure. It conjures a whisper of the woman I believed my mother to be before she had my father's blood on her hands.

I clear my throat, swallowing past the lump that forms.

"I can't wait for you to see the apartment, Mom." Freya steps in to give me a moment to compose myself. My little one is observant, always looking out for me.

"Yes, I would love for you to see it, Daphne. The place had been lacking since I moved in, but Freya has turned a once cold, functional apartment into our *home*."

"It wasn't cold." She grimaces. "Not totally."

Her mother lets out a little laugh as she considers us. "Home isn't the place, it's the person."

"Well, I can honestly say my life was cold before your daughter came into it, shining brighter than the sun. I simply bask in her warmth. A trait I'm sure she gets from you."

She tilts her head ever so slightly. "You bring it out in her. Freya had a singular mind growing up. She wanted to be a surgeon, and boyfriends weren't worth her time. I can voice it now…" she says, reaching out to clasp her daughter's hand, "… that I worried she may not find someone to share her life with."

"Really?" This is clearly the first Freya is hearing of her mom's concerns.

"I know what it is to go through life without a partner who understands and can shoulder the burden with you."

"You made it look so easy."

"I had you, and that's all I needed. You made me a better, stronger woman, darling, and I feel so privileged to have watched you grow up into the incredible person you are today. Man, or no man." She gives me a soft smile. "Though I am thrilled you found a man to love and appreciate your journey so far and yet to come."

We raise a glass to the future and family, even though the word feels odd on my tongue.

I never imagined that Freya would give me so much more than a submissive to care for. She's given me love, support, and hope for a future I'd long since given up on. I believed myself too broken to ever be enough for a woman. The fact I found my soulmate just blows my mind.

The rest of dinner is spent in jovial conversation as I probe

Daphne for stories of Freya when she was small. I'm promised albums of photographs and happy memories. The things people take for granted—a lifetime of Christmases, birthdays, and other holidays.

When Freya moved in with me, she asked me for pictures to hang on the walls. The look on her face when I told her I don't have any of me growing up broke my heart. Whatever evidence there was of my dysfunctional family was lost when I got shuffled from place to place. She made it her mission to make new memories worthy of being framed on the walls.

Our friends at Venom now take up space where there was once nothing but vast expanses of cream paint. There is laughter, silliness, candid moments captured, and my favorite—selfies of Freya and me. Fun days in Central Park. A snapshot of victory after saving a patient's life. She makes the smallest day-to-day moments significant, full of joy and wonder.

By the time the evening comes to an end, I've almost convinced myself that I'm good enough for Freya. I'm not too proud to admit she could do better, but a worthier man would have to snatch her from my cold, dead hands. She's mine, and I'll ensure it stays that way.

I have my driver take Daphne back to her hotel while Freya and I take a stroll in the cool evening breeze.

"My mom loved you," she says as she nestles against my side.

"You think?"

"I *know*. Trust me, she doesn't hold back if she thinks something, or in this case, someone, is wrong for me. I'd already have been pulled aside and given some sage words of wisdom."

"Okay," I breathe out a sigh of relief.

"Were you really that worried?"

"Yes. She's your mom. If I made a terrible impression on her, I would never ask you to choose between having a relationship with your mom or me. The bond you have is sacred."

"It is, and I feel truly blessed to have had a happy childhood." She interlaces her fingers with mine as we leisurely walk back to our place. "But, my mom always taught me that her job was to get me safely to adulthood, and as much as she's my champion in everything I do, there comes a time when you have to make a choice about who your family is going to be. That *if* I met someone who sets my world on fire but would also be there in the quiet and sad moments, I would need to put that person above even her."

"That's so... selfless."

"She may not have gotten her happily ever after with my dad, but she has a man in her life now who loves her the way she's supposed to be loved. I could never fathom anyone even coming close to how much I love her, and then you walked into my life, and everything changed."

"How so?" I push her for more, eager to understand how she sees me because tonight felt different. Official in some way. Confirmation that this is really happening. This woman has picked me to navigate this life with.

"Because no matter what, I choose you. It's always going to be you, Daddy."

"Say it again." I stop her in her tracks, pulling her into my arms.

"It's always going to be you, Daddy." She pushes herself up onto her tiptoes, planting a kiss on my lips. "*You're mine.*"

I pick her up and throw her over my shoulder. "Change of plans, little one. We're not going home. I'm taking my fiancée to the club."

She squeals with delight, and it's music to my ears. I'll never tire of the way she makes my heart take flight, and I'll never stop loving her with everything I have.

Chapter 24
FREYA

Time has seemed to fly by these past six months. My fifth year of residency is almost at an end. I adore working with Pierce, savoring every word of wisdom he has bestowed on me, but now is the time for applying to other hospitals.

I don't know what's going to happen, but we'll figure it out. Pierce encouraged me to apply to hospitals in other states, assuring me we can make it work. It's not like we aren't committed to each other. We're engaged and have set a date for the wedding.

I've been going to interviews across the country, but my heart isn't in it. Every hospital I visit, I'm acutely aware that I left a part of my heart behind in New York with Pierce. He's open to moving if I get the right offer, but in truth, I don't want to move out of state. We have a life here in Manhattan. Friends. The club.

We spend as much time in the club as we do in the hospital. Pierce takes my submissive training seriously, adamant that I should continue to learn and explore the lifestyle. We had a long talk about the night he brought Flex to the playroom. I love him for allowing me the opportunity, but I love him even more for the sigh of relief he heaved when I declined.

Recently, I discovered that I really enjoy it when Daddy hog-ties me. We've tried everything on the original list he had me fill out, except for anything involving another person. It's special to me that Pierce is the only man I've ever been with, and I know he loves it. When he tells me how precious I am as his submissive, it makes me so proud and happy that I waited.

I know so much of it came from a place of discomfort. There was always something missing. Something I worried was *wrong* with me. Since meeting Pierce, my life has become a rich tapestry, finally allowing me to see the bigger picture. I know where I fit in. I'm not odd or weird. I'm cherished and praised for being unique. Everyone deserves that level of acceptance from the one they love. I consider myself so lucky to have Pierce be the man who loves me unconditionally.

When I emerge from the first surgery of the day, I'm paged to the Chief of Surgery's office. Dr. Milligan stepped in while Pierce was suspended during the trial, and I have grown to admire him. He was Pierce's mentor, so I knew I would learn so much from him.

Unfortunately, they have been interviewing a number of candidates for an attending position here, and they are coming from some of the best residency programs in the country. I didn't expect any special treatment, and I voiced that to Dr. Milligan when I applied for the job.

My pulse quickens as I reach the Chief's office, wrapping my knuckles on the door before entering.

"Come in."

As I step inside, I'm unable to read the esteemed doctor as he beckons me to take a seat.

"I know you're aware I've been interviewing the top neuro residents in the country for a position in Pierce's department."

"Yes, sir."

"And you both entreated me to make the best decision for the hospital and not what suits your relationship, which I appreciate. It isn't my job to play matchmaker."

"Of course."

"That being said, you are an impressive candidate, and I gave you the same consideration afforded to all who applied."

"I understand." This guy has an even better poker face than Pierce. He's giving nothing away.

"I conducted my final interview yesterday, and it cemented my decision."

Shit. This isn't going to go my way. I have offers from John's Hopkins and Vanderbilt, so I won't be jobless, but a small part of me was holding out hope for the position here.

"I am pleased to offer you an attending position here at NYU Langone."

What? I can stay here. With Pierce. *Oh my God.* I'm an attending at the top neurology hospital in the country.

"Obviously, you have time to consider the offer." He pushes a manilla envelope across the desk. "I won't rush you for an answer today, but the sooner you decide, I can make arrangements if I need to contact my second choice."

My logical, surgical side kicks in, tempering the giddy fiancée in me. Yes, this is what I want, but the terms need to be good for my career moving forward. Pierce has taught me to demand the best and have confidence in my skill.

"Thank you, Dr. Milligan. I will read over the offer and get back to you as soon as possible."

"Very well."

With the envelope clutched in my hand, I exit his office and walk as quickly as I can without breaking into a run to the nearest on-call room. They're usually empty at this time of day, and I just need a minute to gather my thoughts and read over the offer.

I twist the lock on the door before sliding my back down the pale wood until I'm sitting on the floor. My hands are shaking as I tear open the envelope that potentially holds the key to my career path. As much as I love Pierce, I won't give up my career to make our relationship easier, and I know he wouldn't want that either.

I gingerly tease the papers from the envelope, my heart racing as I read over the first page. My hand flies to my mouth to hold in the gasp that escapes me.

The offer is good.

The offer is really good.

The hospital is going to pay off my student loans on top of a very generous salary.

My face is sore from smiling too hard.

I pull my phone out of my pocket and fire off a quick text to Pierce, telling him to come find me when he has a minute. I'm so happy, I can't wait to share the news with him. This is the culmination of so many years of tireless work, studying, night shifts, and sacrifices. It almost feels too good to be true.

I transferred to NYU Langone this year because I wanted to study under the best neurosurgeon in the country at the leading hospital for neurology. It was a dream come true when I got news of my transfer. I never could've imagined that he'd be the love of my life.

To have found such love in a kink club only makes me love him more. He has opened my mind and heart to so many new and exciting experiences. I've done things that scared me, thrilled me, and pushed me out of my comfort zone.

I love being his submissive. I respect him as my Dom, and it fills me with pride to know that he chose me and continues to choose me every single day.

There's a knock at the door, and it startles me even though I'm expecting Pierce.

"It's me, little one."

A thrill courses through me as I pull him inside.

He fists his hands in my hair, leaning down to capture my lips in a heart-stopping kiss.

I lean my forehead against Pierce's. "Did you mean what you said?"

"What?"

"That you'll never get enough of me."

"One thousand percent. You're mine. I'll always want more."

"Then I guess it's good that I just got offered an attending position here."

He lifts my chin, searching my gaze for any sign that I'm kidding. "Really? Are you serious? Milligan gave you an offer?"

"Yes. And a great offer at that."

His face sobers for a moment. "You have other offers, though. Is there one that you favor, little one? John's Hopkins is an amazing opportunity."

"Are you trying to get rid of me?"

His brow furrows at the allegation. "Of course not, but I also don't want to hold you back. You have to make the decision that's best for your career."

"I have."

"You've made up your mind?"

"Yes. Take your cock out of the equation for a moment," I jibe. "NYU Langone is the top facility in the country for my specialty. I would be an idiot to turn it down. They are willing to pay off my student loans, and the salary package is generous."

"Wow. That's amazing."

"But the best part, and the part I'm most excited about... I get to continue to work alongside one of the best neurosurgeons in the world. The fact that I love deepthroating his cock is an added bonus."

"You're really going to work here with me?"

"Yes. Why are you so surprised? We're getting married."

"Because no one has ever chosen *me*. I've never known anything else." His words make my eyes well with tears.

"I chose you, Pierce. The job is great, but in the end, there was never any contest for the other offers I've had. Don't tell Dr. Milligan, but I would've taken any offer he put forth because it meant being here with you. I want to start our life together now. No holds barred. No long-distance relationship. I want to come home to you every night in our home. I will always choose you."

He picks me up and spins us around before planting a heartfelt kiss on my lips. "I fucking love you, Freya." His lips descend on mine, but we're quickly interrupted by our pagers going off.

Pierce gives me one of those wickedly delicious grins of his. "How good an offer did he give you?"

"Three hundred."

"That's my girl! Know your worth." He gives me a quick kiss

before grabbing his pager. "You're with me in the ER. You got enough energy for surgery? It's going to be a long day."

"Of course. I've always got the energy for surgery."

"And that's one of the many things I love about you, little one. You are fucking fierce in the walls of this hospital. I'm looking forward to working with you as a colleague rather than a mentor."

"Let's go and save a life together, Dr. Harrison."

He opens the door, holding it for me. "After you, Dr. Perrington. I would follow you anywhere."

"Thank you," I push myself onto my tiptoes before whispering in his ear, "Daddy."

"You're going to be the death of me."

"But what a way to go, right?"

The second we step out into the hallway, we take off at a run, ready to face the world and save lives. *Together.*

What a gift to find my soulmate here at work where and when I least expected it. I had such determination that I would explore the lifestyle while keeping my professional life completely separate. Fate had other plans, and I bow at her feet, knowing I'm the luckiest woman, submissive, surgeon, and soon-to-be *wife.*

I will spend every day of the rest of my life being thankful for the man beside me. For the journey he faced and the hardships he fought to be in Venom that night, my masked stranger. He opened himself up to me and let me find myself in him. A strong submissive, his *little one.* He will forever be my *Daddy Dom.*

Epilogue
PIERCE

My heart is in my stomach right now as I stand at the foot of the altar, awaiting my bride. I'm not nervous about marrying Freya or about being married. She's had me by the balls since the moment we met. My trepidation is for the day. I want everything to be perfect for my little one. She deserves the best.

Celest came to the apartment last night and kicked me out. Even though Freya and I have been living together for months, her best friend insisted on the tradition. I spent the night at Flex's, tossing and turning, eager to see my bride. When you're marrying your best friend, they're the only person you want to talk to.

I've been waiting for this day since the moment I first laid eyes on my lady in lavender. I knew the instant our eyes met that my life was going to change. I never imagined the tumultuous road we'd travel or that loving her would quell the demons that plagued me for decades. If you'd told me two years ago that I'd be here, more than ready to be a husband, a friend, and a forever Dom, I wouldn't have believed it possible.

I shut out anyone who tried to get close. I allowed myself to be terrorized in my dreams by the man who taught me the kind of man I *never* wanted to become. For Freya, I want to be a better man. I want to give her everything my father denied my mother and me.

Flex, Dalton, Ryder, Mateo, and Ford stand to my left—my groomsmen. My family.

When the doors open and Freya's bridesmaids walk down the aisle, I can't help but notice where Flex's gaze settles, a wide grin on his face and a look in his eye I know well. But today isn't about anyone else. It's about Freya and me, joining our lives together as one, willing to face the good, the bad, and the kinky for as long as we both shall live and love.

My pulse is racing as the string quartet heralds the imminent entrance of the bride. I lean over to Flex.

"Have you got the rings?"

"Relax, brother. We've got you," he gestures to the others, and for once, there's no laughter at my expense or anything even close to a joke which is our preferred mode of friendship. Instead, on this most important of days, I see heartfelt support in their eyes.

Today, Freya becomes my family, but she has already given me so much more than her alone. She's giving me a mother-in-law who treats me like her own son—a gift I know a lot of men joke about. The in-laws have a reputation in society, but I can say with absolute conviction that I cherish Daphne. She loves me the way I always picture a mom would.

If that weren't enough, Freya opened my eyes to the family I chose at Venom. I had convinced myself I was a lone wolf in this world, even though I had a glut of friends at the club. They were there for me when it mattered during the trial. There wasn't a moment of hesitation. Freya made one phone call at my behest, and they all surrounded us with their support.

My nerves are getting the better of me as my hands begin to tremble. I'm a surgeon. I was trained to have steady hands even in the most crucial of situations, and yet here I stand, about to see Freya at the top of the aisle, and I have to clasp my hands behind my back to hide the fact that I'm nervous.

The music is ethereal, wisping through our guests, enchanting everyone as we collectively look to the imposing, intricately carved doors of the cathedral as they open, casting my bride in a breath-taking silhouette.

With her mom at her side, Freya begins the walk down the aisle —the picture of elegance. The closer she gets, my breath hitches at the sight of her. She is stunning in an ivory gown flowing behind her as she sashays toward me. I knew she'd make a beautiful bride, but what I didn't anticipate is the intricate ivory lace masquerade mask that adorns her face.

My little one.

It takes everything in me not to take off running up the aisle to close the gap between us. The second her eyes find mine, my nerves dissipate, and all that's left is pure, unadulterated love for the woman before me.

Her long black hair cascades over her shoulders in soft waves, and my cock twitches at the thought of wrapping it around my fist later tonight when I make her mine in our marriage bed.

My heart is hammering in my chest, pounding so hard I almost believe our guests might hear it. I can't contain the grin on my face as she kisses her mom on the cheek before taking her place at my side.

"You look… stunning."

As she stares up into my eyes, I know I'm making the best decision of my life.

"You look extremely handsome," she says for everyone to hear before whispering under her breath, "Daddy."

Fuck me. If one moment were to encapsulate my little one, it would be this. Standing in front of everyone we love, the picture of bridal innocence, with a quiet, fierce, and confident ownership of exactly who we are to each other.

"I decided on a mask rather than a veil." Her smile could light up the room, shining like the rising sun on a beautiful summer's day.

"It's breathtaking."

"It is for you to unmask me."

"With pleasure."

You could hear a pin drop in the cathedral as I reach around and untie Freya's mask, her eyes fluttering closed for just a moment.

As I gently remove it, she hits me with a genuine grin that could launch a thousand ships. I'd die before I let anyone hurt her. I would walk through fire for one more kiss. Knowing we are standing here about to declare our love for one another destroys all my carefully crafted walls, opening my heart for Freya to hold in the palm of her hand.

"There's my little one." I brush my hand over her cheek in a gentle caress. "Ready for forever?"

"Yes."

The priest walks us through the ceremony before giving us the opportunity to recite our own vows, which has me nervous all over again. When he gestures for me to take the ring from Flex's proffered hand, I take a deep, calming breath. As soon as my hand touches Freya's, I know everything is right in the world. I slide the thin platinum band onto her ring finger and clasp her hand in mine.

"Freya." I swallow past the lump in my throat. "I knew the moment we met my life had changed. I didn't know how or why, but every beat of my heart recognized in you what I've been missing my whole life. Family.

"Before we met, I didn't believe in soulmates. That there could be one person in this vast universe who's meant for me. It seemed too optimistic and fanciful for a kid who grew up with no one.

"In you, I've found so much more than a wife. You're my best friend. The person I want to share the highs and lows of this journey called life. You make me a better man, and I will spend every day for the rest of our lives striving to be worthy of your love. I promise to cherish you, love you, and protect you with everything I've got. You are my family, and I can't wait to see where life takes us, but I know with you at my side, I will always be loved, and *you* will have my heart for eternity."

There isn't a dry eye in the cathedral as I hear sniffles all around. I had forgotten that anyone else was here with us. My heart beats only for Freya.

"Freya, you may recite your vows," the priest entreats.

I turn to Flex who steps up to give Freya my wedding band. His eyes are glassy, and when I grin at him, he mumbles under his breath. "This place must be dusty."

Trust Flex to crack a joke in the middle of our wedding.

The moment Freya reaches out to grab my hand, I'm undone as she slips my platinum wedding ring on my finger.

"Pierce…" She struggles to keep her emotions in check, taking a deep breath before she continues. "I doubt many couples meet each other for the first time twice."

There's a soft chuckle from the pews.

"The day I met Dr. Pierce Harrison, I knew I was in the presence of greatness. I wanted to learn everything I could from a surgeon I admired. I knew working under you would change my life. It wasn't until we met again, for the first time, at a masquerade ball, that I knew the mysterious man behind the mask would define a turning point in my life.

"You've taught me so much about myself, professionally and personally. You make me a better woman, and I love the way you love me. I feel safe in your arms, and I promise on this day, in front of *our* family, that I will love you until the end of time. I'll cherish what we have. Champion you in all your endeavors. And above all else, I will *always* be by your side. You are my forever, Pierce, from now until the end of time. My love for you is endless."

My heart is galloping, threatening to break free from my chest like a wild mustang. I can't believe I'm standing here right now with the love of my life. I slip my hands into Freya's hair and kiss her with everything I've got.

"You may kiss the bride." I hear the priest say faintly in the background, and everyone laughs.

I'm breathless when I finally relinquish her lips. She has never looked more beautiful than she does at this moment.

"I now pronounce you husband and wife." We turn to face our guests. "I present to you, Dr. and Dr. Harrison."

Freya intertwines her fingers with mine. "Lead the way, Dr. Harrison."

"With pleasure, Dr. Harrison."

We walk down the aisle to everyone clapping and wishing us

well, and I look at my beautiful bride, beaming, her smile radiating joy.

There's a Rolls Royce outside, waiting to take us to the reception venue, and as soon as I close the door behind us, my lips crash down on hers, claiming her as mine once more.

"Do we have to go to the reception? Can't we just slip away to the club?"

"Not today, little one. Don't worry, I have plans for you tonight. You look too fucking gorgeous in this dress, but by midnight, you'll be wearing your wedding mask and nothing else as you ride my face."

"How am I supposed to get through dinner and dancing now?"

I plant a soft kiss on the tip of her nose. "Because I have a little surprise for you. Take off your wedding ring and look at the inscription." I take mine off at the same time.

"You had them inscribed?" Her face is alight like a child on Christmas morning.

The second she reads the inside of her ring, her eyes well with tears.

"*Daddy.*"

I hand her my ring to let her see what I had inscribed on mine.

"*Little One.*"

"You'll always be mine, little one." I brush away an errant tear from her cheek. "Don't cry."

"I love you, Daddy."

"I love you, too, little one."

As I press my lips to hers, time stops, and the world is only us, in this moment, loving each other completely and without judgment. Freya will always hold my heart until it beats its last. My life, *my wife*, and forever my stunning submissive.

THE END
Preorder THE ASSIGNMENT now

Acknowledgments

To my beloved Sir. I couldn't chase this dream without your unwavering support. You remind me every day what true love is. Thank you from the bottom of my heart for always championing me on this crazy journey.

Ria, I love you more. Thank you so much for the many hours listening to me flesh out my characters and find their voice. You make the process so exciting with your enthusiasm and love for every book boyfriend I write.

Nicki – Thank you for helping me elevate my work to provide readers with the best experience. I know that my characters are safe in your hands.

To my readers I want to say a huge thank you. Without your support I wouldn't get to wake up every morning and do my dream job. I knew I wanted to fly on the pages of the written word, but you gave me wings.

About the Author

I'm happiest when wandering through the uncharted territory of my imagination. You'll find me curled up with my laptop, browsing the books at the local library or enjoying the smell of a new book, taking great delight in cracking the spine and writing in the margins!

I'm a native Scot but live in Texas with my husband, two kids, and a whizzy little fur baby with the most ridiculous ears. I first fell in love with British literature while majoring in Linguistics, 17th Century Poetry, and Shakespeare at University. I'm an avid reader and life-long notebook hoarder. In 2014, I finally put my extensive collection to good use and started writing my first novel. Previously traditionally published under a pen name, I decided to branch out on my own and lend my name to my full back catalogue!

I write contemporary romance with all the feels, sports rom-coms and paranormal romance, and I am currently working on some other exciting new projects.

Social Media

http://www.evahaining.com/newsletter
www.instagram.com/evahainingauthor
www.facebook.com/evahainingauthor
www.twitter.com/evahaining
www.amazon.com/author/evahaining
www.bookbub.com/profile/eva-haining
https://www.goodreads.com/author/show/20271110.Eva_Haining
https://tiktok.com/@evahainingauthor
http://www.evahaining.com/newsletter
www.evahaining.com

41449654R00169